Forever Connected

*The Anglo Arabian infused
adventure continues...*

BOOK THREE

Forever Connected

A STORY ABOUT GOOD ENERGY
AND FOREVER FRIENDSHIPS

BRITT HOLLAND

Forever Connected First published by Arabian Wolf Publications 2021

Arabian Wolf Productions
House of Social Enterprise BV
Geleenstraat 16,2
1078 LE Amsterdam
The Netherlands

Copyright © 2021 by Britt Holland

All rights reserved. No part of this publication may be reproduced, stored, or transmitted in any form or by any means, electronic, mechanical, photocopying, recording, scanning, or otherwise without written permission from the publisher. It is illegal to copy this book, post it to a website, or distribute it by any other means without permission.

This novel is entirely a work of fiction. The names, characters and incidents portrayed in it are the work of the author's imagination. Any resemblance to actual persons, living or dead, events or localities is entirely coincidental.

Britt Holland asserts the moral right to be identified as the author of this work.

Britt Holland has no responsibility for the persistence or accuracy of URLs for external or third-party Internet Websites referred to in this publication and does not guarantee that any content on such Websites is, or will remain, accurate or appropriate.

Designations used by companies to distinguish their products are often claimed as trademarks. All brand names and product names used in this book and on its cover are trade names, service marks, trademarks and registered trademarks of their respective owners. The publishers and the book are not associated with any product or vendor mentioned in this book. None of the companies referenced within the book have endorsed the book.

First edition

ISBN: 978-1-8383802-2-9

www.brittholland.com

Literary Agent: Susan Mears

Contents

Introduction	9
Acknowledgement	11
House on the Bluff	13
Maddie's Arrival	28
Plunging In	34
Cristina	41
Jigged Journey	45
Rude Awakening	54
Crate Ideas	61
Unease Looming	67
Hollywood Humphrey	72
Poolside Paradise	77
Harsh Homecoming	83
Cristina Crisis	92
Slithering Snake	100
Daffodil Daphne	108
Flowing Feeling	119
Daisy Oracle	124
Midnight Merlin	129
Clarity in Darkness	138
Operation Observation	147
Evil Death	159
One Funeral and A Marriage	167
Wedding Witness	178

BUSY BRAIN	185
WRITE IT FORWARD	195
BEEN WITH BEN	204
EL PADRE	214
PORTUGAL POTENTIAL	223
PARTING WORDS	230
EUROPE BOUND	234
VILLA VISTA	238
LIFE'S A BEACH	245
FOREVER CONNECTED	257
INTERVIEW WITH THE AUTHOR	265
ALSO BY BRITT HOLLAND	269

To Sarah

Girls with Curls
Loud and Lovely
Funny and Fearless
Peas in a Pod
Forever Connected

Introduction

Vivika, the hospitality professional from *Between the Sheets* who attended The Grand Reunion in *Mountains of Love*, travels to Costa Rica. Vivika finds herself co-owning a coffee plantation and meets handsome Humphrey. Against the vibrant back- drop of resplendent nature, Vivi embraces every *Pura Vida* day and her forever friendships. When Vivika attends the bi-annual Pussy Posse reunion in Portugal, old flame Bash, revs the powerful engine of his olive golden Aston Martin. Ready to go full throttle.

Acknowledgement

Thank you to Charlotte Mouncey. Without your patience, creativity, kindness and professionalism and unwavering support, I would not have been able to boast the inspirational book covers. Thank you too for taking such care about typesetting my stories. You have taught me so much along my way and I am eternally grateful to Corinne from CWR Talent for introducing us and *Passing it On!*

From the bottom of my heart, thank you Charlotte.

House on the Bluff

The view from The House on the Bluff was the same, though the circumstances were not.

As I looked across the Pacific Ocean, I watched the sun sinking over the horizon. The sky was streaked with raspberry, tangerine and blueberry swirls, like ripples of ice cream as the day melted into the night.

Twenty-five years ago, I first came to Costa Rica with my Pussy Posse pals, Annie, and Hélène, to see Amilcar and Theo. I had met both boys when we attended hotelschool together, in the Swiss Alps.

During our visit, we were invited to see Amilcar at *La Hacienda*. This property had belonged to Amilcar's late father, *El Comandante*, the King of illegal trade in pre-Columbian art.

The coffee plantation was about half an hour's drive inland. The spectacular footprint of *La Hacienda* and its land encompassed green hill after rolling green hill until the land rose into a steep cliff and subsequently plunged into the ocean. The final bluff marked the natural border of the estate as it disappeared into the Pacific and the endless horizon beyond.

Theo was my Dutch friend, a *Token Tico,* living in Costa Rica since he was a pre-teenager. He was like a brother to me, and my hero. He always knew what to do in a time of crisis, or so I thought. Theo didn't take instructions from anyone. Though he responded to the nods and the nudges from Amilcar, who was not the type of person to command others. Very unlike his feared and ferocious father, *El Comandante.*

As well as Theo and Amilcar, I'd met Bash, the son of yet another art smuggler, at the hospitality management school in Switzerland.

Recently, I'd seen Theo and Bash again at a Grand Reunion in the Swiss Alps. Unfortunately, Amilcar had been unable to attend due to his rapidly deteriorating health.

Following the reunion, Theo asked me to come to Costa Rica after a trip to Spain, where I'd experienced some unresolved adventures. Amilcar had also especially requested for me to come to visit him.

To Say Goodbye.

When I arrived, Amilcar was laid up in his bed, placed in the middle of *La Hacienda Sueño en el Cielo's* lobby. He was unplugged from all his support devices. Without words, he made it clear that he wanted to see the jade man, an amulet that Theo had given to me twenty-five years ago, in that very same spot where Amilcar now lay. My little man of wisdom was nestled between my bosoms, as usual. Here, he absorbed the temperature of my skin, and his vibe was in synch with my heart.

I placed the precious piece in Amilcar's upturned palm. He lifted it to his lips with all the energy he could muster.

Without saying a word, Amilcar gently kissed the little man, then put him into my palm and whispered, '*Vaya con Dios*', May God be with you.

Theo and I held Amilcar's hands and each other's.

Rain clouds darkened the sky, and the downpour started, pounding on the roof above and soaking all the vegetation around us.

After some time, Amilcar closed his eyes and drew his last breath as the sound of thunder rocked *La Hacienda*.

The three of us were now reduced to two. In earthly terms, at least.

Theo sobbed like a boy as the rain subsided and the sun came out.

As I looked out over the plantation, a perfect double rainbow appeared and framed the House on the Bluff in the distance. It was then that Theo gave me the letter that Amilcar had wanted to give me himself but had not been able to. Part of the letter read:

'I won't keep talking about the past, especially since I have now left you for a new future. But to make sure that Hacienda Sueño en el Cielo remains loved and cared for, I am leaving the estate to you and Theo. The accumulated riches of art my father stashed here, I give to Theo. It cannot be traded to the network, but it can be sold for good, and to support sound business under the Loving Little Lids Social Enterprise work.

When Theo gave you the little Mayan Man all those years ago, it was by my instruction. I told Theo I wanted him to hang the magical amulet around the neck of the person he trusted and would always. Theo chose you. He has known for all this time that the shared ownership would be with someone he cares for.'

From then on, it was up to Theo and me to continue what Amilcar had started all those years ago. After *El Comandante* had died, Amilcar had gained the freedom to do what his heart desired.

To do good.

Some days after the ashes' ceremony and our final farewell to Amilcar, I stood in The House on the Bluff, gazing into the unknown.

The topmost house was more regal than the other three dwellings dotted around below. The dominant structure stood like a mother eagle watching over her three chicks. Perched on stilts, with dark wooden tropical floors, *Casa Curtis* occupied the most elevated position on top of the Bluff, off the beaten track and hidden by dense rainforest.

Howler monkeys, the largest New World monkeys, voiced their loud calls as they passed by. The spider monkeys, with their disproportionately long limbs, flew like agile and oversized, furry, long-legged arachnids through the sky. Sloths moved as if they were in reversed slow motion and dazzling frogs sat in the sunshine, billowing their cheeks. A host of other creatures, including *serpientes venenosas*, the dreaded poisonous snakes, occupied the dense rainforest as well as an infinite number of insects, including mosquitoes, responsible for the killer dengue fever.

Winston Curtis had lived in The House on the Bluff with his son Arturo, or in *Casa Curtis*, as the house was affectionately known by locals. Father and son had moved from Nicaragua when the boy was in his teens. Arturo had started his early adult life as a coffee picker on Amilcar's estate where he fell in love with the wonders of nature. Amilcar supported the young chap to pursue his dreams to become a conservationist.

Twenty years after Winston and Arturo had moved into the House on the Bluff, Arturo was found face down, at the bottom of the cliff, his satchel and notebook by his side. His binoculars were still around his neck, and there were two clear puncture marks where the snake's venom had penetrated his tanned skin. It would never be clear whether Arturo's death was due to falling down the cliff due to the snakebite or the subsequent effect of the poison penetrating his blood.

It didn't matter; Arturo was dead.

The only consolation to his grieving father was that Arturo died doing what he loved, and that gave him a sense of peace. The rest of Curtis's family had suffered a torturous and unimaginable death all those years ago in Nicaragua.

One day, Amilcar had recounted to Theo and me the story of how he had first met with Winston and Arturo Curtis.

Amilcar had arrived back home from a trip when the family driver gave him a letter from his father. Amilcar had been stunned to hear from *El Comandante*, who never knew the whereabouts of Amilcar and was rarely in contact.

His father never paid any attention to Amilcar. Clearly, he did not care about his only son.

In the letter, *El Comandante* wrote that he needed someone to be employed as plantation manager *urgentamente*. The coffee trade was a decoy for *El Comandante's* Pre-Columbian art smuggling and a Central American base for the underground drug network that spanned continents. Amilcar was told to find a manager for the plantation to strengthen the illusion that there was a legitimate coffee business at *La Hacienda* and avoid prying eyes and investigations.

El Comandante ordered Amilcar to find someone urgently, saying, "Anyone will do. But get it done. I need a Coffee Plantation Manager. There is no time to waste."

For the most part, Amilcar was left entirely to his own devices. If any smuggled art needed shifting for his dad, Theo would take care of it, rather than Amilcar, who suffered terrible health. Theo was both capable and willing to support his friend Amilcar, whom he deeply loved and respected, ever since they had got to know each other well in Switzerland.

Amilcar was the brains and the heart; Theo had the guts and the energy.

As his driver turned into the driveway of *La Hacienda*, Amilcar noticed a commotion at the wrought-iron entrance gates, which were elaborately decorated with monkeys and birds.

Like the gateway to paradise, he mused, though that would be a debatable suggestion.

The guards were shouting at two men.

Perhaps they were looking for work.

It was a frequent occurrence, as coffee pickers were fired at one farm and sought work at the next. Amilcar ordered the driver to stop and told the guards to back off. Amilcar looked at the two men, or rather, an older man and what looked like a teenage boy. They had an air of desperation about them. He saw the haunted look on the older man's face, though he could not see the boy's expression as he was looking down at the ground.

The young chap stood with his shoulders slumped. His head

bowed like a flower that had no water, slowly dying, parched and limp, without the vibrance associated with young life.

Amilcar got out of the car and opened the door, inviting the man and the boy to join him for some food and coffee. With a respectful nod, the older man silently agreed and ushered the boy into the car. Amilcar noticed their lack of belongings. They were dirty, their eyes dull, and their faces grief-stricken. He had seen men like them before, who'd been fired by a slave-driving coffee landowner, desperate for jobs.

But these men were somehow different.

The strong scent of sharp, rank sweat pervaded the car. Amilcar opened the window to let in some oxygen. It quickly became unbearable to breathe in the stale stench that cut like an acid knife in his throat.

Amilcar's heart lifted at the thought that he might be able to do something for the teenage boy and the man, who may well have been close to the age of his father. Or perhaps considerably less. After all, a harsh existence drains a person.

El Comandante needed a manager. And God had presented him with one.

The car snaked its way up the driveway through the hills of green, finally coming to a standstill. Amilcar got out and introduced himself properly. Winston Curtis put his large hand, the texture of sandpaper, into Amilcar's, soft as silk. Amilcar summoned the butler to prepare some food and drink. He stepped away to discretely utter some other instructions that the man and the boy could not hear.

Amilcar's frame was frail, so his clothes would fit the teenage boy but not the older man. He was encouraged by the thought that the man would fit into the clothes of *El Comandante*.

Winston Curtis told Amilcar they were looking to secure work at the *La Pantación de Café* as coffee pickers. On probing more profoundly, it appeared that they had worked in a different plantation further north, just south of the Nicaraguan border. Both Winston and Arturo had failed to pick the daily required amount of coffee. Compared to the other more experienced workers, their work fell short of expectations. After three days, they were ordered to leave.

La Hacienda had never been run as a coffee plantation. Amilcar had sometimes wondered what it would be like to have a successful coffee business. He wished he could help those in need and offer them jobs that would generate an adequate income. Amilcar mused how different this would be to the dirty business that his father *El Comandante* ran, in which greed set the standard.

Amilcar understood that coffee pickers led tough lives. He empathised with the workers, whose sweat soaked into their shirts, leaving their clothes feeling damp, heavy, and cold against their perspiring skin.

Theirs was a relentless and unforgiving existence.

Only the mature, bright red coffee cherries could be picked, and those had to be selected one by one. The ripe red cherries were twisted to the left, then carefully pulled off the branch to ensure the green bud stayed on the tree. That bud would be the next coffee cherry.

Most pickers managed to fill seven to eight baskets a day, equating to eight pounds of coffee, earning the worker around eight dollars a day.

This paltry sum was less than one dollar per hour or one dollar per basket.

Winston explained in Spanish to Amilcar that both he and his son had only been able to pick three or four baskets in their recent workplace. Three days was simply insufficient time to learn the skill and speed of coffee picking, and so they got told to leave. They had walked for days to get to *La Hacienda Sueño en el Cielo*. They were confronted by hostile guards who wanted to turn them away before they even got through the gates. They were only saved by Amilcar's timely arrival.

Amilcar asked Curtis where his wife and the rest of his children were living. It was inconceivable in the Catholic Latin American culture to only have one son, although Amilcar himself was the exception personified. As an only child, he was the object of stigma. Especially as he was not outwardly strong and considered a failure by his father, that bully of a man.

As Amilcar asked about the family, Curtis, and Arturo both looked up. The boy then glanced back at the ground. It was the first time Amilcar saw Arturo's pupils, which seemed to dilate before dying again.

Curtis said, "We have no family anymore, except for each other. In the recent mudslide in Nicaragua, we lost my wife, Arturo's mother, and our three girls. They were swallowed up before our eyes as our house collapsed and were carried down that river of black hell. As the only two men in our family, we were unable to save them. We were coming back from cutting wood, and we saw the nightmare unfold. The rains at the beginning of the season were sudden and torrential. We heard them scream as we saw their bodies engulfed, and they were sucked under into the thick mud, which took everything in its wake. Nobody was saved. We failed them. May God keep them in his eternal peace."

Curtis bowed his head.

Sitting across the table from Amilcar, both father and son looked like ghosts.

They were mere shadows of humans, thought Amilcar. So frail and small. Desperate and sad.

Amilcar felt sick. He lived in the lap of luxury. He may not have his health, and he did not have a family, but Amilcar could only count his blessings compared to Winston and Arturo. These men had lost loved ones, all in one go. Mother Nature had relentlessly taken them. Without warning, discernible reason, or apology.

"How could Nature be referred to as Mother?" Amilcar once asked me. "Father Nature maybe would be more appropriate. At least in times of cruelty, nature should change gender."

I remember feeling horrified when he told me that. My own parents were caring and loving. Different in their individual ways, yet the same in terms of unconditional and expressive love. Not everyone was that blessed, I realised. Amilcar's father was a sadistic bully, greedy, opportunistic, relentless and, in a word, evil. As for his mother, she had been Amilcar's everything. He had loved her deeply, but she had passed.

Amilcar offered Curtis and Arturo jobs, starting the next day. He advised them they could live in The House on the Bluff. Amilcar explained that the house was a long way up but that Winston and Arturo could live there rent-free if they were up to scaling the steps. Amilcar pointed from their spot in the lobby to their new home across the hills of green. It stood majestically against the setting sun, illuminated by a halo of gold.

Winston broke down and wept. Then he kissed Amilcar's hand. Arturo did not respond. He was still frozen by recent events, buried alive in grief.

By the time Curtis and Arturo arrived at their new home, the place was spotless and stocked with food. Clothes had been placed in the cupboard, laundered and clean, straight from *El Comandante*'s wardrobe and from Amilcar's previous closet.

Winston and Arturo worked on the coffee plantation, taking their time to learn the ropes. Amilcar enjoyed having them around. He could see that Winston really embraced the job. He was always trying to improve the coffee, strengthen the shrubs, and condition the soil. Arturo spent most of his time with his nose in books about animals and plants. Amilcar could see the healing in the boy as he engaged with nature. Every day after picking coffee cherries, Arturo explored the rainforest beyond the estate.

One day Amilcar spoke to Winston and asked whether it would be okay for Arturo to spend part of his time mapping the animals and plants on and around the estate. Amilcar said he had wanted to have the logging of species done for some time and would pay Arturo to document his findings. Winston knew Amilcar had spotted his son's passion and was grateful to Amilcar. They had developed a close bond. Amilcar gave Arturo a pair of high-quality binoculars, as well as writing pads, pens, a camera, and a satchel, to keep his work in as he roamed around the estate.

El Comandante came to *La Hacienda* some months after Winston and Arturo had started work. Arturo was in the rainforest tracking animals. Curtis Senior was called to present himself to *El Comandante*. There was no need for it, as the plantation was starting to show signs of progress under Winston's care. Still, Amilcar's father took pleasure in abusing people and putting them down. When *El Comandante* had finally finished his tirade and insults, Amilcar found Winston in a corner. He looked once more like the shadow of a man he had seen when the two men first met arrived at *La Hacienda*.

Amilcar's heart bled for him.

Both Winston and Arturo were now like true family to Amilcar. His father never was. Amilcar vowed he would end the endless torture Winston and Arturo had endured. Amilcar swore he would put a lid on his own relentless suffering at the hands of his father, too.

Within days Amilcar booked a trip to Switzerland, asking Winston and Arturo to take care of the estate in his absence, with the help of Theo, if needed.

It was not long after Amilcar's departure that *El Comandante* was reported missing. Years later, his body was found sealed in a Mayan grave, which *El Comandante* had once pillaged himself.

Karma, Amilcar simply said to anyone who asked.

Amilcar's first 'clean-up' had been accomplished on his journey to creating a better world. Starting at home.

Amilcar knew he did not have a long life ahead of him. However, he intended to make a positive difference while on earth and set up a structure where he could continue what he'd started once he was gone.

With his father out of the way, Amilcar put his mind to developing the *Loving Little Lids Social Enterprise*. An organisation aimed to help people and the planet, using the lids of cans and other bottle tops to make exclusive designer bags, curtains, artwork, and fabric from waste materials. Amilcar's friends, Wai and Usnavy, Nab for short, started working with Amilcar back in 2002.

Amilcar's mission was to provide a means of support to those less fortunate to survive and thrive.

The House on the Bluff was reached by climbing the one hundred and two steps. A small rickety lift chugged into action at the press of a button the size and colour of a ripe tomato. This contraption was only used for luggage or bags of groceries. Unsafe for humans, yet helpful in elevating supplies to the house, the lift had a one-square meter metal surface, allowing for one large suitcase or a few bags. It reminded me of the cogwheel train that used to take us up the mountain from the Rhône Valley during our time at school in Switzerland. Here we had met up recently after thirty years.

Within mere months of the hospitality school Grand Reunion, I had ended up in Costa Rica. On the top of yet another mountain, in a different continent altogether.

The grizzly silver jagged light dazzled in the dark black sky, sending waves of shock through the atmosphere. The deep voice of thunder followed, almost immediately, after the flash had lit up the world, as the gods collided in the pitch dark heavens. Angry skies were particularly prevalent during the green season, from late April to early December. Storms and power cuts were near-daily events. *Casa Curtis* regularly got hit by lightning, and the electricity often failed.

On sunnier days, the elevated and west facing position of *Casa Curtis* allowed for breath-taking views over the Pacific Ocean. At sunset, the perfect golden sun sank like a glowing ball into the vast expanse of water, painting the sky in purples and pinks. Sometimes bold and pronounced, like an artistic, abstract painting. Other times, watered down and diluted like impressionist scribbles across a canvas of sky.

During the morning, the sun rose behind the house through Curtis' east-facing bedroom window. When Curtis used to stand on the balcony, he would look back over the plantation that he considered home, in a place he had grown to love. Both *La Hacienda* and The House on the Bluff had become his sanctuaries.

In addition to finding a home, Winston Curtis felt he had gained a son in Amilcar. Arturo, too, had gained an older brother, who looked out for him and had only his very best interests at heart. Their bond was profound and a blessing to both. And Amilcar, as he told me, got to know what it was like to have a person who loved him like a father.

When Arturo was found dead, Amilcar built a chapel on the grounds of La Hacienda to allow for Winston and himself to pay their respects and for Arturo to rest in peace at home.

Curtis Coffee, as the locals started to call him, continued to develop the plantation and lead an ever-growing team of workers. Some came to *La Hacienda* as skilled labourers. They heard that people who worked there would receive a fair wage and would be treated with respect. Word got out, and coffee pickers from other plantations sought employment in this good place. Those who were inexperienced pickers, just like Winston and

Arturo had been, would be given a chance to gain the skill of harvesting coffee cherries without fearing the loss of their jobs.

Winston groomed a second in command, Merlin, who appeared to be both meticulous and reliable. Merlin had been convicted of murder, but Winston was quite convinced that Merlin had been used as a scapegoat, just like so many others he knew. Curtis wanted to give Merlin a chance, just like Amilcar had given to him.

After listening to Curtis' plea, Amilcar agreed without hesitation for Merlin to join the growing Coffee Family.

A few months later, Winston died.

Curtis went to sleep in his home and never woke up. He died from natural causes, the doctor said.

Winston was buried next to his son in the particular spot, from where you could see the sun sink into the sea. Every day.

Forever. Or until the sun no longer sets in the west.

Maddie's Arrival

"What time is Maddie coming?" I asked Theo.

There were many unresolved questions around Bash. He had been picked up by Interpol and was involved in the illegal art trade in the desert. After our bizarre adventure in Southern Spain, Theo told Maddie she needed to come to Costa Rica and regroup.

Theo said that he would communicate with Bing, who was still in Morocco. Theo and Bing would fix the Seven Star Glamp Camp there, which served as a meeting post for illegal art traders. In addition, Theo aimed to try and sort out what could be done about Bash's predicament.

Maddie was delighted at the thought of flying to Costa Rica. She and Theo had been an item since way back, from our hospitality course days in Switzerland, not that I knew it at that time.

Since the recent Grand Reunion, the electricity between them was entirely back on.

Maddie was now making her way over the Atlantic. Theo had invited her. And Maddie had said yes. Perhaps she was answering an unspoken question to more than just simply a *Costa Rican rendezvous*. We would find out.

"I am so glad Mad Maddie is coming over to join us. But what happened to Bing?"

"I told Bing to stop all reservations and ensure that the coast is clear to wrap up the *Al-Trab*. The mission is to ensure the camp disappears. Since the big dealers came recently, they will not return within the next month. That is our window to move. It will happen in the next weeks, and I want Maddie here. Away from any possible calamities and repercussions that may pop out of nowhere, as the desert tam-tam blows un-whispered plans across the Moroccan sands. If word gets out that we are rolling up every inch of the camp, then we will have big challenges on our hands. Best to disappear overnight, without a trace. Bing's right-hand man and head honcho in the local tribal network proved himself trustworthy. He will support Bing and me to complete *Operation Blow Over* or 'O.B.O.' on the ground. All the gear and equipment will be taken to Spain and kept in storage, until the time that we open our own *Glamp Camp* in a place where we control the movements and operate on our own terms, based on our own interests and ethics."

"Wow. You and Bing have not wasted any time," I said. "As you mentioned, I guess you needed to move fast. As for your reference to ethics, were you going to become pure as the driven snow?"

As I pulled my little Mayan emerald-green amulet out from between my breasts, I kissed him demonstratively while smiling teasingly at Theo. "I was sure your way of getting me my little man was controversial, but you are my darling brother from another mother. I put my trust in you to do whatever is needed."

"Ethics are not principles, Viv. Ethics are about doing the right thing even if the circumstances are tricky. Or doing the best thing you can to bring joy, relief, new opportunities, or fix things that need dealing with. It all goes together. Let us not be judgemental about good or too analytical about bending some rules as needed."

"You are my Robin Hood Hero, Theo. You have a good heart. You do good even though at times the used method may be slightly dodgy."

I went over to Theo to give him a hug, but I leapt back and jumped on one of the chairs, "What the hell. Where did he come from?"

Theo turned to see who or what I was looking at, "He is she," he simply replied and started to stack the plates in the sink.

"Is it the same one as when Hélène, Annie and I came to see you and Amilcar twenty five years ago?"

"This is *Nana*, number three. They only live for around ten to twenty years. But they are all called Nana, so I don't make mistakes. I would hate to insult the crazy creature."

"How do you know that she is a girl?" I asked. "They all look the same to me."

"Female iguanas normally have longer, slimmer bodies than males. They also have smaller heads and do not have bumps on top of them. Plus, Nana laid eggs, so that is a bit of a dead giveaway," Theo laughed.

When I looked back to where I had spotted the pre-historic looking reptile, Nana had disappeared without a trace.

Just like the camp would do, I hoped.

"I have been thinking about what business we can run and

was thinking about fractionalising the coffee crop."

"Fractionalisation?" Theo asked. "Isn't that a real estate thing, a bit like timeshare?"

"The principle is derived from real estate, though you could apply the idea to almost anything that people wish for. It makes me think about how you could share homes, art, clothes, handbags, cars and even horses. It has become a relevant thought related to coffee- particularly the crop we have here at *La Hacienda*. The idea is, rather than timeshare, to *Coffee Crop Share*. By appealing to those who want to have their own homegrown coffee but don't want to run a plantation. We will be mostly dealing with HNWI, high net worth individuals."

My thoughts travelled back to General Salim, with his massive ego, explosive character, and deep pockets. It had been a long time since anyone had pulled my heartstrings like the General used to do. I was unexpectedly and strangely stirred by the memory of one of the only two men who had captured my soul and my imagination during my life so far.

I had said goodbye to Salim in my mind, though just like a dormant volcano, I knew that one day the bubbling lava may stir and erupt again.

I had done what was impossibly hard for me. I had kept my distance after we reconnected. After all the seemingly endless weeks of silence and pain and not knowing what had happened to him. Whether he was dead or alive.

The other man I loved, the Captain of my heart, was dead. Literally, James passed away some years ago, and there was no danger of reliving more than memories.

As for Salim, I was half a world away from him, though if I let myself go I could still imagine his heat against my skin, his warm breath on my neck. His tribal dark eyes flashed before me once more. That charming, charismatic smile made my stomach tumble.

How was that possible? A figment of my imagination, igniting my heart and awakening my loins? Be careful, I thought to myself.

Theo interrupted my musings, "Viv, the fractionalisation idea is an excellent one. How about you explain a bit more about the concept when Maddie arrives to allow us all to engage our minds and plan our way to a bright future. I need to leave for San José within the next ten minutes or so. Maddie's flight is due early morning, and I will go and crash with Wai in the capital and catch up with him. Then I'll pick Maddie up after a few hours' sleep. We should be back here around noon tomorrow, at the latest. If you need anything, Nab, whom you know now, is on standby to take you anywhere or do anything. And if you feel like a swim at *Si Como No*, then you know you are always welcome to crash the night there, too. In any case, looking forward to being with my two favourite girls in the world by tomorrow."

"I think it's best to stay here with Merlin. I don't yet know the first thing about coffee, and perhaps I could spend some time with him today to ask him about the plantation, the harvest and what is needed. As far as understanding the coffee business, I am about as useless as a chocolate coffee pot. It is a great blessing that Winston took on Merlin as his second in command sometime before he passed. Merlin is key to our continuity and pivotal to propelling the business forward. You pick up Maddie, and I will quiz Merlin, then we can map and mastermind and write our story forward."

"You are poetry in motion, Viv. You always make my heart smile. Now let me get my act together and pick up Wonder Woman Number Two and bring her home."

With that, Theo touched the bridge of my nose with his index finger and planted a kiss on the top of my hair, "*Ciao, Chica*," he smiled and went off to pick up our much loved Maddie.

I was happy to be left alone with my thoughts. And my laptop.

Indeed, a little message to Salim, miles away in the Middle Eastern sands, would just constitute a friendly 'hello'...

Plunging In

"Bussi! Where are you?" I heard Maddie say as she walked into *La Hacienda*'s entrance.

She let go of Theo's hand and skipped towards me, like a young gazelle in love. She was all smiles as she hugged me.

"Can't believe we are both here. In the very navel of the Americas. Where Columbus landed all these years ago. I am so happy to see you, Viv!"

"And me, you!"

Maddie took a step back and looked at me. "Enough of those tears, darling Viv. We cried in Switzerland when we hadn't seen each other for two decades, but the last time I saw you was less than a month ago. You are a funny old moo."

"You look blurred to me, and I don't even have jetlag like you."

"Once you recover from the bliss of seeing me and stop blabbing, your vision will go back to seeing reality. The three of us are now in one place. You two are my favourite people in the world, along with my darling girls. And as for jetlag, I don't think I have any. This hero here booked me a flatbed on the flight over from Madrid. After a few glasses of bubbles, I simply slept all the way across the Atlantic, direct into San José. I am ready for the day, darling Viv. Totally up for our adventure."

Theo popped out to bring Maddie's luggage inside. He returned ten minutes later, with three colourfully painted ceramic mugs filled with hot, strong coffee.

We settled around the exquisite table made from an old church door with flora and fauna carved into the tropical wood and covered by glass. The table had twelve chairs around it, all in different styles. Eclectic and colourful and most of all comfortable.

"A cup of Amilcar's coffee before you freshen up Maddie? Which one do you fancy?"

"I love a man who asks which cup I would like."

Maddie picked her preferred mug from the tray and cupped it, smelling the coffee, closing her eyes as she inhaled the aroma.

A deep sound came from her inner soul. One that could only spell the sense of satisfaction that knows no words.

"I think I just arrived home," Maddie said.

With her eyes still shut, she took a sip, savouring the flavour and smiled. She took another and swallowed the luxurious liquid.

"So, this was what dreams are made of," she said. "I hope I never wake up from this paradise."

She opened her eyes and looked at Theo and me.

"Thank you for bringing me here," she said to us both. "I can feel there is much more to this beautiful country than hills of green."

Moments later, *La Hacienda's* lobby was filled with Louis Armstrong's beautiful song; *'I see trees of green, red roses, too, I see them bloom for me and you.'*

"You smoothy, Theo," I laughed.

Having switched on the surround system from his phone, Theo now stood behind Maddie. His mug of coffee in his right hand was clasped close to his chest. In contrast, his other hand rested gently on Maddie's shoulder.

"Happy to have my *chicas* in *La Casa*," he smiled. "I am thinking about where you would like to stay. *La Hacienda* naturally has enough rooms, but I think you girls may enjoy having a bit of your own space. If you like, you can move between here and *Casa Curtis*."

"*Casa Curtis*?" Maddie asked him.

I pushed my chair back from the table, "Bring your mug and come on over to see *The House*."

Maddie walked over to join me. From the wall-less lobby, she could see the expanse of *La Hacienda* in all its splendour for the first time.

"Talk about trees of green! And red berries, too. I see them brew, for me and you, and I think to myself, what a wonderful world. My Lord, guys," Maddie said as she turned towards Theo and me, "This is *Paradise Lost*. Or should I say *Paradise Found*? I saw my fair share of coffee plantations in Ethiopia, but this is truly tremendous. All this is the coffee estate that Amilcar entrusted you to look after?"

"Every inch of it, until where it spills over into the Pacific Ocean," Theo said.

"See that hill in the far distance with the building on it? That is *Casa Curtis,* or the House on the Bluff, as I call it. Theo sent in the cleaners, so you and I can spend time at *Casa Chicas,* the Girls' Zone."

"You are a *'caballero de verdad'*, Theo," I said.

Maddie smiled at Theo. "A true gentleman, albeit in a bit of a Robin Hood Rogue style. And that is what I so sincerely love about you. Generous and kind, naughty and nice. And full of surprises."

"On that note, I have a surprise for you," Theo said. "Rather than have a shower Mads, are you up for some effervescence in nature?"

"I have no idea what that means, but you make it sound tempting, so I won't ask, and I shall simply say yes."

"How about you, Viv. Up for some bubbles?"

I knew what Theo meant; I had been there before. Twenty-five years ago, and always I recalled the magic of nature.

"Is it still the same?" I asked.

"Totally unchanged," Theo said. "I have towels. Why don't you slip into your cossies up here, and then we'll drive down?"

Maddie opened the zipper of her suitcase, rummaged around, and pulled out an emerald-green bikini. I was already wearing mine, as I had had an early dip in the pool.

In fact, it was the same pool that Hélène, Annie and I swam in twenty-five years ago when we came here on our Pussy Posse trip. That was the day when Theo gave me my magical jade man amulet, which was a sign to Amilcar that Theo trusted me. I was chosen by Theo. I never knew that until Amilcar told me in that letter that I was given after he had passed away.

Amilcar supported Theo's choice for me to partner with him to support the estate and the business after Amilcar no longer could.

The car was waiting outside, and Merlin, the plantation manager, whom I did not know very well at that time, greeted us. He placed a wicker basket in the back of the 4x4 beast of a car that looked like it could devour any terrain, one red fertile soil chomp at a time. After a ten minute drive, we arrived and spilt out of the car.

"Come on, Mads," I said, having to raise my voice for her to hear me. "Once we are in, we will swim slightly downstream, and the sound of the waterfall will be less."

Maddie raised her big brown Liza Minelli eyes to the skies above, opening her arms as if she was embracing the sun, the flowers, and the birds.

We were in a magical world.

The serenity of the place was interrupted as Theo flew past us and splash bombed into the pristine waterfall pool.

"Come on, missies! Get yourselves in here!"

With that, Maddie and I stripped down to our swimming costumes and jumped in. The water was cold. The air was full of oxygen and birdsong. The dramatic outpour of water from the cliff above pounded down, battering the rocks. In its liquid form, the water appeared to have the upper hand over the solid rock, which was perpetually pummelled and shaped by the force crashing down from an inexhaustive source.

The waterfall was living proof of abundance and infinity. A sentiment that resonated with me still.

I came up for air as the sun shone down on us and exhaled. I felt the surge of nature's energy around. Then I put my head under the water and breathed in the sound of silence. My body recalled the very same magical experience, etched in my brain, from all those years ago.

Back above the water, Theo caught my eye, and gestured me to follow. Maddie was not far behind him as they half waded, half swam, downstream in the path of the meandering riverbed. After some time, the water rush calmed and the sounds of the cascading water lessened. Maddie looked at me as I caught up with her and Theo, who was just a few meters ahead of her. Then, she turned around and panicked.

"Where is Theo?" she yelped.

She sounded like a dog with its paw trapped. She looked around, checking the river's edge and the expanse of water as it gently trickled downstream, dancing and splashing on its way.

I caught up to Maddie.

"Viv! I can't see Theo. He was right here!" Her voice was strangled.

"Don't worry, Mads. Theo is totally okay."

"But where is he? He was here, and now he's gone! He might be trapped. It's been like a minute or two now. No one could stay underwater that long. This is not funny, Viv. Maybe he is pranking us, and it all went wrong."

"Mads. He is fine. I know where he is."

"What are you talking about?" Maddie's eyes were wide with fright. "Don't mess with my head, Viv. This is Theo. I know he always saves us, but maybe this time he is the one in danger."

"Calm down and come over here."

I swam up to a rock in the stream that appeared flat with the water's surface.

"Take a deep breath and follow me." I held my hand out to Maddie. I looked at her. Her eyes were wide, but she nodded.

I then took a deep breath and submerged. I checked behind me and saw that Maddie had followed. Her large eyes wildly searching under the water until she came up for air.

"Hi there, ladies. Welcome to the 'inner circle secret cave'. A little hideout for some peace or a hideaway in case of danger. Remember that." Theo's words sounded soothing, yet ominous.

But for now, it was a blissful and beautiful hidden bubble of air caused by a rock formation that couldn't be seen from the water edge. A naturally formed sanctuary had been created under the water level. You had to go down under first to come up into the hidden space.

Maddie swam up to Theo and clung to him. "Please don't let me feel that way ever again. I thought I had lost you. My heart felt sick."

"Sorry, Mads. I should have thought twice. Forget the fright and check this out."

He put his head under the surface, enclosing the water in his mouth and billowed his cheeks like a frog. When he came back up, he teasingly squirted some onto Maddie's face and swallowed the rest.

"Triple grade A drinking water. You will not find anything purer. This is the source of life. And all who drink from it will feel Mother Nature's true energy."

"Positively biblical, Saint Theo," I laughed.

Then Maddie and I ducked under and drank from the source. Now submerged in the water and ingesting it, I could feel my soul awaken.

The prosecco feeling of bubbles once again coursed through my veins as my body and mind remembered. I could feel a surge of goodness as it ran through me.

Cristina

Following our swim in the waterfull and our rendezvous in the secret underwater cave, we made it back to where Merlin dropped us off a few hours earlier. Merlin was nowhere to be seen, though there was a small fire, a rug on the cut grass and comfortable cushions. The picnic basket was closed, but the plates and glasses had been set out on the top of an upturned coffee harvesting basket with a slab of wood on top. Though the impromptu table wasn't practical, it looked a treat. Over the small smouldering fire, a grill with six doubly stacked parcels wrapped in banana leaves, steaming away.

"What are those perfect little pouches," Maddie asked. "They smell amazing."

"*Tamales*. The outside is a banana leaf, which you don't eat; it's just used as a wrapper to cook the food. Inside are veggies, pork, and a few other bits and bobs. Tied together with string," Theo explained.

"They look delish," I said. "I could murder a few of those tempting tasty *tamales*. I am beyond peckish."

"Here you go, Viv, take these for starters and add some rice if you like," Theo said and presented me with a covered dish, kept hot by aluminium foil, with a cloth around it. He passed me a spoon. "Dig in Viv."

"Wow, did Merlin prepare all this?" I asked.

"No, Cristina did. She helps around the house sometimes. She needs the work, and she does a good job. Here is the *Salsa Lizano*, which I know you love Viv."

"Why don't they sell that internationally?" I asked. "The flavours are so good. It's a secret recipe Theo, isn't it?"

"In 1920 the big boys at Unilever bought the rights to the brand, and the whole sexy story lost its charm," Theo told us, as he opened the first of two thermoses.

"How much caffeine are you expecting us to drink, Theo?" I laughed. "Two steaming steel bullets of coffee?"

"No, *chicita*. You have a choice of chilled *Caipariña* or frozen Margarita. These babies heat up, as well as chill. A bit like my good self," Theo joked.

"You are the god of bliss, Theo," Maddie said. "I am not sure I can go back to reality."

"Then, stay in paradise, Maddie. You are my guest if you would like to be. Forever, if you so choose."

"Aw, you charming thing," Maddie said, but I could tell she was touched by Theo's words.

"Forever is a long stretch, and I hope all will be brilliant. For now, let's toast tomorrow. We need to put our heads together and make some sort of sense of business. We'll never get to heaven in a rocking chair, as the Lordie won't have no lazybones there. As my grandfather used to sing," I said.

CRISTINA

"Agreed, we need to get our skates on," Theo said. "Time is running, and opportunity is knocking. How about I drop you girls at *Casa Curtis*, so you can install yourselves there. Cristina has cleaned the house and stocked the fridge. The place hasn't been used since Curtis passed away. Merlin picked Cristina up and took her over to yours to open the house. Hope all is good, and you will be comfortable."

With the second mention of Cristina, I saw Maddie's expression change. She seemed to be getting rather fond of Theo, perhaps even a little territorial.

Theo told me about a *'Tina'* many moons ago. I recalled I'd heard that name before. She was a native Costa Rican who lived in the jungle. He used to enjoy more than just a canoe ride in the hollowed-out tree with her. It was the time when Theo was the young Blond Chief of Entertainment. He catered for illegal traders of jade as they passed through the rainforest, seeking some illicit fun with women and drugs. Theo, in essence, was the pimp who looked like an angel with his blond locks and bright blue eyes.

I would never have credited Theo with sourcing both angel dust and women to satisfy traders' lust.

Theo had had a colourful past. Maddie, too, had done her fair share of living, especially with her caramel-eyed man in Ethiopia, who was a model and the father of her two girls. Maddie had kids. Manu was the father. He had been beautiful, though later, he'd become monstrously abusive. Eventually, Maddie escaped from Ethiopia and raised her teenage girls in Germany.

I knew less about Theo's past apart from the fact that his dad, too, like Amilcar's, had been an illegal artefact trader.

And as I said, Theo was naughty, though I did not think of him as 'A Baddy'.

Our friendship went back for thirty years now. Theo was solid.

Surely.

Jigged Journey

After a great lunch, having enjoyed delicious food and booze, we gathered up our things. Theo called for Merlin, who appeared, and we put our stuff into the car.

We drove back up through the coffee plantation to pick up our gear at *La Hacienda*. We said goodbye to Theo as he had a call planned with Bing.

"I have an 'O.B.O.' call. I will deal with Bing and make sure 'Operation Blow Over' is on track. You girls go and chill. I am pretty sure the jetlag will catch up with you, Maddie. So, let's meet tomorrow for breakfast at *Si Como No*, which borders our land and is only a ten to fifteen-minute walk or so for you guys, albeit uphill. I can send Merlin to pick you up, or if you prefer a morning stroll, it's up to you. I will give you a mobile phone that works, and there is also a landline at the house so we can stay in touch. As they have a great pool at *Si Como No*, I suggest you bring your swimming gear. Wai may join us, too. He is up from San José, and it would be good to have him included in a think-tank session.

I told Maddie about Wai and his involvement in the Loving

Little Lids Foundation.

You know him already, Viv, so if agreed, let's kick off the day over a Gallo Pinto breakfast at Viv's favourite eco-resort."

Merlin put our bags into the same 4x4, which we had taken across the terrain earlier. We set off for The House on the Bluff. Merlin seemed agitated somehow. His demeanour had been pleasant until now, but I sensed a change in him. I couldn't put my finger on it. Anyone could perceive that the air had turned heavy very unexpectedly. Though I speak Spanish well enough, I decided not to make conversation and leave him be.

Something told me not to ask.

Merlin took us down a route leading beyond the bottom of the hill, where we had the ashes ceremony for Amilcar. I looked up to see the little chapel, bathed in the sunshine.

I sent a brief hi to Amilcar in heaven.

The car snaked in the shadow of the taller trees. Their roots caused bumps in the road as they crossed underneath the track in pursuit of nutrition. Additionally, the back route was full of potholes, and the shrubs audibly scratched the car's sides. Merlin did not appear concerned as nature's needles teased the lacquer off the 4x4's perfect coat. He forced a way through the overgrown path.

Merlin appeared to be a man on a mission.

Eventually, we left the estate through a rickety, rusty-looking gate that hung off its hinges, like a drunk clasping onto a solid fixture before inevitably collapsing and falling to the ground. It was just a matter of time.

The exit contrasted starkly with the primary and grand entrance to *La Hacienda*. That one was sculpted out of fancy iron, depicting birds and monkeys. It reminded me of the magical Queen Elizabeth Gate that gives access to Hyde Park from Park Lane in London. Apparently, Giuseppe Lund, the designer, intended it to be feminine and fresh with the charm of an English Garden. I recalled the walks that Captain James, Mike, and I had in Hyde Park, after our Bloody Mary and Eggs Benedict Breakfast, when we met up in London. We could have crossed into Hyde Park from The Lanesborough Hotel, where we traditionally brunched when the boys were in town. Yet, we would always enter Hyde Park through the Cinderella Gates, as I called them. They indulged me. Each held my hand as we strolled, across from The Lanesborough, through the magical gates into Hyde Park.

I recalled that past and precious era.

I remembered those masculine men with a smile in my heart. They had certainly treated me like a Lady. Captain James and General Salim were the only two men who I had ever truly loved. Nobody had truly sparked my attention or ignited my fire, apart from Bash recently, though was a harmless flirtation. Nothing much.

And Bash had disappeared, into the hands of Interpol. On the same day I had boarded the flight to Costa Rica.

The main entrance to *La Hacienda en el Cielo* looked like The Gates of Heaven. They blended the masculine and the feminine, the natural and the magical, and the divine. The main entrance exuded grace. The backdoor, which Merlin had just hurtled us through, spelt doom.

Why had we gone this way?

I tried to ignore the unsavoury feeling. I didn't ask and attempted to tell myself that this was simply a shorter route to the coast and to *Casa Curtis*. Opening the front gate would require the guard; maybe he was on a late lunch. Whatever the reason, at least we were on our way. We would be at the house before sunset. Maddie would love it; I was sure of that.

Merlin continued the journey across the river, which, to be fair, was not as high as in the thick of the green season, though it still seemed a bit deep to be wading through. I felt he was taking a bit of a risk, but he probably knew what he was doing. I had only ever arrived and left *La Hacienda* over a road and a bridge and, as I said previously, through the main gate.

Twenty-five years ago, we had crossed the old railway bridge. As Hélène, Annie, and I trundled over the steel construction in our rental car at the time, the rickety 4x4 made a noise like a train as we drove over the river above the old railway track. This time the same bridge was fully tarmacked. The experience was safer though it has now lost its railroad charm. I particularly remembered the last bridge before getting to *La Hacienda* territory.

It was known as 'The Bridge of Death' or the 'Oh My God Bridge'.

The narrow bridge was located on the road from Jaco, where Theo lived and went to Quepos on the central Pacific Coast. You couldn't imagine it as safe for a bicycle, yet thirty-ton lorries made the crossing. The loose slats of the roadway clanked loudly while the bridge shook under the weight of the vehicles. It was a terrifying yet thrilling experience. As you looked down into the river below, you could see a discarded train carriage and a train cog. It felt like adventure was everywhere, the first time we crossed that bridge. Nicknamed the *Puente Paquita*, it was built in the 1930s by the Bananera Company. The train moved the bananas to the port of Quepos.

Quepos. That was where we hung out. At *Arco Iris,* meaning rainbow, which was the local disco.

I recalled the fresh fish, hauled out of the ocean for that day's menu at the Gran Escape. The waiters were as cute as punch and could be found surfing on the beach before their shifts. I befriended and dated one of their team; he was a surfer by day and a bartender by night. He was beautiful and a very nice guy indeed. He came to stay with me in London. I remembered going to buy a few pieces of clothing in Harrods for him. The July sale was on. My *Tico Beau* did not have formal clothes with him. We were due to attend the baptism of my cousin's baby in the countryside. We went to buy my guy a shirt and some chinos. The dedicated assistant in the Men's department got very excited when he saw Eduardo. His testosterone levels surged as he looked at Eddie's firm, young and athletic body entering his domain. He had his measuring tape around his neck at the ready to take Ed's inside leg measurement. Eddie disappeared into the changing cubicle, then he beckoned me with only his face showing around the burgundy velvet cubicle curtain.

"Mi Amor," he called out to me.

I went to see what was going on. Eduardo was wearing jeans without underwear, and he was worried about having his inside leg measurement taken. I advised the extremely effeminate and overexcited shop assistant in Harrods that we would simply take the selected chinos and that the shirt in pink would be fine. The look on the face of the very attentive assistant spelt disappointment with a capital D. Eduardo the gorgeous individual, was relieved beyond *palabras.* I kept in touch with Eduardo, until he got married. I heard he opened his own car wash. When I heard Rose Royce's hit *Car Wash*, I always thought of Eduardo el Guapo, the most handsome and kind-hearted soul.

I hoped that I might see him again one day.

Merlin didn't say much. He received the occasional phone call, and his dark raspy voice cut conversations short, it seemed. I felt stressed in the big black beast of a car. Maddie had dozed off. The rhythm of the rocky road had put her to sleep, like a baby in a buggy on cobblestones. I was sleepy too after our swim and the delicious lunch. But I kept my wits about me. I had to stay alert. We couldn't afford for both of us to snooze. After twenty minutes of driving, I recognised the minor road with the Pacific gently lapping on each side. Golden sand stretched for a few meters on either side of the tarmacked track. Many of the beaches in the area had dark grey volcanic sand. However, *Bisantz Bay* was blessed with golden fringes that graced the tropical green trunk of the peninsula before it rose into a steep hill. The bluff was covered in trees and all types of tropical vegetation. The narrow road that traversed the brow between the twin beaches came to a sudden stop at the point where the cliff rose steeply like a fortress before it plunged into the ocean. The car couldn't go beyond that point. Maddie was still fast asleep. We had arrived at the foot of the Bluff where *Casa Curtis* was situated.

Merlin took the luggage, putting the two cases and one roll-up bag onto the luggage lift.

"*No para personas,*" he said. Not for people.

He then pressed the big red tomato-shaped button to send the luggage off to the top of the hill. The cogwheels chugged into motion, and the baggage stuttered unsteadily as it slowly and very noisily made its way up in between the trees and out of sight.

"*Vos tiene que caminar.*" You must walk.

He pointed at the steps leading up. I remembered the hundred and two steps. I knew I would have to get used to them again, just like when I first went there with Annie and Hélène. This time with Maddie. With the slamming of the boot, Maddie woke up and stumbled out of the car, trying to get her bearings. Merlin handed us two door keys on a key ring and reignited a stale cigarette stub he'd retrieved from the ashtray. Then, without bidding us farewell, Merlin turned the car around, leaving Maddie and me to our own devices.

"Charming chap. Not. What is that guy's problem? He seemed fine this morning. But now, you could cut the air with a knife; it's so tense."

"He seems very grumpy," Maddie agreed.

"Never mind about Merlin. Maybe he has magical qualities, but they were certainly not on display this afternoon. This morning he seemed okay when he took us to the waterfall. This afternoon, however, I was uncomfortable with him. Almost to the point that I felt like texting Theo. But Merlin would likely have been instantly sacked if I said anything. You know what Theo can be like. He is a sweetheart but also a hothead. I am sure Theo has let heads fly for less. Robin Hood with Latino blood, even though he is essentially a Dutchie. Quite a concoction. Anyhow, Mads, we need to brace ourselves for those steps that meander up to the top of the hill. The luggage should be up there when we reach the summit. Merlin put it on the little cogwheel platform and said it was not fit for people."

"Okay, Bussi, let's do this," Maddie said. "One step at a time, as they say. We will get to the top in the end. We always do. We met on a mountain, you, and I in the Swiss Alps. We were next-door neighbours then and will be housemates now on top of another high place. We always scale heights. Onwards."

We made a few stops on our way up. Maddie was happy when a pair of parrots flew overhead, and she saw a sloth clutching a tree. Doing nothing, or so it seemed.

"Oh God, I feel like that creature," Maddie said. "What is it?"

"It's a sloth, Mads. It eats leaves, and it takes about a month for its food to digest."

"I know the feeling Viv. I am about to balloon out of my pants, but that may just be the perfect steak I had in business class, then the *tamales* and rice I ate at lunchtime. But why is it hanging upside down?"

"They do that because sloths can't run. So, they hide. If a predator is after them, they are less visible. They spend so much time upside down that their fur lies the opposite way to other furry animals, growing upward from their paws and up their bodies."

"Honestly, Viv, I feel my fur is upside down too right now. I really thought I would not get jetlag, but I am exhausted, if the truth be told. Think I need a siesta, then I will be right as rain."

"Almost there, bushed Bush Baby. Just under halfway there. Another sixty-nine steps or so."

It must have taken us at least ten minutes to climb the steps up to the house. The luggage was waiting for us on the cogwheel platform. I took one of the two keys Merlin had given us. One for me and the other for Maddie, I presumed. I tried to open the door, but it wouldn't open. Then I remembered that locks on doors, gates and pretty much anywhere in Costa Rica turned backwards. The lock responded.

The house was simple in design. Large windows made you

feel like you were part of the habitat. The beams and floors were all made of tropical wood that shone as if someone had really buffed it. Perhaps this was Cristina's work.

The view still took my breath away. Over the treetops to the ocean beyond, I felt I could sense infinity.

Now was not the time to take in the splendour and remember the past. Maddie was my priority of the moment. She was cooked and needed some care.

"Fancy the hammock on the veranda, Mads?" I asked.

"Oh, Viv. What a view. I am on top of the world."

"You are, my lovely. Now come over here and have a little swing in the hammock."

Maddie centred her bum in the middle of the netting as if she were perching on a chair. As she tried to lie down, she almost fell out as she hadn't yet figured out the knack of hammocking safely.

"Easy distribution and no sudden movements, Mads. Like getting into a canoe. Once you are in, you are safe as houses."

A colourful butterfly landed on the rocking chair next to the hammock.

"Don't worry about the butterflies, bugs and bees. They live here and really it is best to go with it. Let me get you a rug, so you can be snug as a bug in a rug."

I gently pushed the hammock to start its soothing back and forth motion. Maddie smiled lazily. Her eyes half-closed; she was going into a trance.

I went off to find a light throw to cover her. When I returned, Maddie was fast asleep, like a babe in her cradle, gently swaying in the tropical breeze.

Rude Awakening

Maddie slept in the hammock as I snoozed in the rocking chair on the veranda, until dark descended, and I came inside. There were three rooms. One of them was locked. The other two rooms were fully prepared with fluffy towels and clean sheets. I slept in Curtis Coffee's old room that faced east and overlooked the plantation inland.

I realised you could signal from *La Hacienda* to *Casa Curtis* using a mirror and sunlight.

My mother had taught my brother Martin and me when we were small how to signal if you were in danger, whether by sight or through sound. I recalled she told us what an 'S.O.S.' signal was and explained that it means 'Save Our Souls'. With her knuckles, she hit the wooden table three times at equal intervals. Then she did the same but in quicker succession making the knocks sound shorter and followed with three longer ones like the first sounds she had made.

"Long-long-long, short-short-short, long-long-long," she said.

"Now you have a go," she encouraged us.

It took us a little while until we got the hang of it, and she asked us, "Now, how else do you think you could let someone know you are in danger?"

We went through a scenario as if you were underground, perhaps you could tap, or in a house, you could use the radiator's metal to carry the sound. We had fun clapping the S.O.S. code, hitting a pan with a stick and using a mirror to reflect the sun. We felt like little adventurers, ready to take on the world of danger. Little did I know back then that my mum's little lesson in life might come in conveniently one of these days.

At this moment, there was no sunlight and no immediate danger of any sort. For now, at least.

I woke Maddie up. Sleeping overnight in the hammock would make her feel wrecked the next day. It was something you needed to get used to, and then you might get a better rest than in a bed. She was not really in a fit state to understand what was going on. I showed her the bathroom and prepared her toothbrush. After she finished, I guided her to her room next to mine. She fell into bed and continued where she'd left off.

At around three in the morning, I woke up. It was raining, and lightning lit up the darkened room. I had left the shutters open and the window ajar. I closed them as the rain was blowing in, landing raindrops on my face as I lay in my bed positioned under the sill.

I then heard a piercing sound I could not place, followed by howling. The noise subsided, and I settled back down to sleep. Then I heard cries and more howling. My bed shook as the floor underneath me vibrated. I jumped out of bed, and switched on the light in the hallway between Maddie's and my room. I threw open the door, and there Maddie was rolled up in a ball like an embryo on the floor, trembling and shivering. The light from the hallway filtered down, gently glowing on her. She was in utter distress. I didn't know if she was still asleep or awake. I cautiously went over to her and knelt beside her.

"Maddie," I whispered.

She pulled her knees closer to her chest.

"Maddie, darling. It's me. Viv."

I took the throw she had taken into her room from outdoors and placed it round her, and gently stroked her arm and her hair. Maddie started sobbing. I kept talking to her, until she finally became conscious and sat up, slightly bewildered, and clearly frazzled.

"Mads, it's okay. Why don't we get you back on the bed?"

Maddie uncoiled herself and hung onto me for support, as she lugged herself onto the double bed. I tucked her under the cover, then I switched on the nightlight next to her bed. It was a gentle golden hue, which seemed to soothe her.

By now she was fully awake clutching her covers to her chest.

"Are you okay, babes?" I asked.

"I am sorry Viv, so sorry to put you through this."

"Shh, sweetie. All is okay. You are safe and all is okay. You must have woken up suddenly and not known where you are or something like that. All is okay now. All is totally alright."

At that time a major lightning flash lit up the room and killed the electricity. Moments later security lights came on as the back-up generator jumped into action.

"Well, blow me down Mads," I said. "It seems that the house has been upgraded. Twenty five years ago, the lights would simply have gone out. There was no back up system then."

Maddie seemed to be okay now and we were both wide awake.

"How about we check out what is in the fridge darling and fix ourselves a cup of something? We had lunch but nothing for dinner so maybe a midnight snack is in order."

"I am sorry Viv, for what happened," Maddie said again.

"I hope you will let me know what happened Mads. Are you up for that over a bite to eat?"

Maddie nodded slipping out of bed and covering herself with the throw as we went into the open plan living room. I brought in the rocking chair and installed her in it.

"Now let's see what we have here."

I opened the fridge which had fresh fruit, cheese, cold cuts, bread, and chocolate in it along with fresh pineapple juice, butter, and macadamia nuts. I opened the small freezer compartment, which was empty, apart from what looked like a black brick.

"What the hell is that?" I asked, lifting the rectangular shape out of the cold space.

It looked like compressed wood, like a briquet my parents sometimes used to light the fire with when the logs were wet. I held the brick up to Maddie.

"What the hell?"

"You don't know what that is?" Maddie smiled, from her spot in the living room.

"Smell it," she advised me.

I put the condensed block to my nose and inhaled.

"Oh Lord!"

"Yup. Exactly. But that is a pretty darn perfectly packaged piece of ganja. That may be just the ticket for me to open my appetite, as well as my heart to you. I used to have some every day in Ethiopia when I walked with the dogs around the rustic compound where we used to live. And I miss it. After decades of a daily dose, I have to say Viv that I am pleasantly delighted to be able to smoke a Dutchie in the presence of a Dutchie."

"Feel free, my dear. I am not into it, but it has been put there by someone for a reason. I presume on instruction of our *Tico Dutchie*, Theo."

I placed the cannabis on the work surface and noticed some roll-up papers that were still perfectly intact, as well as a pack of loose tobacco.

"Seems like he thought of it all."

Maddie slipped off the rocking chair and crumbled off some of the dark brown compressed weed. She expertly blended it with shag and rolled a perfect joint or that was how it looked to me. Then she struck one of the long matches in the box on the kitchen windowsill, inhaled deeply, blew out five perfect circles and moseyed on over back to the rocking chair. She looked like another person now. Chilled and happy. Relaxed and calm.

Thank goodness she's recovered from what seemed like a hellish nightmare.

I decided not to press her and to leave her to enjoy her funny smoke behind me, as I prepared some snacks from the bounty stacked in the fridge.

Maddie relaxed and opened to me about the recurring nightmares she had been experiencing ever since she had left Ethiopia. Manu her ex-husband had beaten her up in the past both physically and mentally.

The pain trapped inside her soul was now popping its head up even more clearly.

"I think the fact that I was received by you and Theo so amazingly, made me subconsciously let my guard down. And when I am not aware, the demons come. That is what had happened when you found me on the floor. They haunt me when I am sleeping. That is when they catch me. Normally, I manage to keep myself to myself. My girls are deep sleepers. But you found me. For that I am so sorry Viv."

"Bussi. Listen. Bad things take time to heal. It's a process. But good things are happening, and both Theo and I are by your side. Try and accept the oozing of the old. Much as it will taste like poison and feel like hell. Let us embrace it and work through it. Anytime you have a sinister thought or anything reach out. I will not crowd you out nor expect you to share if you don't want to or are not ready, but the sooner you heal the sooner you will be able to trust and love again. Properly. Without reservation. And I don't necessarily mean someone else. I mean yourself and life itself. That is what matters most. During our time in Costa Rica let's make sure that we have fun, do good and heal what is needed. Address what we can and deal with what we should. For the sake of tomorrow."

My words were muffled by a tremendous pounding on the corrugated iron roof.

Maddie's Liza Minelli eyes flew open. I smiled and signalled that all was well. Then I put my hands under my armpits and jumped around the living room like a monkey, while pointing to the roof; Explaining to Maddie that the creatures were migrating very noisily overhead on their set path. No *Casa Curtis* could stop them in their wake. Minutes later they would be pounding over the guest room *casitas* at *Si Como No* and no doubt leaving their guests in shock.

Just like Annie, Hélène and I had done during the *madrugada*, the onset of dawn, when we first stayed on the Central Pacific Coast all those years ago. We were so shocked when we heard them for the first time. The second time we felt like afficionados who were *in the know.*

"As the Howlers wake up, we should get some sleep darling Mads. I will text Theo that lunch is better than breakfast, or perhaps even sunset cocktails. There is no point in getting into a think tank with hazy brains. Or maybe we will leave it for the next day."

I messaged Theo who responded quickly:

'No worries, Viv. Take your time. We will be in touch later. I too was up all night, talking online with Bing. Things are moving but have not yet landed. Will talk to you and Maddie later. Hasta luego hermana. Get some rest and make sure Mad Maddie lands properly. I left her a little gift to make that happen. Check the freezer. Catch you later.'

I simply write back:
'XXX.'

Maddie and I crashed as the sun rose from the east over the hills of green and as the beaming rays of light poured into my bedroom.

Crate Ideas

Around ten o'clock I woke up to the aroma of fresh coffee. I slipped into a T-shirt and joggers and wandered into the living room where Maddie, clad in a sarong, was fixing a fresh brew.

"Good morning, my dear. Did you manage some shut-eye this morning?"

"I fell into a perfect sleep, Viv. I did have some colourful dreams, but they were about parrots and peacocks in paradise. It was heavenly."

"Happy to hear Buss. And thank you for what smells like a great cup of coffee."

Maddie handed me a mug. It had a brightly hand-painted sloth on it staring at me with his huge eyes wrapping his three-toed paw around the cup as if he was hugging it. Maddie's one had a monkey swinging from a tree by his tail as he looked out into the world.

"Funky mugs," Maddie said, as she looked for the name of the artist on the bottom. "It's signed *Mike Romero.*"

"Oh, how cool," I responded. "That was the artist who used

to live here when we came during my first trip to Costa Rica. He had a gallery at *Si Como No* as a visiting artist. Annie fell in love with a bust he sculpted from petrified wood. A resplendent male torso. Annie was so enchanted with it that she simply put the amount on her credit card, believing that anything she bought in Costa Rica would probably be of excellent value. It was only after she lugged the statue all the way back to London that she calculated the crazy amount in *colones* and worked out that her little purchase had set her back over two thousand dollars. She reminds me of it to this day. Annie has always been very organised in terms of what will happen after she dies and that includes leaving me that male torso in her will. For now, the sculpture sits across from the massive Buddha in her London living room."

I went to the cupboard and was delighted to find four more pieces that belonged to the same collection. Each animal was painted in the same way with their eyes staring right at you. One was a dolphin, the next a frog, one a jaguarundi, a wild cat native to the Americas, and the last one was a turtle with eyelashes that make him look dreamy.

"I love turtles," I said. "When I was in Costa Rica with the girls we were invited to an island where the turtles nested. I was so excited as I had not seen them hatch before. The guys who took us to this island were good looking dope heads. We had met them in the real estate office in Jaco when we dropped in on Theo. We were so excited about Costa Rica that we really wanted to see if we could extend our growing real estate portfolio and get a small place here. Little did we know about the squatter issues over here though that's another matter. We went over to the island and it was a magical experience.

It was just like in the movies.

The little lovies cracked open their eggs and then trundled as fast as they could to the ocean, leaving a scuttled trail behind them. We had to keep our distance as it's a conservation area with high level restrictions but it was amazing. We stayed too long and missed the sunset departure. As a result, we were stuck on the island.

The stretch of water between the mainland and Turtle Island was only about fifty meters or so. It would have been easy enough to swim so I did not really see too much of an issue. Okay we would be dripping wet but we had dry clothes on the other side. However, the real challenge was that in that part of the estuary there were crocodiles. Naturally once we knew that we would rather have stayed on the island, even though that was highly punishable as turtles were the citizens of the island and humans were not allowed to stay the night. In the end one of the dope heads called a friend. I use the term 'friend' lightly. We had to have a whip round and each of us had to pay fifty dollars for this guy to bring his boat out and take us back to the other side. That's two hundred and fifty dollars for the five of us. I wondered whether they had intended this scheming plan from the outset. It's easy money and we were in no position to argue. We never saw them again."

"What would you say are the things you love most about Costa Rica Viv?"

"The coffee, the water, the views, the nature, Salsa Lizano, pineapples, surfer boys, the scent of flowers, the rain as the mist rolls in from the sea, the blue butterflies the size of plates, the monkeys, the rivers, the whales and dolphins, the ants that protect their nests, the sunsets, the smiles on the faces of people, my little Jade man and most of all Theo and our joint adventure in this gorgeous land."

"Excellent. Now how do we turn some of those into business opportunities? More coffee?"

"Yes please, Mads. Wouldn't mind a top up." I held out my mug to Maddie which she filled to just over half.

"Mads, I love the fact that you don't top up the mug to the very top. I love a cup of coffee just so. When eating in a diner in the States when they fill up your coffee for free, they don't stop till the coffee hits the rim, making it impossible to enjoy the experience. Anyhow. What strikes you most about Costa Rica from a business perspective? Where do we start?"

"Coffee. Naturally," Maddie said. "We have a tremendous opportunity to sell the coffee. And with our marketing minds, Bussi, we should be able to come up with some great ideas."

"Or, some crate ideas," I quipped.

"Crate ideas?"

"Yes, I was thinking, we could get people to prepay for their part of the coffee. That way we would have sales upfront and keep the people working on the estate. We could design amazing, personalised packaging for those who have bought into buying crates of coffee. We would only sell per crate rather than per kilo. I was quite sure that wealthy New Yorkers would love to have their own coffee to gift to friends or impress guests with. Perhaps even hotels or other organisations would like to buy coffee with their own stamp on it. Or wealthy LA'ers. The owner of *Si Como No* has close connections with Hollywood and perhaps he could give us an angle or even the database from the Little Lids Foundation."

"Great thinking, Buss. If you just take some time to consider the pockets of opportunities, then I think we may well tap into some promising veins to float our coffee boat. Theo has already given us the green light to move ahead so there is nothing stopping us."

"Here's what I propose. We get the names and postal addresses, send personalised letters printed on coffee paper and with a few freshly roasted coffee beans as well as a few untreated red ones. When the high net worth contacts receive their post and open the envelope the aroma will dance directly up their unsuspecting nostrils. That way we have them at first sniff as they *Smell the Coffee.* Sending a scented message will allow us to give them a call and find out who has an appetite in the coffee scheme. Good that databases are all 'opt in' and we can just go ahead and do our thing. Meanwhile we will review the packaging and all the other necessary bits and bobs to create *Crate Lift-Off.*"

"As always, beautiful ideas flow from your gorgeous brain darling Viv. Can't wait to get started."

"Let's trundle up to *Si Como No* to see if we can get some Hollywood contacts to start the day. I will give Theo a ring and see if we can meet him there. Will slip out of my sloppies into something a little more jungle chic. You may not even have to change out of that gorgeous sarong, Buss. You look great in it. You fit right in with the colour and the vibrancy of our hilltop paradise. Though thinking about it we will lose Theo for sure if you rock up looking like his exotic Bird of Paradise."

"Berliner! For a Dutch-British girl you do talk a hell of a lot of twaddle, darling."

With that Maddie started to unknot her sarong, "Will jump under that exquisite outdoor, tropical, rain shower. I love the fact that it was built so you can simply soak up the cold water, in the warm air, in the buff, on the bluff. This is paradise at its best."

Unease Looming

"Ready to rock 'n roll', Mads?"

"Well, kind of, though I feel a bit uncomfortable Viv. I couldn't quite put my finger on it, but when I was having my shower, I felt like someone was around. I could not see anyone, then I thought I heard a thud when I was standing on the outdoor shower platform. It seemed to be coming from under me. Since the house was built on stilts it could be anything and it might just have been an animal. I couldn't rationalise it. My intuition said there was something not quite right."

"How weird, Buss. Should we go and check it out?"

"It was probably nothing and maybe it would be better to simply mention it to Theo. I love being in the house, but I don't know whether it was my nightmare on the first night or something else, I just have a sense of unease. Don't get me wrong, I adore this place. Maybe it was only that I was not used to the noise of the jungle and subconsciously still on high alert since my bad days with Manu though he was in Ethiopia. Strange how your brain can imagine someone right with you, when you know you're a world apart. That's nice when you want to be close to someone but not when you're happy to get away from them. Anyhow, let's get going to *Si Como No* and forget about my musings."

"Okay darling, we will let Theo know."

I had taken one of the keys off the keyring that Merlin had given us when we first arrived at the house. I handed the other key to Maddie and picked up the bag that contained our swimming costumes.

"Could you lock the door behind us Mads?"

Maddie was happy to oblige however she couldn't fit the key into the lock.

"It won't go in, I think."

"How odd. Let me see."

I put the bag down. I slipped my key into the lock and there was no problem. It locked. I took the key from Maddie and compared the two. They were almost the same, but not quite.

"I think Merlin may have thought he gave us identical ones though he clearly must have taken a wrong one by mistake. Never mind. We will ask Theo for another one and give yours back since it was useless."

"Unless…," Maddie said, as she took her key back. "Viv, could you please open the door again. I want to check something."

"You sound like your usual investigating self, Mads. What are you thinking?"

"I'm thinking this key must be related to the house, or it would not have been on the keyring. The only other locked door is the third bedroom. Let's just go and check."

"That is for storage, Mads. No big deal. Let's get going to *Si Como No*. Theo must be arriving soon and it will take us twenty minutes to descend the bluff and climb the road up the cliff to the hotel."

"Just let me satisfy my soul, darling Viv. Won't be a minute. Wait here if you like."

I unlocked the front door and Maddie went inside.

A minute later I heard her say, "Viv, that key fits the door. Come and see."

I wandered into the house and joined Maddie at the open door. The room was gloomy. The shutters were closed and it smelt musty. I could make out shapes of boxes with drapes over the top. I tried to switch on the light but the lightbulb seemed to be missing.

"Maybe we should just close the room up again Maddie and ask Theo for another key to the front door."

Maddie took out her mobile, switching its torch light on, which reflected off an old mouldy canvas that looked worn. She lifted the cover and beckoned for me to come over.

"Check this out Viv. Seems the family of your jade man resides in this crate."

I went over and looked down on at least fifteen artefacts made from emerald green jade and a little figure which looked very similar to my amulet. Mayan and exquisite. The energy from the stone was palpable, even without touching it.

"Oh, my Lord, Mads. What do you think this is all about? Do you think it is what Amilcar referred to in his letter to me before he passed? He mentioned that the illegal trade artefacts which were already robbed could only be used for good. And that naturally, all illegal sourcing and trading of new relics should cease."

"If that is the case, why are these jade pieces of pre-Columbian art here and not at *La Hacienda*? Let's not mention anything to Theo for now Viv. Let us go and meet him and then when we come back, we will think about what to say or do. Let us not discuss it and forget it for now. My brain needs some oxygen to look at this from a logical point of view, rather than react in the heat of the moment."

With that, we closed and locked the door, then we set off on our steep climb up the hill to *Si Como No*. Having arrived at the top of the hill, the eco hotel was only a five minute walk along the tarmac road.

Theo was just parking his car as we got there.

"Hola, lovely ladies," he greeted us. "I wish I could have you in my morning every day. This is what I would call *True Morning Glory*."

He winked at Maddie and took the bag I was carrying.

"How about you go and take a dip in the pool while I order a hearty breakfast of Gallo Pinto?"

"Sounds perfect," I said, taking back the bag with our costumes in it, as I hooked arms with Maddie. "Rice and beans for breakfast. It may sound odd but it's great, especially after a dip in the pool."

Maddie and I jumped from under the poolside shower into the infinity pool.

"What do you think the story of *The Closed Room* is?" I asked her.

"Something is going on, Buss. But before we draw any conclusions, we need to see what we can find out. Only then is it sensible to ask Theo. Clearly the few artefacts we saw have been stored there for a while if we consider the musty cloth. Though of course that is an assumption. We don't know."

From the far eastern rim of the pool, we both leaned over a

little and could just about make out the bright blue corrugated iron roof of *Casa Curtis*, as it popped up between the thick canopy of trees on the bluff.

"Why did they use such a bright colour that doesn't blend with the jungle?" I asked.

"Maybe it was simply the only iron that was available," Maddie replied.

"Perhaps. To be fair how often would anyone look down on the roof of the house on the bluff?"

Though as it turned out, Maddie and I were not the only ones observing *Casa Curtis*.

Hollywood Humphrey

"Well ladies," Theo greeted us as we arrived still damp from our swim. As we took a seat at the table where he was sitting, he asked, "How about a Mimosa, chicas?"

"You know us so well darling Theo," Maddie said.

"Bubbles are always welcome, with or without vitamins," I added.

Just at that moment a tall, dark, and handsome stranger came over to our table. He raised his eyes to Theo and then smiled at us and asked, "May I?"

Theo got up and hugged the guy. He was clearly pleased to see him, a broad smile on his Dutch face. They appeared easy in each other's company. Theo pulled out the fourth chair from the round table.

"Have a seat, bud. Very happy to see you again. Unexpected. But great!"

Maddie and I were confused. I looked at her quizzically. I had to admit, I was rather taken by the tall handsome stature, A fine specimen.

"Join us," Theo invited. "Glad to see you in the house, Humphrey."

He added, "Maddie and Vivi meet my main man, Humphrey. My brother from another mother. But that is an entirely different movie, isn't it, *Hollywood Humphrey*?"

"Hollywood Humphrey?" I quipped. "I can see the smile is fit for the screen, but what is your story Mr H?"

"Oh, nice!" Humphrey exclaimed. "A live wire! I like those. Not easy to find and a total delight when fate blesses your path in the middle of the jungle. It is my pleasure to meet you."

"This is our Marvellous Maddie," Theo introduced Maddie who was smoking her morning cigarette of the day. She exhaled, giving Humphrey her welcoming Liza Minelli smile. Demure, but warm.

"And, this is Vivi Vivacious," Theo followed on with my introduction.

"I can see that is a befitting name, Ms Huge Blue Eyes."

"Actually, they are neither blue, nor green, nor yellow, nor grey," I quipped. "They are a bit of a mix, a bit like my good self. I am Dutch, British, International, and all stirred up."

I had no idea why I was babbling.

Just be quiet. What's the story with you? I asked myself.

Humphrey slipped smoothly into his seat, between Theo and mine.

"What do you fancy for breakfast?" Humphrey asked, addressing none of us.

Oh, I would not mind a bit of you, Mr Crumpet, I caught myself thinking. *You are some delicious dish.*

"Gallo Pinto, naturally," Theo answered. "It has been a while since we had breakfast together, my friend."

"With *huevos fritos*, sunny side up. I remember our jungle breakfasts well."

"You mean you guys have known each other before you met Maddie and me, Theo?"

"Yes ma'am," Humphrey jumped in. "I met this Dutch Chico when we were both around twenty-three. I came to Costa Rica from LA and met this awesome guy. He showed me sights that my young and vulnerable brain will never be able to forget."

"That's just because you are a visual man, Hump," Theo said. "I was never quite sure how you combine making movies with your wildlife photography and then that modelling you used to do so much of. What brings you to Tico Land on this occasion?"

"A bit of filming. Some relaxation and a good cup of Costa Rican coffee and hopefully some time with Charlie and two of his rather lovely angels," Humphrey said, flashing his Hollywood Smile.

His eyes shone as he exuded a sense of genuineness that made him seem very likeable. I must admit, I was instantly attracted to him in a soothing and profound sort of way. He looked like he might have modelled for Annie's sculpture, the one she bought from Mike Romero.

This man was a work of art. His torso toned and tantalising.

The Gallo Pinto and fried eggs arrived with the Salsa Lizano and fresh pineapple juice in a jug. The chilled bottle of Champagne was kept cold in an ice bucket placed between Theo and Humphrey, along with four champagne flutes.

"Thought we would have *Piña Mosas.* Instead of orange juice, I ordered fresh *jugo de piña* with champagne. If you allow me the creative license to adapt our Mimosa moment."

"All is good, if it bubbles," I said.

"You look like you are *Effervescence Personified*," Humphrey responded, locking eyes with me, still smiling in a slow, happy kind of way.

"Well, who knows? Maybe you will find out. Maybe you won't. I don't typically play my cards in the jungle with a stranger I have never had the pleasure of meeting before, even though he had apparently known my surrogate brother for well over three decades. That makes me a little suspicious."

Then, turning to Theo, I asked him, "What's the story, bro?"

"Nothing Viv. Though Hump and I spent holidays together, he lived in the US. When Humphrey is here, we simply pick up where we left off. There is nothing more to it."

Then turning to Humphrey, Theo asked him, "So big H. How long are you in this land for?"

"I need to scout a location for a movie. I need hills of green, so what better place than to check out the locations in Costa Rica."

"Depending on what you need, I may be able to help," Theo said, looking at me.

I nodded and smiled, "Tell him what we have."

"Let's dig in and keep Big H here in suspense a little longer. He is always in control, so while we have him wait a bit before we spill the beans, let's enjoy our rice and beans."

Humphrey smiled as he picked up the colourfully painted jug of pineapple juice, "I am quite able to wait for anything that is worth waiting for." He shot me a look, "Shall I be mother?"

"Oh Lordie," I said, trying to suppress a grin. "You must have spent some time in the UK. That is such a British Expression."

"I did. I went to boarding school there. Many moons ago. May I?"

"Yes please, pour me in," I said, looking him straight in the eye.

I felt a little surge of energy. I did not have the nerve to hold his gaze for long. My blood was rising. I averted my eyes and caught Maddie looking at me.

Surely a little banter and bubbles couldn't hurt, could it?

Poolside Paradise

Breakfast turned into lunch and ended up with us lounging by the pool at *Si Como No*.

"Well Ms Vivi you somehow managed to keep me from scouting locations."

"Mr H. You are entirely free to get up and leave whenever you like. Nobody is stopping you from doing your work."

"You are stopping me Ms Vivi. You stopped me right in my tracks. Unexpectedly but without a doubt you pulled me up short."

Maddie and Theo were in the pool, having a great time. It was so good to see Maddie happy. They seem to be getting on well. As for me, I was enchanted by Big H. He was charming, eloquent, and very British in some ways though clearly American.

He had the British gentleman side about him, yet the LA confidence. Quite a powerful combination.

No doubt he had wooed many a woman in his time. I could not help wondering whether he was married or in a meaningful relationship. Now was not the time to ask.

Why would I? We were simply enjoying each other's company by the pool.

"Tell me about your first trip to Costa Rica when you met Theo," I said.

"I met Theo on the beach at Jaco. I was always interested in health and after university where I studied photography, I took some time out to visit the world's Blue Zones."

"Blue Zones?" I asked, not quite understanding what Humphrey was talking about.

"Dan Buettner was a National Geographic Fellow and multiple *New York Times* bestselling author. He discovered five places in the world – dubbed blue zones – where people live the longest, and were healthiest: Okinawa, Japan; Sardinia, Italy; Nicoya, Costa Rica; Ikaria, Greece, and Loma Linda, California. I decided that, after I graduated, I wanted to travel the world a bit. Being interested in both health and photography, I decided to visit at least one of the Blue Zones, with a view to travel to them all.

The concept of blue zones grew out of the demographic work done by Gianni Pes and Michel Poulain outlined in the Journal of Experimental Gerontology, identifying Sardinia as the region of the world with the highest concentration of male centenarians. Pes and Poulain drew concentric blue circles on the map, highlighting these villages of extreme longevity and began to refer to this area inside the circle as the blue zone. I started with the Nicoya Peninsula in Costa Rica. This was the closest to home and ticked all my emotional boxes, in terms of nature."

I stared at Humphrey.

"What's the matter?" he asked.

"It's just that what you say has such resonance with me."

Humphrey smiled. "I know," he responded.

"Sometimes Fate, or Mother Nature, plays cards that allow stars to perfectly align."

"I don't feel you are a stranger, but rather someone I have known all my life, but was never yet introduced to."

"Meant to be Ms Vivi if you ask me. Let me get you a cooling drink. What is your tipple?"

"You really are quite the Brit, Mr H, under that Hollywood facade of yours."

"*Mojito*, *Caipariña*, Frozen Margarita, Bloody Mary, or other?"

Bloody Marys reminded me of another time and place. More London than rainforest. My mind jumped momentarily to the Bloody Mary breakfasts I'd shared with James and Mike in a bygone era, now just retrievable through my treasured memories of my first true love.

"You may be surprised that Costa Rica has a drink that resembles a Bloody Mary, known as *Chilguaro*. It is the most well-known shot throughout Costa Rica, made of tomato juice, *Tabasco* hot sauce, lime juice, and *guaro*, with a salt and pepper rim. All in all, not a million miles away from a Bloody Mary."

"I wouldn't mind one of those for breakfast in that case but for now I really fancy a Mojito, but with brown sugar, not white. Brown makes all the difference." I realised that I was flirting with H and he knew it, too.

"Coming up," he said, looking like a lion who'd just got up from his sunny spot on the African plain after an afternoon siesta.

Big H was of Big 5 calibre and Big Game. A rarely

encountered creature, I was looking forward to getting to know better.

Humphrey returned brandishing four Mojitos. He dropped two of them off to Maddie and Theo who were still in the pool and then settled back next to me on the wooden sun lounger.

"Can't believe we are in May and we haven't had any rain all day," I said. "Normally the rainy season or rather the green season as we used to refer to it for marketing reasons, brings quite a lot of rain by this time of year."

"Maybe *La Niña* is doing her thing," Humphrey said.

"La Niña?" I asked. "Are you changing the gender of *El Niño* just to make a political point?"

"No, no," Humphrey laughed, "La Niña has the opposite effect to El Niño. During La Niña events trade winds are even stronger than usual. Because of that warmer water is pushed towards Asia. Upswelling increases off the coast of America bringing cold to the surface, pushing the Pacific jet stream forward. During a La Niña year winter temperatures are warmer than normal in the South and cooler than normal in the North."

"Well, well, Mr Humphrey, Sir. I am impressed. So, tell me this. I understand why La Niña is called what she is, as an opposite to *El Niño*. But why is it called that?" I sipped my Mojito with my bamboo straw and look defiantly over the rim of my glass, both aiming to tempt and tease Humphrey.

"El Niño as perhaps you know means *Little Boy* or *Christ Child* in Spanish. South American fishermen first noticed periods of unusually warm water in the Pacific Ocean in the 1600s. The full name they used was *El Niño de Navidad*, because El Nino typically peaks around December. In those years the period between March and June would be much wetter."

"Who you be, Mr Humphrey?" I joked, though I must admit I was impressed. I loved the fact that he knew these details. He wasn't showing off, thank God. I hate Know-it-All's and preacher prats, but Humphrey simply conveyed wonderfully interesting stuff in such a nice way. And as for his voice... well, I could get lost in it. Maybe it was the Mojito after the pineapple Pimosas as Theo had named them, that was making me giddy.

One thing was for sure, this guy sent me spinning in a very lovely and natural way.

"I thought you studied photography not environmentalism."

"I said I came to Costa Rica after I completed my university and yes, I did study photography, but I never said I didn't continue studying," Humphrey held my gaze as he spoke. "I love learning about those things and people that interest me. I want to understand them, know what makes them tick, what creates a shift in weather pattern and what makes their waves topple over onto the beach as the ebb and tides take control."

His smile lingered.

If I could drown in that look, I would be happy forever.

I recovered from my musings. I realised that I had closed my eyes in an ecstasy like fashion. I may even have made a sighing sound.

I must get a grip!

"Could I get you a coffee Ms Vivi?"

"No gracias," I murmured. "Let me stay in paradise for now. Sipping on my Mojito."

I sucked my straw and looked at Humphrey, who laughed and passed me a cold glass of water.

"Just a little bit of $H2O$ goes a long way to keeping a

headache at bay."

"You are a poet but don't know it."

"I know trouble when I see it. And right now, you are heading for some. And so, I suspect, am I. Your beautiful face has turned pink Ms Vivi. It may be time to call it a day."

"It is simply the reflection of the setting sun, Mr Humphrey. I may be a little sun kissed, but not burnt."

"I hope that you will always be kissed and never burnt. I like you."

"I like you too, Mr Humphrey. You are a wonderful environmentalist, a great conversationalist, quite the naturalist and I would also say an optimist. Those are my observations, though I admit by now I may be a little pissed."

I took my time to look him up and down and frankly I don't think I had been able to conceal my admiration and interest.

Out of nowhere I could hear myself asking Humphrey, "Are you free, Mr Humphries?" Just like in the British TV programme I used to watch when I was growing up. We used to love the reply from the camp chap, who always replied, "Yes, I'm free."

"Yes, I am free and I would very much like to serve you." He started laughing. "It reminds me of the days at Sherbourne where I went to boarding school. We used to love watching that programme but if Matron caught us, we would be in trouble. I would imagine I would be in far greater trouble if Matron only knew what was on my mind now."

"Naughty Mr H!" I smiled. I felt a warm glow flowing up from my toes to my heart.

I felt like I was in paradise. With a wonderful man.

Harsh Homecoming

"Cristina will be cleaning the house tomorrow," Theo told us. "She asked me to let her know when you would be out. I think she finds it difficult to have people around who are not Spanish speakers, though I know you can speak the lingo very well Viv. It may just be an excuse. I think perhaps she is shy, though I have not ever seen that side of her before. But I guess I should respect that."

I noticed Maddie flinched just like that first time when Theo had mentioned Cristina.

"It's okay, Theo. Viv and I can clean the house for as long as we are staying there. No need for Cristina to come."

"I know you are able to do the *casa* cleaning Mads, but if the truth be told, Cristina really needs the money. She looks after her family in the jungle and though I have no responsibilities in that regard, I somehow do feel I should offer work for pay whenever I can. Half the time I don't really need her to cook or clean but the income helps her."

"Okay, understood," Maddie said, then dropped the subject. I could see she was uncomfortable with the Cristina

Connection.

"Merlin will pick you guys up tomorrow morning to take you to *La Hacienda* if you agree. After that you guys can pick up Humphrey from *Si Como No* and come on over. We can spend the day together. Big H can check out the plantation from a film scouting perspective and we can perhaps wrap our minds around the business angles and move ahead with some plans for the coffee plantation. How does that sound?"

"Sounds good to me," Maddie responded.

"I think that is a great plan," I added.

"Merlin will pick you up around 9 and then you guys should be at *La Hacienda* by 9.30 or just past. We can have coffee and breakfast and schedule our day."

We said goodbye to Humphrey and then Theo dropped us back at the House on the Bluff.

"What is that smell Theo?" I asked. "Whatever it is, it smells delicious."

"I had the guys in the kitchen make you some grouper and some mango salad. You guys need a bite as we didn't have dinner. I think some of us may need a bit of blotting cloth to soak up some of the alcohol we poured into our systems around the pool today. It's lean and clean, and will not upset your stomach, just give you some needed nutrition. I want you back in fine shape tomorrow for a great day at *The Ranch*."

"That is a rubbish cowboy accent, Theo," Maddie laughed. "You sound better when you call it *La Hacienda*."

"Fair enough my fair maiden. *La Hacienda* it will be henceforth until eternity. For you, I will speak any language you ask me to." With that he squeezed Maddie's hand. "Go carefully up those steps."

The solar powered torch lights came on automatically at sunset, lighting the hundred and two steps. The bulbs were like oversized, glowing, yellow fairy lights, dangling on wire above our heads. It looked as if someone had decorated a giant Christmas tree as the lights zigzagged up the bluff, towards the house. Theo handed me the carton with the food in it and Maddie carried the bag with our wet costumes. We said goodbye to Theo and made our way up the stairs. I had to take a breather every so often. My head was pulsating. Too much sun and alcohol. But the day had been epic. It was all good. As we went up, neither of us spoke. We needed all our oxygen for the ascent.

Around three quarters up, I whispered to Maddie, "I can't. I need to sit down."

"No worries," she whispered back. "Let's take a pew on this concrete slab and open that delicious smelling food box. I am starving. We can have our takeaway and then have a shower when we get to the house."

We sat down and I opened the box. We picked at the fish in silence and took out the juicy mango from the salad. Neither one of us talked, as we softly munched on the food. The bluff however was alive with noise. Frogs, rickets, and nocturnal animals of all sorts were making a tremendous racket. It was never ever quiet in the jungle.

I once came out to Costa Rica with a group of clients who organised incentive travel. One of the agents also came with me to Jordan where we visited Wadi Rum, a place with total silence filling the day and the night. There was no sound apart from the wind blowing the sands and whistling between the majestic sandstone rocks that stood majestically in the red golden dune landscape.

At the time when he joined me in Costa Rica he simply said, "How could one bear all the noise of the jungle? Give me the desert anytime over this madhouse."

I had often considered his words. I loved the jungle if it was bordering the Pacific. Having the noise and the colour of the rainforest, with the expanse and solitude of the ocean was to me the optimal combination of elements; The desert was too solitary, the jungle too social. The Pacific was the soothing force. Quiet, passionate, refreshing. I loved the sea.

A jungle fringed beach was my idea of bliss.

Maddie and I sat there listening to the animals as we snacked on our food; the flies and mosquitoes zooming overhead attracted by the lights.

Then I could smell the rain. The first drops started to fall and I smiled at Maddie. The drops came faster and thicker. I packed up the box and we were ready to scale the final heights. We went from dry weather to full on rain in no less than two minutes. The sharp precision of lightning cut across the night sky, lighting up all the trees and animals around us for a split second. I counted... twenty one... twenty two... twenty three... twenty four... the inevitable voice of thunder followed from four kilometres away, one kilometre for every second counted. We were now soaking wet and started to laugh.

Suddenly another *bang* filled the air.

"Vivi. Stop!" Maddie pulled me by my top and gestured me to be silent.

And there in the dark just beyond the shrubs, almost by the front door, we heard the lift chugging into action.

"Lie low," Maddie whispered.

She gestured me to stay in place while she made her way up towards the front door on all fours, keeping parallel to the cement slabs as she found her way up. I could see her peeking around the corner towards the moving platform. Within seconds the lift stopped. Then it started again. Someone honked their horn. I decided I should join Maddie; in case she needed my help. I left the box and the bag on the steps and joined her. She was now at the lift platform. I saw Maddie hitting the big red tomato sized button to make the lift come up again. It trundled into action and responded. Then it stopped and started to descend again.

Someone was controlling the button at the bottom of the bluff!

What was going on?

The rain continued to pour down. More honking could be heard from the place where Theo had dropped us off. Eventually two headlights could be seen disappearing down the tarmac road between the beaches and the luggage lift arrived as intended by Maddie at the top of the hill. I leapt back down to get the box and the bag where I had left them and to find the key to open the front door. Drenched, I put the key in the lock and switched the light on. Maddie came in brandishing a crate that was full of what looked like wet magazines.

"Whoever wanted this down the hill, did not get it."

Maddie took the wooden crate into the living room and placed it on the tropical wooden floor. National Geographic magazines lay like limp, lifeless and sodden leaves as they oozed out across the tropical floor. I went off to get a bath towel to absorb the water.

"What the hell? Who was so keen on a load of National

Geographic mags?" I asked Maddie. "Don't get me wrong, I love them, but really, *why would you take those from the house?* And more importantly, *who* would do such a thing?"

Maddie began to remove the wet papers that were now falling apart, placing them into a pile next to the box.

"Here you go," she said, holding up a little Mayan amulet in her hand and placing it next to the disintegrated paper. "Check the pile Viv, in case there's another one in there."

I felt my way through the slimy paper and indeed I found another amulet. Maddie continued her search and found five more.

One had cracked, and its head was disconnected, like a decapitated soldier fallen in battle.

"Let's check the third bedroom," Maddie said. "Bring the torch from the kitchen drawer Viv. I will get the key."

We let ourselves into the third bedroom.

"Someone has definitely been in here," Maddie deduced. "Those Mayan figurines were taken from those we saw this morning."

"Why would anyone not take them all, Mads, if they were going to steal them?"

"We don't know if they were working on instruction Viv, or on order. If only seven were required, then it would be best to leave the others in situ."

"Why hide them in a crate and not put them in a pocket or a pouch?"

"Maybe wherever they were going to go has regular inspections and body searches. Spot checks are done relatively often even for loyal staff. It is par for the course."

"Do you think that is why Merlin took us down the back

route out of *La Hacienda* when he dropped us here the other day? To avoid a potential search?"

"Now you are starting to use your brain Viv. That is what we need more of."

"But why National Geographic magazines, Mads?"

"Well, those particular publications never raise any suspicion. Everyone trusts National Geographic," Maddie laughed.

"So, when faced with National Geographic in unusual circumstances make sure to double check the circumstances."

"Are you kidding me? Don't say that Mads! Humphrey told me he had done work for that organisation. Should I be distrustful of him too?"

"I don't know Viv. Right now, nothing makes sense. We need to get our minds around this. We know we should not have access to the room and we know that these amulets are stolen artefacts. Just like the one that Theo gave you all those years ago. The question is who was moving what? And in the name of whom?"

"Let's call Theo, Mads," I urged.

"No. Let's think this one through a bit first. Amilcar wrote in his letter that the stolen artefacts could be sold for good by Theo. So, if he was behind this and, for the right reasons, then all would appear okay. However, I am still not sure why they would no longer be in *La Hacienda* but in the House on the Bluff, which had been closed ever since Curtis Coffee passed away. Only because we came did Theo have the place opened as he thought we may like to have our own space together. So having these artefacts stored here seems odd. However, we must be careful not to assume or *ass-u-me,* as that *makes an ass out of you and me.* There must be more to this. Let's go back to the living room and I will roll up a happy ciggie and puff some wisdom into the situation. Relock the door Viv. Just in case."

"In case of what? Mads, I am very uncomfortable with this whole situation."

At that moment the lightning lit up the dark sky beyond the veranda. A split second later we were plunged into darkness. Then, the bang came. It always did.

Maddie rolled her joint.

"What if they come back tonight?" I asked her.

"They won't Viv. They are not such doughnuts. Those Berliners will need time to figure out what to do. We have at least until tomorrow. This is not the work of professionals. And it would not have been anyone who knows that we are staying here. Those people would be Theo naturally as well as Merlin who dropped us off; he is a bit suspect due to the route he took us on and how agitated he was acting. And then there is Humphrey though he only knows where we are as Theo said he would have us picked up from this house. Next we have Cristina who cleaned the place before we came."

Maddie dragged on her joint making the orange glow light up like the red hot tip of an iron rod.

"You could brand a herd of cattle with that joint of yours," I laughed.

The tip lost its vibrance as Maddie exhaled.

"This Cristina woman," she said. "I don't like the sound of her. I don't know why Theo still engages her at *La Hacienda* as well as here. Who knows what else he was paying her to do?"

"Maddie! What are you insinuating? Am I detecting some jealousy? Theo may have dated her in the jungle a gazillion years ago but now he is clearly very much into you. So why worry about Cristina?"

"Because hell hath no fury like a woman scorned. Theo never told me the whole story about Cristina. I am sure of that. And with the story untold, something is sure to unfold. Mark my words. I am expecting a *serpente venenosa.* A poisonous snake."

Cristina Crisis

The pounding of the Howler monkeys woke me up around six in the morning. At seven the Costa Rican national anthem blasted out of the radio, along with an announcement that the government wanted to share with the entire population. I switched off the radio, choosing rather to listen to birdsong.

The world was fresh and vibrant, washed clean by the downpour the night before.

Life looked colourful and bright, yet thoughts of the night before gave me a chill. Maddie was still asleep. Perhaps the ganja had knocked her out in addition to the full day of sunshine we'd shared and the events of the night before. I needed to wake her up. Soon Cristina would be coming and Merlin would be taking us to *La Hacienda*.

My heart did a little salsa move, thinking of the prospect of seeing Humphrey again.

I poured a cup of hot brew for Maddie and knocked on her door.

"Morning Mads, rise and shine. Here is some caffeine to get

you going. We have a date with your mate Theo."

I opened the shutters and the window. The oxygen laden breeze travelled in. Maddie sat up in bed with two pillows tucked behind her, opening and closing her eyes as she became accustomed to the daylight. I passed her the cup of coffee.

"Welcome to the day, darling," I say. "How are you doing?"

"Not sure yet Viv. My night was almost hallucinatory and busy. I thought I would simply conk out, but that didn't happen until an hour or so ago. I am sure I will be fine, though perhaps I need a bit of time."

I responded, "Tell you what, how about I meet Merlin and we go to pick up Humphrey? I will let Theo know we will be at *La Hacienda* a little later. We will then come back to pick you up. That way you have a bit more time to organise yourself. An hour later will be fine and we'll make sure you find a spot this afternoon to have a siesta so you'll be able to handle the day. Don't forget you may also still be suffering from a bit of jetlag which is mixing up your senses."

"Okay sounds like a plan Viv. Thanks. An extra half an hour or so would be perfect."

"I will gather our things from the washing rack in case we need them so don't worry about bringing your costume or a change of clothes. I will chuck a few things together for us both."

With that I went off to grab a bag and bundle together the usual items we might want including my laptop, reading glasses and a bottle of sun cream.

Having said goodbye to Maddie, I opened the door and noticed the lift was moving upwards. Within seconds I spotted a crate stacked with cleaning products arriving at the top of the platform. I remembered that Theo told us that Cristina would be expecting to work when we were out. At that moment I saw her. She was making her way up the final steps to the house. I looked down on her gleaming black hair, head bowed as she climbed the final metres up the cliff.

"Hola Cristina," I greeted her.

She raised her head and looked up at me. She was stunningly beautiful; a cross between an exotic, indigenous South Pacific girl painted by Gaugin, and a panther on the prowl.

Feminine, sensual, and dangerous.

She didn't smile or say anything until she reached the top.

"Buenos," was the sole word she spoke.

Then she went to the platform, picked up the crate of cleaning materials, pulled out the key from between her breasts and opened the door without looking back at me. She closed the door behind her. I was stunned. Both by her beauty and her blatant disregard for me. Her attitude did not suggest shyness to me as Theo had suggested. Rather she seemed rude, disinterested, and completely removed from wanting to engage in any way. Baffled I made my way down the steps with my bag, letting gravity take me to where Merlin was waiting by the car.

"Buenos días," he gave me a diluted smile. It seemed genuine but submissive.

"Hola Merlin, que buen día!" What a great day!

I explained the slight change in plan to Merlin. Merlin followed orders, simply nodded and off we went along the road that traversed the peninsula. A wild horse was walking on the golden sand to my left and on the other side there were boys who looked as if they should be in school, kicking a football on the beach. When we reached *Si Como No*, Humphrey was on the phone. He greeted me with a kiss on the cheek and gestured me to follow him for a coffee. Merlin waited by the car. We sat down in the open lobby which was built like a ship open to the elements from both sides and positioned above the green canopy. The reception overlooked Cathedral Point, where the House on the Bluff's roof could be seen a lot more clearly than from the pool.

As if by magic two steaming cups of coffee arrived. Humphrey ended his call.

"Good morning, Viv, you are a sight for sore eyes. You look wonderful. You have an energy about you that makes me want to embrace the day. And you."

"Morning Mr H. Happy to see you too."

We chatted for a bit and I explained we would be picking up Maddie on route to *La Hacienda*. Humphrey had been up much of the night as he was working on an ecologically inspired theme park in Bali and was up late talking about the deal.

"The time difference is a killer but needs must, so sometimes we have to get by with little shut-eye."

"Sounds like you and Maddie could both do with a siesta this afternoon. I called Theo on the way over here to let him know we shall be coming a little later."

Humphrey and I got into the car and Merlin drove us back down to the end of Cathedral Point, back to the house.

"Wow, what a jungle hideaway."

"Come on up if you like Humphrey. The views are to die for. You accused me yesterday of interrupting your scouting. Today, I would like to make up for that and support you in your quest. It is a bit of a climb but you look like the fittest man on the planet, so if you would like to scale the dizzy heights towards amazingness, I invite you to come with me."

My implied flirtatious ramblings clearly hit a chord as Humphrey's butterscotch eyes twinkled.

"I will follow you anywhere," he said. "Lead the way."

Having done the steps several times now, I was getting used to them. When I spent time in Jordan, I stayed in a glorious roof terrace that looked out over Amman. There was no elevator there either I would climb fifty five steps multiple times a day. It was strange how your body somehow remembers. Your mind knows too that you could do it and that conviction helps you to deal with the challenge more readily.

I set off up the steps.

We didn't talk on the climb. No need to waste energy. Humphrey had little problem moving up the hill. He was clearly fit as a fiddle, glowing gently, and smelling divine.

Not a trace of sweat on this yummy person.

I was about to open the door when I heard raised voices inside. That did not bode well. Theo's females were colliding it seemed.

"Allow me," Humphrey said, as he took the key and pushed the door inwards.

"They would never allow doors to be constructed like this in the US," he said and added, "Fire hazard. But anything goes here."

The voices subsided.

We entered the living room where Cristina stood with a broom in her hand and Maddie with a smouldering cigarette in hers.

"*Hola* Cristina," Humphrey said. "*Qual es el problema?*"

I was taken aback. I did not know Humphrey had met

Cristina before nor that he spoke Spanish. Then again, I had only met him twenty-four hours ago so who was I kidding, thinking that I knew this man.

Though in my heart I felt I had spent a former life with him. A crazy notion.

Maddie politely nodded at Humphrey, making her way out onto the patio. I joined her, leaving Humphrey and Cristina inside. Humphrey's soothing voice sounded deep, as he settled into speaking to Cristina. The ravishing beauty held her broom across her bosom.

"Witch," Maddie said, under her breath. "She is a bloody *bruja,* that is the word Theo once used when he talked about her when I met him in Holland all those years ago. And he was not wrong. She is a witch. Ever since that time I have suspected her to be trouble and it seems I am right."

"Do you think you may be a little jealous of this female rival Mads?"

"I am trying to ascertain whether she is a rival or a relic. According to my findings, I shall decide whether my path with Theo will end or continue. I will never be someone's second woman again. Manu sowed more seeds than Selassie the gardener in Ethiopia and I am not planning on being a flower in a shared bed. She can have him if that is her plan."

"Hang on, Mads, what happened?"

"I woke up and I'd forgotten that cow was coming here. I dropped off to sleep again after you left but woke up to a loud noise followed by a scream. I was totally confused and disoriented. I jumped out of bed in my undies and saw this woman bending over the mirror in the living room which had fallen off the wall and crashed on the floor. Next to it lay a picture of me and Theo taken at our reunion recently. He was holding me under his left arm with a beer in his right hand tucked under his armpit as is his hallmark. I came in to hear her repeat the words *Mala Suerte* and pulling at her hair like she was deranged. I went over to her and she hissed like a snake and pulled back, holding a piece of jagged mirror at me as if she was fending off evil and then pointing at the picture, shouting *Puta!* I think we all know what that means."

Maddie inhaled deeply before she stubbed out her cigarette as the filter caught light almost burning her fingers.

"*Mala Suerte* means *bad luck*, Mads. That is a Costa Rican superstition. Broken mirrors are believed to bring doom. Maybe you just caught her in shock."

"That picture was in my things Viv. She clearly went through my stuff when I was still sleeping, clearly unaware I was in the house. Or maybe she didn't care and is just on a higher mission to find out whether you or I might be bedding *her man.*"

At that moment Cristina's voice, high and shrill, shouted, "*Es mi medio naranja.*"

Now I was flummoxed.

Why the hell was Cristina shouting about half an orange?

Moments later, Humphrey walked onto the veranda.

"Seems we have a hot headed person who has lost her sensibilities. The best thing to do is to take ourselves off. Anything of value, bring with you. Theo will have to deal with her. Best just to remove ourselves."

I looked at Maddie.

"Give me a few minutes to get my stuff," she said.

"I have your things Mads, I gathered them before I picked up Humphrey. Maybe you didn't register when I told you."

"I need just a few minutes. I will see you outside."

Cristina was now on the veranda. Humphrey told her to take a seat there until we left the house. She listened to him, thank goodness.

"Why were you talking about oranges?" I asked Humphrey, while Maddie was collecting her things.

"*Medio naranja*, means other half or soul mate. As in a couple. Cristina was referring to Theo. Basically she's claiming that he is hers."

"Blimey, that doesn't bode well. Hope this jungle doesn't become any denser than it already is. Maddie couldn't be hurt again. Not after bloody Model Manu."

"Manu, the model?" Humphrey said.

I was about to explain in a nutshell when Maddie came out to join us. She looked cool and in charge. It was a mystery to me how you could deal with such a horrible situation and minutes later collect yourself. I was proud of Maddie but also very aware that she was able to manage herself through troubled waters as she had had to survive an emotional tsunami that swelled and fell, repeatedly over a span of two decades, in Ethiopia when she was married to model Manu, who had gone from lover and father to sexual exploiter and sadist.

With her colourful cross-body bag picking out the turquoise of her multi-coloured freshly pressed blouse, Maddie smiled at us and said, "Shall we?"

Slithering Snake

Merlin pulled up at the resplendent gates of *La Hacienda*. Today we were coming in through the main entrance. Merlin was asked to get out and the guard frisked him. Maddie had dozed off in the car and when we came to a standstill, she suddenly opened her eyes clutching her bag tightly and seemed instantly wide awake.

"Just weird how they don't trust their own people. Seems like everyone is considered a back stabber or a crook," I said.

"They apparently have good reason to think that Viv. Look at that snake we left in the house."

"Humphrey, I know it is a bit much to ask but would you be kind enough to have a word with Theo about what's happened? You probably could better convey the situation, especially since you spoke with Cristina. Coming from you it may be less inflammatory."

"Sure thing, ladies. My pleasure to serve you."

I knew Humphrey was linking his response to our conversation the day before by the pool, offering to serve me. My heart warmed. I liked this guy.

Theo greeted us at the entrance and invited us for brunch around the pool.

"It's a beautiful place you have here, Theo," Humphrey said.

"Thank you, my friend, but it equally belongs to my sister now. Amilcar our great friend who recently passed, left us to make the most of it and do some good in this world."

"I like that Mr T. Maybe I can contribute in a humble way if you allow me to think with you."

Humphrey looked at Theo and me.

"For sure, great minds in partnership can move mountains. And as for a green scene, *La Hacienda* may work for your movie," I said.

"I love it and everything about it, Viv. Utterly heavenly," he winked at me and held my gaze.

I recalled how the General used to do that. Stopping me dead in my emotional tracks. I should heed Maddie's warnings.

This man Humphrey, on the face of it, appeared faultless, interesting, astute, kind, funny, intelligent, academic, well-travelled, interested, with the right vibe, handsome, competent, well-mannered, and delicious. But the only thing that seemed to be a question mark was that he had worked for National Geographic. And that might mean some sort of a cover-up.

Oh, why had Maddie said that? Now I could not un-hear it.

"Breakfast is a bit DIY, I am afraid," Theo said. "Cristina cannot be in two places at the same time and she is the only one I trust to do a good job in sensitive surroundings."

If instant ice ages could occur then that was what I experienced now. Maddie froze over. Theo did not notice but both Humphrey and I did.

"Let me help you with that DIY Theo," Humphrey offered.

"Let's leave our chicas to chill and let us make that awesome omelette that sets any tongue on fire. I think both Maddie and I need some heat to burn off lack of sleep."

Humphrey looked at Maddie and closed both of his eyes briefly in a competent and caring way that said, *"I have your back."*

"Let's go for a stroll Mads. Just walk it off a little. Then we'll have some breakfast and take it from there," I said.

Unconvinced, Maddie slowly stood up. I hooked arms with her.

"Theo will sort this lousy situation out, Mads. I am sorry you must go through this, but one way or another you will know what stand Theo takes. In the end, truth is what matters, as well as managing expectations. I don't want to sound like some matron but my wisest, loveliest, maddest, and most magical friend always tells me that no one can take your power unless you allow them to. Are you going to allow the witch to snitch your force?"

Maddie looked at me. I could see her reflecting. Struggling with her anger, frustration, and the confrontation, not knowing her exact place and rationally aware that she should live by her own wisdom.

After a few minutes' silence she opened her bag, took out a cigarette and her lighter. She sat down on a rock that protruded between the pineapple plants around the side of house. It was high enough not to be scratched by the spikes of the fruits which could easily rip open her skin. The hostile scales and spikes on the outside of the fruit protect its soft, sweet centre of yellow flesh. As Maddie sat on the rock inhaling her cigarette, the pineapples seemed to dance like flames under a large cooking pot.

I could not bear it. Please *Dios* keep Maddie safe and let Theo be the one she needed him to be.

Maddie stubbed out the cigarette and leaned forward to take off her bag over her head.

"Hold this please, Bussi," she handed me her pouch.

I thought she needed assistance to jump off the rock and offered my hand to her like a cavalier prince, "Allow me to help you down, dearest."

"You are a hoot Viv. Always making up fairy tales and being the sweetest person. I need to roughen you up a bit. And now is the time before you fly head over heels into a thing with Mr H. He seems like a good guy but you told me he worked for National Geographic in his time. So, remind yourself he may be very good at reading people. And you my darling Viv are an open book. A dream story. That many would like to read. Like you tell me not to let anyone take my power, please don't give yourself too easily. To anybody."

As Maddie took my hand and jumped over the spiky pineapples, she said, "No, you little bastards, you don't get to scratch me. I will skin and eat you alive before that ever happens to me again."

Without waiting for me to give her some psychological repost, she said, "Are we alone? You must always check first Viv. Always assume that someone is watching."

I looked around, "I think that we are alone."

"If you think so, you don't know so. Follow me."

There was a small shed with a door that was open. The structure was well maintained and had a proper lock on it. A manual sliding bolt could be secured both from the inside and the outside.

"In here," Maddie said.

I followed her. "Whatever are you up to Mads?"

Maddie switched on the light and closed the door, securing it and checking it twice.

"Now we can know that nobody can see us. Open my bag," Maddie instructed me.

I opened the turquoise bag which had a tangerine lining.

"My favourite colour combination Mads. I love it."

"What is wrong with you, Berliner? Do you think I brought you into a secure place to show you the colours of my bag? For goodness' sake girl, get a grip and put your paw into the pouch. Feel around and pull out anything that you don't recognise as a pen, a key, my lighter, or packet of cigarettes."

I fumbled about and pulled out something the size of a large USB. I looked at it.

"What did you go and do Madster?" I asked.

"That bitch will not get away with her sly seduction of Theo. I plan to expose her wicked ways. And I will do so slowly and painfully. Watch me. While Theo plays his flute, this Cobra is snaking her way back into his life. She tried to exploit him all those years ago in the jungle. He told me he was seduced by her and under her spell. One day, just before he was due to travel to Switzerland, she told him she was pregnant and that she needed money. While Theo was mesmerised by her feline beauty, he realised that Cristina or Tina as he called her, was the cat that wanted his cream. In more ways than one. But she also hunted for other juices in the jungle. If the providers had money. The illegal art traders all wanted a piece of what *La Bruja* had to offer. Theo told me that in monetary terms, she did very well."

"Yuck, Mads. That is a grim sticky picture you paint. What did Theo do?"

"We talked about the sorry saga when we met in Holland. After I'd given up on having a relationship with Bing and when Theo and I had our reconnection rendezvous. Theo told me there was no way of knowing if *La Bruja* was speaking the truth. She didn't look pregnant when he'd said goodbye and she continued to drink heavily on the day before he left for Switzerland. He gave her five thousand dollars to take care of herself in his absence and said that he would stand by her. Either to have an abortion or to have the baby and in that case, he would support her."

"Wow. So, what happened?"

"Theo did not go home during his two years on the Mountain in Switzerland. He did not hear from Cristina and did not see her again after that. He assumed it was all over until the day when Theo was visiting Amilcar at *La Hacienda*. *El Comandante*, Amilcar's ferocious underworld father, was still alive at the time. He made a rare appearance at the estate, brandishing an exotic beauty on his arm. Drunk and inappropriately fondling her breast and kissing her neck. Theo told me he instantly recognised her as Cristina. The young tribal woman who used to wear nothing more than a simple cloth wrapped around her was now dressed up in a mini-skirt and a low plunging top studded with jewels. Her scarlet red lips left marks all over *El Comandante* on his drunken face, on the collar of his sweat-sodden shirt, and just under the belt of his open unzipped khakis. Theo managed to avoid being seen. He told me he felt sick and revolted seeing his former belle in a state of *Pura Puta*, rather than *Pura Vida*.

Theo told me that he'd felt a sense of responsibility as he had been the Blond Chief of Entertainment in the jungle and Cristina had been the one who'd gathered her girlfriends to satisfy the lust of the low life as they migrated looking for new treasures.

After *El Comandante* was reported missing, Theo set out to find Cristina to ensure that she could survive without the work which died when *El Comandante* disappeared and was eventually found dead. As if nothing had happened Cristina skipped straight back into Theo's life. Amilcar agreed that Cristina could work at *La Hacienda* after his father's passing. I think Amilcar had a sense of replacement shame. His father was a swine and he should make things right. One way or another Cristina never mentioned any sons or daughters to Theo. She made herself comfortable, knowing that Theo's and Amilcar's guilt would keep her in good stead. And that applecart she would not want to upset.

Even though she was still beautiful, younger generations of *Gaugin lookalike beauties* were being exploited now and her days as a *Prima Puta* were marked. She had been given a new way to manipulate and to secure what she could to guarantee the luxuries of life to which she had become accustomed."

"Jeez Maddie. That is quite a story. But I cannot imagine Theo telling you all this as it sounds deeply disturbing and makes it sound like he was not the sharp and wise guy we both know, who's always making bold decisions and taking charge. He does not put up with nonsense."

"My rendition is how I see it Viv. I read between the lines when he told me. And yes, we have always seen Theo as our head honcho in terms of leading our pack but even Theo is fallible. You know I adore him - that is exactly why I intend to reveal that underneath this beautiful flower lies the deadliest snake.

I will find a way to drain her fangs from poison, to skin her beautiful scales and hang them to dry in the sunshine so she can cover her own expensive heels with them, the ones in which she still walks all over Theo. The slithering must stop. Theo always protects us. Now it is he who needs to be kept safe and be loved. Wholeheartedly and truthfully. Let's end the lies. Now and forever, until death us do part."

Daffodil Daphne

The table was set with juice, omelette, fresh bread and sliced pineapple. Humphrey was filling the glasses with a papaya and mango blended smoothy.

"Thought we'd lost you but glad you are back. Ready for some soul food?"

"So ready!" I said.

Theo called Maddie over to where he was standing in the kitchen doorway.

"Mads, I just had a chat with Humphrey. He told me that there was a clash with you and Cristina. I want you to be sure that you are my priority. If you allow me let's talk this through later? I want you in my life and I am sure we can make this work."

"Whatever *this* is," Maddie said.

"Come here my Mad Maddie."

Theo pulled Maddie into him and kissed her head. She resisted at first, but then hugged him back. They stayed there for a while in silhouette at the doorway. Like they were meant to be home together.

"Don't let's wait for them Viv," Humphrey said. "Allow me to serve you some pineapple. Try it with some hot sauce. You will be amazed what sweet and hot can do when they get together." That smile again.

"If you like to play with fire, be prepared to get sizzled," I said, as I held the bottle of thick hot sauce at forty-five degrees, while looking at Humphrey. A big dollop landed exactly where intended. I picked a juicy chunk up with my fingers smothered it in sauce and placed in between my lips. "Yummy," I said.

Humphrey stirred, bit his lip, stretched his back, and rolled his shoulders as if he were readjusting himself ready for gentle battle.

"Hmm," he said, in his deep dulcet tones. "Just hmm..."

I took a sip from my glass trying to hide my blush behind the pink drink.

"How did you meet Cristina, if I may ask?"

"You may ask anything you like dear Vivi. The more you ask, the more you will know who I am. I, if I may, would like to know all about you. As for Cristina I was trying to call Theo via Skype on his mobile. I hadn't spoken to him for a while and dialled his number. I was very surprised to see a woman answer. As soon as the video came on, I apologised as I obviously must have misdialled. The woman asked me whom I was looking for. She only spoke Spanish. She told me she was Theo's other half and I had no reason not to believe her. She told me that Theo had moved countries and that she was in trouble. It sounded like a can of worms. She said she was not able to get hold of Theo and that he had fathered a child. A boy whom he did not know about. And that she needed money. I knew about a jungle beauty who Theo also called BC, *Bruja Cristina*. He'd told me that this young voluptuous bombshell had cast a spell on him. I could easily deduce that this woman on Skype was the same person.

But from the minute I heard her speak and from her ways I smelt trouble. I politely excused myself and did not contact her again. Although I must say that she tried to contact me. I was a potential ATM for her just like I feared Theo may have been. Though I must say Theo told me they had fun too. But hey having fun is just another tool to tap into the money source. Sex and fun are a powerful combination for those looking to escape. Some pay dearly for that. And in this case, I think Theo paid with more than his credit card. The Cristina chapter took an emotional toll on him. He was telling me about it just now when I raised the issue of what happened this morning at your place. I told him that he might lose Maddie if he succumbs to Cristina's manipulation. I didn't hesitate to call it that because I recognise manipulation when I see it. Cristina herself had shown me what she was made of on that call and again, today, the second day I have ever spoken to her."

"Wow," I said. "I could never have guessed that. The way she immediately acted subserviently to you."

"That is all part of the manipulation Viv. She is seamless and I fear Maddie is correct, Cristina is trouble. But tell me all about you."

"What would you like to know?"

"Everything. I simply want to drink in everything about you. I am utterly parched and so ready to quench my thirst with the most exquisite soul."

"What makes you so thirsty Mr H? What is your story if I may be so free as to ask?"

"It's probably an accumulation of things, I guess. Life happens, love happens, and then unfortunately so does loss. My partner Daphne was British. She was my first love when I attended boarding school in England. She was at the girls' school. I first set eyes on her when she dressed up as a boy wearing the uniform of our school or rather a choir cassock and found her way into our section. She had come with two of her friends for a bit of a giggle but had lost them along the journey as they were trying to duck out of the way of the teachers. Daphne's long hair was trapped under the school cap she was wearing but a long strand of her golden hair escaped and tumbled down her back. I watched as she took her cap off behind the coat rack. I was so intrigued that I went to see who this exquisite creature was. Not a boy, I could sense that a mile off. I poked my face between the coats and she spotted me. As she took off her cap, her glorious mane tumbled out like an unbridled waterfall of spun gold. I tried to hide my sixteen year old face behind the coats but she grinned at me. Her skin was pale and her cheeks glowed pink. Her huge blue eyes shone.

'You came to see me it seems and now you are shy Humphrey?'

I had no idea how she knew my name. I was the only one at school with caramel coloured skin in this privileged, secluded institution which cost a bomb.

'How do you know my name?' I stammered.

'Everybody knows you over at the girl's school,' she laughed. 'You are the one milk chocolate we all want to taste.'

I can only describe the feeling of embarrassment tainted with a hint of thrill and blended with an unmistakable sense of excitement. I had not before considered the energies that can happen between two people. And now it was palpable. The rush of blood reached my cheeks and my loins and my heart. I felt as if I was on *Cloud Nine*. The words of William Wordsworth danced into my brain, '*I wandered lonely as a cloud. That floats on high o'er vales and hills, When all at once I saw a crowd, A host, of golden daffodils; Beside the lake, beneath the trees, fluttering and dancing in the breeze.*' She was a daffodil.

I remember trying to get a grip. With every ounce of guts, I had in me, I walked round the coat stand to face her, 'You know my name. But what was yours?'

'Daphne,' she said. 'My name is Daphne Leighton-Moore.'

'Daphne the daffodil,' I said.

Looking at me with those huge eyes, she said, 'Humphrey the Handsome.'

And in that instant, our worlds seemed to fuse. Locked in the moment and blissfully unaware of the rest of life around us, we stood looking at each other. It couldn't have been long. The spell was broken by Matron and the unmistakable tick tock sound of her heels which sounded alarm bells. She was the only woman in a school full of boys and men. Mrs Orinoko, or Mrs Origami as we called her as she was always so precisely pleated and finished, appeared in sight.

'Got to go,' Daphne said, as she scooped her golden locks into a bun and tucked them under the cap she had stolen or borrowed from somewhere.

Rather than run, she turned to see Matron hastily coming towards us. She stood on her tiptoes and kissed me right there on the lips; 'I like you,' she said. 'I will see you again.'

Then she hitched up the choir cassock and skittered off like a lamb in spring dancing through a flowered meadow with her cape flying behind her.

I watched her go until Mrs Origami grabbed me by the ear, saying, 'What the hell do you think you are doing? What did I tell you about girls? Don't go near those vixens until you are old and wise enough to bear the consequences. Now get out of my sight and control those troublesome hormones. You are here to make your parents proud. Not to waste your time on female distractions. Now get on with it, Humphrey. Continue your day.' But I was sold."

"Wow that's quite an encounter Mr H! Why did Mrs Origami not come down on you? I would have thought you could have got into serious trouble for dealings with Daphne. Seems she went easy on you."

"I don't know why but Ms O. had a thing for me. She once put me on detention, and then, when I look back on it, she had flirted with me. It was before the Christmas break when most of us returned home for the holidays. My friends and I had been up to some mischief, nothing crazy, just breaking into the kitchen to help ourselves to fresh mince pies. We got caught with the whipped cream still on our noses and the crumbs on our lips. Josh and Gerald were sent out to Mr Preston, the sports teacher, and ordered push-ups in the snow. But Ms O. kept me with her and sat me down in her study. It was warm in there and smelled like Japanese Jasmin, or maybe it was just that she looked oriental.

Anyhow she gave me an intent look and said, 'Humphrey, you and I are different to anyone else. You fit in, yet you don't. That will be the way for the rest of your life, especially in conservative England. Unless you spend your time in London, where life is more cosmopolitan, but that is superficial. Finish your school and find what you are passionate about. And then let your passion take you to where you want to go and want to be. If you know who you are, you will always succeed. I know that from experience.' With that, she took one of her earrings out of her pierced ear. It was a black pearl. She took my hand as I stood in front of her; she opened my palm. She placed the jewel in my hand. Then she closed my fingers as if she were securing the pearl within the oyster.

She continued, 'Pearls are made from grit. The oyster covers the irritating particle with pearl. Layer upon layer, and eventually, you have a pearl. It is beauty born out of pain. I want you to keep this with you and remember that you know something beautiful can become of it anytime you hit grit. Something exquisite is always in the making if you open your eyes to it. Even after a moonless night. The sun always rises.'

I remember feeling disoriented. I simply nodded as Mrs Origami opened the door and let me back into the real worlds of boys, books, and bullies. I would stand up to them now, I thought.

It was a weird experience but one that still resonates today. If there is one rotten apple in the applecart, you must face them. If there is one thing that is stopping you from being, you must tackle it. Only then can you breathe the oxygen you are entitled to and take your place on God's glorious globe and live life as it is intended. I think I haven't been living my own truth for some time. Some events in life take longer to digest."

"That sounds profound. Were you referring to anything, Humphrey?"

He moved in his seat. "More coffee?"

He took the thermos and refilled the cup I held out to him; "It is time to replenish my cup," he said.

I remained silent.

As we had learned at school all those years ago. If you want to know more, be quiet and still.

Humphrey took a sip from his coffee.

"Did you ever see Daphne again?" I asked.

"At school during official events, the boys and girls got together for religious and other occasions, though not often in between. Daphne would sneak the odd note to me. I was not quite as creative. After school, we lost touch, but she for sure was the first flower of my heart. I often thought of her.

I moved to LA to study photography and lived my life. I had my friends and a healthy number of relationships. Some good, some less, and overall, my life was good. I travelled and spent time with my parents in both the UK and the US. My adoptive parents lived in the UK, and when I was eighteen, I reconnected with my parents in the US. That was another story for another time if you allow me to tell you about it someday."

"Of course," I said.

"On one of my trips to Africa when working on a National Geographic gig, I went to Uganda. We were shooting at Lake Victoria when I met a lady from the local church who asked me whether I would come with her to see the recently refurbished orphanage. I offered to take pictures to raise awareness and to be used in their fundraising campaign. I agreed as I like to combine doing my work with some impactful support whenever possible.

It was clear that the Flower Meadow Orphanage set high standards. The place was clean, the children were being engaged in play and gardening activities. A group of children were digging with their trowels in the flowerbed. A teacher was guiding them. There was a positive energy about her, though I could not see her expressions under her Boater. I remember us wearing those at school back in the day. When we went to the Henley rowing event with the school, we would all be dressed up in pale blue and white striped blazers and grey slacks and bowties. Describing it to Americans, I simply call it an *English Panama*. Boaters were derived from the canotier straw hat worn traditionally by gondoliers in Venice. The Venetian canotier had a ribbon that hung freely off the back. They were often edged with a matching ribbon. Because of this, boaters were identified with boating or sailing, hence the name. Apparently.

Anyhow, I wanted to have a shot of the teacher and her brood with the flowers around them. I preferred taking pictures of potentially sad situations within a context of optimism. I find that the right energy attracts the correct response. Sob stories sell, but energy moves mountains. That was my theory anyway."

"I fully concur," I said. "There is nothing more powerful and positive than aligned good energy. Did you get the picture you were looking for with the kids and the teacher?"

"I got more than the shot, dearest Ms Vivi." Humphrey paused and seemed momentarily lost in his thoughts.

He then smiled as he told me, "I found my English Rose in the garden of the orphanage. Some of the kids helped me to bring my photo gear over. They were so excited to be allowed to move the equipment. I walked over to the bed, and the woman under the hat looked up. The broad brim cast a shadow over her face as she sat on her knees in the soil.

I greeted her. 'Hi there, I am Humphrey, the photographer. I would like to take some pictures if you allow me.'

The woman dropped her trowel, put her head, hat, and all in her hands, and started sobbing. I was taken aback. I got down on my knees beside her and touched her hand.

'Are you alright ma'am,' I asked.

She then tipped her head forward without touching it, and the Boater landed rim up in the soil. I took the hat to save it from getting dirty. As I looked up, the woman who gazed back at me had huge blue eyes with tears running down her rosy cheeks, and a full mane of golden hair streaked with silver.

'Humphrey. Of all the gardens in all the world, you walked into mine.'

'Daphne...Daffodil Daphne...'

Right there and then, we simply embraced each other, still on our knees in the soil. The children gathered around us and were laughing and pointing while they danced with joy, while Daphne and I hugged and cried."

"Wow..." I sipped my coffee. "What an incredible story."

Humphrey looked at me.

"Don't cry, Vivi. It was all good. It was extraordinary, and there was no doubt that destiny played its finest hand. I took you the long route, I am afraid. Daphne and I became a couple. She continued to live in Uganda with Anthony, the son we adopted from the orphanage. I managed my work and met her as often as possible. I helped with the set-up in any way I could and made sure to send funds for education and support the lives of those kids so much less fortunate than some of us. We were good together whenever we were together. Perhaps it was not a conventional arrangement though it was a deep, loving, and valuable one. I felt like I had a partner and a son even though we never married. We travelled together when we could and explored the plains of Africa. On some occasions, Anthony would join us, and it was the closest I ever felt to having my own family. Until seven years ago.

Daphne and Anthony were crossing the road in Kampala. At that moment, a drunken fool careered into them and did a runner leaving my loves like migrating animals hit by a car, splattered over the tarmac. Roadkill, they called it."

Humphrey stopped talking. His eyes were darker than before. His face tormented; he looked like a different man. The energy that had made him shine had now been sucked from his soul. Limp and lifeless.

The damage that grief can do.

Flowing Feeling

We spent the day at *La Hacienda* talking and swimming. Maddie and Theo went off for a siesta, and Humphrey fell into a deep sleep, too, on the lounger under the palm leaf roof of La Cabana. Though we had planned beforehand to scout and discuss business, it was clear that today was not the day to force it.

I was feeling exhausted as well. I was aware of the way Humphrey's emotions were already influencing me. I had felt his pain so very strongly when he spoke about his loss, and that was something that had never happened to me before. I'd only known this man for less than forty-eight hours, and he was affecting me. I told myself to be vigilant.

I wandered over to the hammock and sat in it. From the vantage point, I could see Merlin working with the men on the plantation. There were fewer workers now. The coffee picking took place between December and March or April. It was more about maintenance, ensuring the soil was nurtured correctly, and fixing fences. In addition, the house's shutters needed painting and other odd jobs that a great estate always requires, needed doing. I was grateful for Merlin to be running the logistics. He seemed very competent though my suspicions had been raised when we drove out through the back exit, and I observed that his mood changed when he dropped us home. I realised it was impossible to know what was going on in Merlin's mind. Each person had their stories and their lives. Perhaps he was having a hard day, or the front gate was being maintained, and that's why we took the back route. I had no idea.

As I lay gently swinging back and forth in the hammock, looking out over the beautiful green hills that lay in front of me, I tried to think like Maddie. She had an investigative sort of mind. There were quite a few unanswered questions.

Was Theo still into Cristina, or was he serious about Maddie?

Who was Cristina, and was she the snake Maddie said she was? Certainly, Humphrey seemed to think she was a manipulator.

What was Maddie's plan in taking the remaining artefacts from the locked bedroom?

What role did Merlin play in this whole situation? Was he, in fact, the criminal that people said he was when he first came to La Hacienda and Curtis Coffee had believed in him and given him a job? Was Merlin a con merchant, or was he being played by someone else?

And as for Humphrey, was he genuine? After all, he had done many jobs for National Geographic, and Maddie warned me about that.

My head was spinning as I slowly slipped into a deep dream. I must have dozed off for some time. Maddie and Theo had not yet reappeared when I woke up, though Humphrey had just begun to stir. The sun was setting, allowing for a distant view of Cathedral Point, where the House of the Bluff stood. When I heard his voice, I was lost in my thoughts, sitting sideways in the hammock, and touching the ground with my feet to keep up a perpetual rocking motion.

"I slept and woke up. You must have given me some peace. I never sleep in someone else's company. You quietened my soul. It is an extraordinary feeling. One I have not really experienced before," Humphrey said.

The solar lanterns hanging from the roof of *La Hacienda* began to glow. I smiled up at Humphrey.

"Good little siesta, Mr H? I think you really needed that after your late-night phone calls with Bali."

"I am not sure this was Bali related Vivi. I suspect that as I confided in you, I felt relieved but drained. I have not shared what happened for over seven years. It has been my deepest pain. I did not want to talk about it for fear of not managing my emotions. But I told you. While I felt exhausted, I was also strangely lighter for sharing events with you. Thank you for simply listening. Sitting here looking at you, I am wondering whether you are my Kintsugi."

"Your what?" I asked. "Is that something Mrs Origami taught you?"

"No, I came across it when I was in Japan with National Geographic. I combined my assignment with a trip to Okinawa. That place is also considered a Blue Zone, with women living the longest on the planet. That is where I learned about *Ikigai*, too."

I interrupted, "I think Ikigai resonates with me because of my strong belief in social enterprise, running businesses for good. It is of immense significance to have a direction and purpose in life. Only then can you have a sense of fulfilment and a sense of meaning. Working towards what matters is the most valuable thing you can do with your life. Only then will you get satisfaction and meaning. Working the sweet spot. But what is that *Kingi Thing*y you were referring to earlier? Sorry, I interrupted you. It is a weakness of mine, especially when I get excited about the topic."

"In that case, I am not at all offended. I am happy we enjoy our conversations."

The rain started coming down.

As a colossal raindrop burst on my nose, I laughed and said, "Let's go under the Cabana for now until those sleepy heads Maddie and Theo make an appearance."

We settled into a rocking bench that looked like two or three rocking chairs had merged to form an extremely wide one. It had comfy pillows.

"Can't believe I went from swinging to rocking. From the hammock to the rocking couch. I must admit I am feeling a bit guilty for this level of laziness."

"Tomorrow, we can do what is needed," Humphrey said. "For now, let's just go with the rhythm that life is showing us."

"Like a metronome, giving us the right beat per minute for our music."

"Very poetic, Viv."

"Did you know that the word metronome is derived from the word *némo*, meaning: I manage or I lead? I remember that from my classic Greek class."

"Nice," Humphrey said. "I like these golden nuggets. Talking of golden nuggets, Kintsugi is the centuries-old Japanese art of fixing broken pottery. Rather than re-joining ceramic pieces with a camouflaged adhesive, the Kintsugi technique uses a particular tree sap lacquer dusted with powdered gold, silver, or platinum. Once the broken pot is fixed, no matter how many pieces it had been broken into, it shows the beautiful seams of gold glinting in the obvious cracks. While the piece will never be the same, it gives it a special appearance that can be equally beautiful."

"That is such a wonderful way of looking at fixing things that are broken. Repairing them with purpose and soul. I find it touching."

"You have healing energy, Viv. You may very well be the golden glue between my broken pieces."

With that, he put his arm around my shoulder. Humphrey and I sat as we rocked together, listening to the rain.

Daisy Oracle

That night we crashed at *La Hacienda*. Having slept a large part of the day, we came alive at night. Theo created combustible cocktails while Humphrey took charge of the barbecue.

"We have plenty of space here. Shall we chill out at *La Hacienda* tonight?" Theo asked, to which we all agreed. "Tomorrow, we will move you, girls, to *Si Como No*, so you don't have to worry about any noises or nuisances. I want you both to be comfortable. Knowing Humphrey is in the same place will put my mind at rest though you better behave yourself, Big H. You are engaging with my baby sister, and she means the world to me. Don't go blowing it."

He gave Humphrey a broad smile and took his beer from close to his armpit so he could make a toast, "*Pura Vida*."

We raised our glasses, "*Pura Vida*," we toasted in unison.

"Talking of *Pura Vida*, does anyone fancy a *porro puro?*" Theo asked as he retrieved a pre-rolled joint out of his pocket and went over to the barbecue to light it up.

He dragged on it and then passed it on to Maddie, who was sitting on his left.

"Here, darling," Theo offered her the joint. "Smoke the peace pipe with me."

"You are so smoking hot I cannot resist that offer," she smiled, putting her lips around the *porro,* and ingesting the smoke as if she was drinking it in.

I recalled how the Arabs talked about drinking an *argileh*, the traditional hubbly bubbly, and now I could imagine why they said that. I visualised Maddie walking around her Ethiopian compound at sunset. With the dogs by her side and smoking her way out of the day into the night. With the threat of Manu's atrocious threats and abuse looming after dark.

As if Maddie had just read my mind, she got up from her place on the comfortable shabby chic sofa in the Cabana and held her hand out to Theo.

"Come walk with me."

Theo got up and took her hand. They sauntered off beyond the pool and out of sight.

Once again, I was alone with Humphrey. He was upbeat and talented, gorgeous inside and out, though he too had a most traumatic story with perhaps still more to be known. I thought about Theo and his past, challenges, and strains that even I didn't know about. In the end, I realised that everyone lived both good and bad times during their lives.

Without pain, there were no grooves, and without tracks, there was no music. At the same time, you should be vigilant. You should trust and believe in better. But you should also take care not to repeat a pattern of pain if you can avoid it. If lessons were sent to live through, we should remember to learn rather than repeat them.

"Where is your mind at Viv?" Humphrey leaned over my

shoulder, putting some freshly grilled shrimps in front of me. "Do you want me to peel those babies for you, or you prefer to deal with them yourself?"

"Thank you," I look up. I could not see Humphrey's handsome face as the light was shining from behind him.

"You are lit up from behind like an angel," I smiled. "I always peel my own prawns."

"Fully understood, ma'am," he said as he slipped into the seat next to mine.

"Shall I check your steak?" I asked. "It seems to be sizzling. It smells divine."

"Don't worry about the meat *guapa;* it is temperature-controlled, unlike my good self."

I felt my blood heating up and my cheeks blushing. For the first time, I felt a bit uncomfortable. Humphrey couldn't see, but he noticed anyway.

Humphrey may not be married, but he clearly had some unresolved issues and emotions. I enjoyed our time together and thought very highly of him, but I began to see that he was perhaps, not yet, the guy for me.

I leaned across to grab the cut lime off the wooden slab that served as a chopping board. I placed my fork in the middle of the fruit and squeezed it. The lime sap sacks burst, allowing the explosive scent to infuse the air. I drizzled the juice over the tiger prawns. Humphrey's nostrils flared.

"Powerful stuff you have there, Missy. I can't argue with that scent. I can only imagine how good it will taste if only you will let me try it."

I put a sliver of butter on my plate which melted, as it fused with the lime juice.

"Here you go," I said as I prodded the shrimp onto the fork and presented it to Humphrey. "If you play your cards right, I will give you a few more."

"I am not a gambler Viv," Humphrey said. "I only place my bets when I am totally sure I am going to win."

"Don't count your money when you're sitting at the table," I said as I started to hum the tune of *The Gambler* by Kenny Rogers. I went on singing a line or two very softly as I wasn't a confident singer, yet somehow, I was fine doing it in front of Humphrey. "You've got to know when to hold 'em, know when to fold 'em, know when to walk away and know when to run." Then I was quiet.

"I won't run," Humphrey said as he cupped my face with his firm, gentle hands and kissed me briefly on the lips. I did not kiss him back, nor did I shrug him off. I liked him, but he needed to sort out his through his pain and his loss. He would not be the person he could be until he did. I was quite sure that Humphrey had all the makings of a hero, but he needed some healing first. I wasn't ready because Humphrey himself wasn't.

Who knew what the future would bring? But, for now, my mind was clear. I would not be going there. For him, but also for me. I wanted truth and happiness. Only on solid ground.

"That steak really will be ruined if you don't take it off the grill, H. You strike me as the person who would deliver the steak *à point*."

Humphrey left me and went over to the grill. "Speaking of which, I think you just made the point, in your lovely way, that I was not yet ready to be served to you.'

"Now, who's cooking with words?" I said.

"You're a tease, my squeeze," Humphrey replied as he carried the steak over to the slab of wood on the table.

He was bending over it just like an artist would do over his work. Full of dedication, knowledge, and appreciation for the creation of something extraordinary. The meat oozed as he laid the slices on a colourful glazed plate that was blue around the rim, gradually becoming a bright yellow in the centre. Humphrey presented to me the flower with its carnivore leaves.

"We will have to let it rest for a little while to get the best out of it. Time makes it better, much as it is difficult to restrain yourself when the delicacy is there, right in front of you. You can appreciate it, smell it, almost taste the grandeur of the promise already. Your mind has already gone there. Your body is already responding." His butterscotch eyes turned to chocolate as he looked at me.

"Looks like a daisy," I smiled, trying to lighten up the situation.

"Yes, it does," Humphrey said, "This calls for the *Effeuiller la Marguerite*. Those French always come up with the most romantic games. Let's see what the future has in store."

Humphrey picked up the first slice of succulent steak and popped it into my mouth.

"She loves me," he said, licking the juices from his fingers.

Then he took the next piece and pretended it was the next petal of the daisy, "She loves me not."

And so, he continued until we had made our way around the plate, and he presented me with the final bite, completing the *Daisy Oracle*.

Humphrey looked at me as he dropped the ultimate succulent morsel into my mouth, concluding the game with a sad half-smile, saying, "She loves me not."

Midnight Merlin

Humphrey and I had talked about the reasons for me not wanting to fall for him. I knew I was in danger of doing so, as I told him. He still needed to find his peace with the past. And I did not want to lose myself and plant my heart in soil that was not yet ready to nurture a healthy relationship. We decided that friendship was a most incredible opportunity between us. We got excited about sharing parts of our lives in that space as firm friends. Having talked to our hearts' content, we fell asleep, in total comfort.

We woke up to a commotion an hour or so later when Theo and Maddie returned, followed by Merlin, who had his head bowed and looked as if the world had come crashing down on him. I felt my heart sink. This did not bode well. Theo asked Humphrey to join him and ordered Merlin into the kitchen.

"What happened, Mads?" I asked my friend.

"We saw Merlin round the back of the house loading up the car in the dark. He did not see us. Theo wanted to go over to him and enquire what the hell was going on, but I suggested we watch from behind the rock with the pineapples around it.

Sometimes you can learn so much more through observation. I could see Theo was really agitated and hardly able to contain himself. I tried to keep him quiet. Merlin was moving things that seemed to have been placed in the shed earlier, the place that I showed you. It's where I placed the amulets, I smuggled out from the House on the Bluff on *BC-day*. I wish *Bruja* Cristina had never shown up. I believe that she is the central snake to anything untoward. Anyway, I will bide my time and prove that. Going back to Merlin, he brought out a few crates just like the ones we saw in the locked bedroom at the house. They were full of magazines, too."

"Are they National Geographic magazines?" I asked her.

"Why is that important, Viv? Who cares what they are?"

"It is just that you said that National Geographic is often used to cover up a scam. I am worried about that as Humphrey has done multiple jobs for Nat Geo. Every time he mentions it now, I feel suspicious, and I think I should be like you and doubt everything."

"Good God, Viv," Maddie said. "The level of Berlinerdom you let yourself in for is stratospherically bizarre sometimes. Of course, National Geographic had nothing to do with anything. Some people just use anything great and magical to try and cover up for their untruths, lies and lowlife quests. Like that *Bruja* Cristina who wants to milk Theo for all he's worth."

"Now, who is getting sensitive," I laughed.

"You are right, Bussi. You got me. I must get a grip on the venom I feel for that vixen. She is pure poison. I think Merlin is caught in the dirty web of lies of that Black Widow. I am not suggesting Merlin is attempting to mate with her, though he may well have been under her spell or at least under her power."

"Humphrey said to me that he thinks Cristina is a definite manipulator. I asked him how he knew Cristina, and he told me the story. Remember when you met up with Theo again after you broke off with Bing all those moons ago? When you reunited with Theo, he told you the story about Cristina saying she was pregnant and that he didn't know if it was true? Humphrey said that when he connected with Cristina via Skype, she tried to find a way to get money out of him. Cristina told Humphrey, *'Yo di a luz a un niño',* which literally translated means 'I gave light to a boy'."

Now Maddie's eyes were wide, "You mean to say she said Theo fathered her child? And that he had a baby while he was in Switzerland? He never told me! What the hell? If Theo knew this, why didn't he tell me, even if he didn't know this when we reconnected after school. He should have told me during the reunion in Switzerland a few months ago."

"Hold your horses, Mads. Calm down. Listen to me. First, Cristina is held together by lies and is driven by opportunism and greed. She has lived that life ever since she met Theo and perhaps before that time, too. Whether it is a survival mechanism or just her hideous character, who knows? But think about it. When Theo told you that story, he said Cristina did not look pregnant and never mentioned any son in any conversation to Theo ever again. In fact, he did not see her when he returned from Switzerland, not until she was in the dirty paws of *El Comandante.* So why would he think Cristina had a baby?"

I could see Maddie moving from right to left. Her mind was racing.

I continued. "Mads, I have been thinking about this and trying to do so with your mindset. I reckon that perhaps

Cristina decided to milk the situation of having a child if indeed she did give birth. Theo gave her five thousand dollars to either have an abortion if she wanted or have the money to look after the baby in the early days. He had no evidence of her being *embarazada* as she told him. No proof that she was pregnant."

"Embarazada! That word should mean in Spanish what it means in English. She is an embarrassment to herself. She is continuing her spiteful spider's journey, biting one partner at a time. Then, before she even finishes mating, she devours that male and goes on to mate with the next. Even if those unsuspecting males try to get away, she continues to tempt them into her web. And so, her sorry cycle continues! I intend to put a stop to that!"

"We can only do that if you put your logical thinking cap back on, Mads. I understand your utter frustration and pain in not knowing and projecting what might be, but let's take a step back. I have been pondering why Cristina stopped contacting Theo for money. Whether she had a child or not, she could have continued to exploit him. Theo is a softy on the inside, and she locked her fangs into him when he was a young adult. Those first amorous encounters in life can stay with you forever. As we all know."

Maddie lit a cigarette. I knew her well enough to see she was trying to compose herself, create some distance between her emotions, and regain her logic.

After a few intense drags, Maddie said, "Viv, what is your theory? I need you to step in and make some sense of this. I know that is usually my job, but my clarity of thinking fails me when it concerns me. Help me to get back on track so we can stop this bloody train before it inevitably crashes... I don't want to lose Theo. Ever."

She lit another cigarette with the now burning filter of the previous one.

"Here's my theory," I said. "Whether Cristina did or did not get pregnant, she saw the opportunity to make money. She had quite a few illegal artefact traders coming through the jungle. They were, it appears, mesmerised by her. She was clearly the *Prima Puta*. Any one of those many men in the jungle could have been the father of her offspring. Maybe as I suspect, Cristina herself didn't even know who *'embaraza-da-d'* her. Maybe the fact that Theo gave her five thousand dollars presented a new business model to her malicious mind. Taking hush money from these guys to keep their secret even if they might not be the dad. How could they prove that they weren't? Throwing money at a problem to make it go away was perhaps the easiest option for those men. If Cristina was able to convince any of them and get money, why wouldn't she?"

"I don't know, Viv. If she really did have a son, Theo would have known about it by now."

"Perhaps, but what if she really didn't know who the father was? If Theo wasn't the boy's father, Cristina would stand to lose Theo's funds and the money she could bribe from the other potential men.

If Cristina presented Theo with a son, he would have a DNA test done. What if he wasn't the father? He may then ban her for life, which would be the end of Cristina's ability to exploit Theo. Today, Theo makes sure Cristina is looked after. He gives her jobs and makes sure she is okay. Theo is her *Life's Security Plan*. In the meantime, Cristina can do as she pleases. At the same time, that scheming woman can top up her fund by shifting artefacts. She certainly has a great source here to tap into. She is highly connected with the underground network. And *La Hacienda* houses both the man who pays for her and the illegal stock that fuels her trade."

"Okay, so let's assume Cristina had a son. You said that is what Cristina told Theo the day before he went to Switzerland. He was around twenty-five when we met in Switzerland, which was thirty years ago this year, so if the boy really exists and is still alive, he would be thirty by now."

Humphrey came out of the kitchen.

"Mind if I join you ladies?" he asked Maddie and me. "We are not getting very far. Merlin is not saying much and not letting on why he was stacking crates in the back of the car. I stayed with Merlin while Theo went to check the crates. They are full of magazines but nothing else. So, it is a bit of a mystery as to what is going on. Theo had a phone call scheduled with a chap in Europe, so I thought I would come out and join you. Merlin has been ordered to stay in the house until tomorrow when we can perhaps make more sense of things in the bright light of day."

I looked at Maddie, and without saying anything, she gave me permission to share what we had discussed. Humphrey listened intently as we told him about the third bedroom in the House on the Bluff and the amulets Maddie had taken after the Cristina Confrontation.

"The problem is that it was a big thing to raise the topic to Theo about having a potential son, and the fact we think Cristina should be investigated. It seems she was siphoning off artefacts from *La Hacienda* and keeping them in the House on the Bluff as an interim storage place until she could shift them. Merlin, who was perfectly amicable since the first day I arrived at *La Hacienda*, has not been the same since lunch on the day when he dropped us at the waterfall."

I continued to tell Humphrey about Merlin putting boxes in the car and leaving *La Hacienda* via the back gate instead of the main entrance. How the car got scratched and the general weirdness of the trip, having said goodbye to Theo.

"We didn't tell Theo as we thought it was odd and wanted to find out more. But now, the web is terribly tangled."

Humphrey was quiet for a while; then he spoke, "I think you girls may be on to something. More evidence is needed. I also think it is important to gain a bit more clarity before we tell Theo your theory. This is a potential can of worms if ever there was one."

"I don't know how relevant this is, but I recall Amilcar, may God rest his soul, saying that Merlin was suspected of murder. Merlin turned up at the plantation looking for work. At the time, Winston Curtis told Amilcar that he thought Merlin was a good soul. And that he should be given a chance to join him in running the coffee plantation. Amilcar did not hesitate and never questioned Curtis, who had become like a father to him. Curtis died a few months after Amilcar and Merlin then stepped up to run the plantation. He really did a great job building on what Curtis achieved before him. Through hard work and dedication. Workers seeking jobs were welcomed even if they had no experience, just like Curtis and Merlin, neither of whom had been in the coffee business before. They had both been given a chance and seemed eternally grateful for the opportunity to restart their broken existence. Their work ethic cannot be faulted. Nor can their support of Amilcar, I recalled Amilcar telling me that. I was touched at the time that peoples' lives could be turned around by the kind stance of single souls, in this case, the souls of Amilcar and Theo. I really think there is something that Merlin is not telling you and Theo, Humphrey. He may be too scared to speak for fear of being labelled a criminal and to be sent packing, or worse, to end up in jail."

"Viv, you did well. You took your brain to a whole new place when I wasn't able to," Maddie said. "You are talking sense, and you have helped me see more clearly. I agree. I think Merlin holds the key. In fact, now I wonder if Merlin gave us the key to the locked room on purpose. There are two keys on the keyring that he gave to us. We were surprised when my key didn't work in the front door lock. And then I tried it on the third bedroom, which we unlocked and found the amulets under the canvas. I am still confused about why we only found about half the amulets when we went through the sodden magazines. Why weren't all of them being shipped out of the House on the Bluff?"

"Sometimes doing things in smaller steps is less noticeable. One step at a time. Feeling your way until you know you have solid ground underfoot. If you are trying to hide something, nudging forward is safer. Suppose your intentions are right and honourable, and you have firm ground underfoot. In that case, you can take bigger strides forward," Humphrey said, then looked at me, and I knew he was referring to us in the last part of what he just said.

"Nothing but the truth matters," he continued. "Let's see what we can do. Since Theo is on the call with this Bing guy,

I will talk to Merlin to see if I can dig deeper. I agree Merlin seems like a decent guy on the face of it, but he is in a very shady position. I will bring him some food and a hot drink. He seemed utterly shattered when Theo was giving him a hard time. Theo's reaction is totally understandable, but, in the circumstances, perhaps his offensive approach is not the best way to go about things."

Humphrey went back inside. Maddie and I decided to call it a night. We mumbled *buenas noches* to Humphrey and Merlin as we went through the kitchen. We continued down the corridor and walked past the salon where Theo was talking on Skype to Bing. The bright blue light of the screen reflected on Theo's drawn face. We knocked on the open door and gave him a brief wave. Theo managed a tired smile and continued his call.

The energy had seeped out of the day.

The arms of the hallway clock held hands at midnight and chimed as the moon disappeared behind the clouds and the rains broke.

Clarity in Darkness

It was the second all-nighter for Humphrey. First the Bali call and now the Merlin situation. While Theo was speaking to Bing, Humphrey continued talking to Merlin. Humphrey's ability to speak multiple languages was exceedingly helpful. Whether it was playing The Daisy Oracle in French or talking to Cristina or Merlin in Spanish. He was a problem solver. He appeared both kind-hearted and caring, in an intelligent, non-show-off kind of way. I wished he would be able to work through his own emotional blockages and come out the other side. Humphrey was a good guy.

"Good morning, Ms Vivi," he greeted me, brandishing a pot of freshly brewed coffee. "What do you fancy?"

I smiled at him. What a guy. Up all night and not a hint of complaint.

"Yes, please, H. Are you okay?"

"All good, Viv. I made some progress with Merlin yesterday during our nocturnal chat. When Theo finished his call, he looked drained. I told him I would sit with Merlin if he agreed. Theo simply nodded and made his way to bed. He is still out for the count, it seems. Anyhow, the storm and lightning were crazy last night, and the electricity short-circuited."

"Really?" I said. "I had no idea. I must have crashed and slept immediately."

"As it happened, it is a good thing. I knew there must be a fuse board somewhere, but I decided to keep Merlin and myself sitting in the dark to shed some light."

"Can't believe you said that. I had had some of my best conversations when there was a lack of physical visibility."

Once, on the night flight, after they dimmed the lights, I had a chat with the CEO of a hotel company in the Maldives. We had spoken freely with honesty, and I still remember that conversation. Then I recalled talking with Fredric, who came with Captain James, an old friend of mine, to stay at my place in London when they were running the Marathon together. Fredric was blind. He and James had completed the distance with an elasticated link joining them. While James was soaking in the bath, I talked to Fredric. He made me see things more clearly than most. Not being able to see, in certain circumstances, could help to shed clarity.

"Where is your mind at Viv?" Humphrey said. "You seem to be on memory lane somewhere. I have seen you drift off before."

"Sorry, Humphrey, you are right. Tell me how you got on with Merlin. Did he loosen up a little and let out some more?"

"Yes, after Merlin had his meal and a drink, the atmosphere was less loaded with just one person talking to him. Then he opened-up. I had some key information about when he was accused of murder. A bit more context about how he arrived at *La Hacienda* and his relationship with Curtis helped me gain his trust. And eventually, at around three in the morning, as I heard the grandfather clock strike the hour in the hallway, Merlin spilt the beans. Naturally, we need to consider that this is just his side of the story. Still, nonetheless, his perspective allows us to build up the situation to be investigated."

At that moment, Maddie sauntered in. "Good morning, Viv. Hi Humphrey," she said as she pulled out a chair and joined us at the kitchen table.

"*Buenos días niña*," I said.

Humphrey smiled at her, and as he poured out a cup of steaming coffee and handed it to her.

"Morning dear Maddie, I was about to tell Viv about last night. Am I good to go, or do you need a bit of waking up time first?"

"You were up talking to Merlin through the night, and yet you're still so considerate to offer me coffee and to check whether I am ready to listen? My goodness, you are a rare man, Humphrey." Maddie looked at me approvingly. "Please tell us. I have my coffee, and I'm ready to listen."

She settled on the colourful, which Humphrey had pulled out for her, while holding her colourful ceramic mug.

"Merlin told me pretty much everything I already thought about the situation. He realised that the alternative of not confiding in me would put him in a worse position. However, he warned me it was *una historia muy mala*. Merlin is a deep soul who has a sense of loyalty as well as a reverence for God. I think he is a highly emotional man though not used to express himself."

"Sounds like a long night, Humphrey," Maddie said.

"I'll top up your mug," I told Humphrey and then I settled

back down at the table.

Humphrey recounted his talk with Merlin. "In a nutshell, Cristina had been coming to *La Hacienda* on regular occasions when she was paid to do so by *El Comandante*. He let her roam the house and the grounds when he was sleeping off his stupor, so Cristina knows every inch of *La Hacienda*. After *El Comandante* disappeared, Theo asked Amilcar if she could do cleaning and cooking to earn some money. Maybe he was unaware that Cristina had a roaring trade in both the *Puta* business and illegal trade. She knew where to look for the illicit treasures that *El Comandante* had amassed over the years. A few pieces at a time would likely go unnoticed, especially since *El Comandante* was usually inebriated and high when he was at home. In addition to offering jobs at *La Hacienda*, Amilcar also asked Cristina if she would like to clean the House on the Bluff where Winston Curtis lived with his son Arturo.

Clearly, it was not the cleaning jobs that Cristina was after. She now had both sourcing and storing bases within thirty minutes of each other. Cristina was allowed to stay over at either place whenever she wanted to. Amilcar gave her a choice of either. He was known for his generosity. The workers knew how Amilcar had helped Curtis and Merlin too. Merlin said he was petrified of being convicted for a crime he hadn't committed and sometimes got up at night when he couldn't sleep. On numerous occasions, he noticed light signals from *La Hacienda* or the House on the Bluff.

La Hacienda was on the highest point of the plantation, and the House on the Bluff was almost at an equal height to it, albeit quite a distance away. Merlin recalled that there were two codes he saw repeatedly. I asked Merlin to translate the first signal into sound by knocking on the kitchen table as we sat in the dark. Merlin did not appear to know what either signal meant. Merlin said the first light signal, translated into sound as DAH-DAH-DAH-dah-dah-dah-DAH-DAH-DAH. I recognised the distress signal. Usually, that means SOS, but it could also be used as a warning, I suspect. The other signal was dah-dah-dah-DAH. I remembered that from my lessons at boarding school at Sherbourne, back in England. It was not from my history teacher but from my music teacher that I learned that this morse code could be found back in Beethoven's Fifth Symphony, though it spelt 'V' for Victory. I remember Churchill from my history lesson making the V sign for Victory. I was fascinated at the time by how music and history were so intertwined. I deduced that the letter V in morse code must have been the counter code for success, or we have the green light."

"Oh my God," I said. "That is a golden nugget I've never heard of before. My mum taught my brother and me the *Save our Souls* signal when we were little. Still, I never knew about the Latin sign for five, the V. I wonder how Cristina and whoever she has worked with as part of her gang knows those codes?"

"Every illegal trader who needs a shorthand code finds their way. And it is easy to remember. You now know the capital of your name, Viv. Tell me what V sounds like."

"Dah-dah-dah-DAH," I said.

"Exactly. Easy peasy, lemon squeezy as Mrs Origami would say," Humphrey said.

"Fascinating stuff," Maddie said. "Please keep going, Humphrey."

"Merlin confronted Cristina on the coding. She immediately had him, figuratively speaking, by the short and curlies. She told Merlin that now Curtis was dead, he had no protection, and she would make sure he was hunted down for something he had not done. The Prima Puta slept with the police and most of the underworld, and for a romp in the sack they would not think twice about throwing Merlin into jail and keeping him there. Whoever locked Merlin up on the request of Cristina would have access to her well-oiled gates of paradise for as long as they could stand up to go through them."

"Wow," was all I could muster.

Maddie was less baffled and was seeing the logic clearly now.

"Cristina is ruling those dicks with her pussy," she said. "Boys will be boys, and to Cristina, they make her business happen. That manipulating witch."

"As for possible evidence of a son, Merlin said Cristina's son was the *novio*, the boyfriend, of Sylvia, the daughter of Eduardo. Merlin said he does not know if Alejandro knows that Cristina is his mother. Eduardo told Merlin that the boy is smart and has a heart of gold. Cristina is smart in a manipulative manner, though her heart is certainly not made of goodness. He added that Eduardo is happy Sylvia will be Alejandro's wife and hopes they will be blessed with children. Merlin was told that Alejandro was an orphan. Parentless. So, there is a disconnect, if Alejandro indeed is truly an orphan, but Merlin seemed to doubt that."

When dawn broke," Humphrey continued, "I told Merlin I believed his account of events and that we will work together. If Merlin is still here at *La Hacienda*, it means he spoke the truth, and if he is gone, it means he did not."

"Isn't that a bit of a risk to have taken?" Maddie asked.

"Perhaps," Humphrey added. "But I trust my gut, and I sense that Merlin is genuine.

We will have to set up a scene to frame Cristina and unmask her. I am afraid I have not yet figured that out entirely."

"I have," Maddie said. Humphrey and I turned towards her with some surprise.

"You are back to taking on your role of Inspector Clouseau, Mads?"

"Yup. I am over my procrastination and no longer taking events personally. Here is what I recommend we do. May I?"

"Please do," Humphrey and I said in unison.

"We will not tell Theo. I know it sounds absurd not to, as he truly is our rock. But my deep belief is that he simply won't believe us. If we are truthful with Theo, I think we may lose him and drive a rift between us; That is the last thing I want to do where it concerns the person, I believe now I genuinely love. The only way is to provide proof and to show Theo the evidence. He is a man of fact. That is the only way we can convince him of Cristina's evil ways. It makes me feel sick to go against him, but in the end, it is an act of love and truth that may impact our entire life. So, it must be done. We need to keep our emotions out of it, as Theo himself would say.

We will rig up the house with hidden cameras and my spy pens, of which I have brought six. I was expecting to need them. I never travel without them following our Glamp Camp Intermezzo."

"Spy pens and Glamp Camp Intermezzo?" Humphrey said.

"Ah, hm, yes. That is another story altogether, and I am sure you will hear about that. For now, let's concentrate on the current conundrum of Conniving Cristina.

The pens are easy tiny cameras I can leave to film what is happening and what is said. We can put them in various places in The House on the Bluff."

"Sounds like a good idea. I also have some film equipment I can rig up and disguise to add to our evidence. Perhaps a little more hi-tech," Humphrey said. "I must say I am very apprehensive about not including Theo and feel very disloyal. Though, in the circumstances, and having seen the powers of Cristina's manipulation, I think you have a valid and forceful point, Maddie. Our intentions are good, so perhaps we have to bite the bullet and live with our discomfort of not involving our main man Theo."

"Agreed, Humphrey. This is the only way to get our proof. Theo cannot under any circumstances know what we are up to. Though he is a tough guy, he seems to protect Cristina at every turn for some reason. Offering her work and accommodating her needs. He will not condone a covert set-up. We will rig up the house and keep one of the pens with Merlin too, to wear in his pocket," Maddie said. "We won't tell him it records as we need to be sure that his motives are clean and he is not telling us lies. I agree with you Humphrey, I don't believe he was, but still...

Let's leave a note for Theo, who is still sleeping and say we will be going to *Si Como No* but may have some breakfast in Quepos on route. We will pick up my gear from *Si Como No* and go to Cathedral Point to put our cameras in place. We will ask Merlin to take us; however, we will not let Merlin know what we are doing. We will simply instruct him to take notes with the pen we give him. I have a notepad I will add to the pen, so he will think we are simply supplying him with tools."

"Shall we disguise ourselves when we go up to the House?" I asked.

"Viv, seriously? Humphrey let's leave Viv by the pool at *Si Como No* and let you and me get the place set up. Darling Viv thinks she is in a movie. With respect, Buss, that is possibly the biggest Berliner load of rubbish I have ever heard you say."

"I guess I was getting carried away," I laughed. "Let's write that message to Theo, gather our gear, and get going. Where do we find Merlin?"

At that moment, Merlin walked in through the kitchen door.

"Buenos días," he greeted us. *"Estoy listo."* I am ready.

Operation Observation

We left a note for Theo on the kitchen table where he could not miss it.

The crates of magazines Merlin had loaded into the black Landcruiser the night before were now purposefully laced with several carefully selected, photographed, and documented artefacts. Merlin knew where the artefact store was, though it was locked. A while ago, Cristina had summoned Merlin, saying she needed help with a key as there was a door, she could not open. Merlin never really entered the house. He oversaw the plantation and had no business being inside. Merlin thought Cristina was unable to handle the lock. When he opened the door without any trouble, Cristina instructed Merlin to place the key on the tissue she was holding. Merlin thought she despised him so much that she did not want to touch the key after he had. Cristina folded the key in the tissue while avoiding touching the metal. She then tucked it between her breasts.

"*Gracias Merlin. Ahora tengo evidencia.*"

From that day onwards, Cristina held the key to Merlin's fate, or so she thought. Cristina pulled a second, copy of the key, out of her pocket and closed the store. Then she walked out of the house, leaving Merlin petrified, like a tree hit by lightning.

Even more disgusted after hearing Merlin's tale, Maddie told us that it was important for the whole operation to have the usual hallmarks. To avoid suspicion and stage *Operation Unmask* seamlessly. Cristina clearly was not in this by herself though Merlin did not know who else might be involved. To avoid the guards at the main entrance, Humphrey instructed Merlin to take the back route, which we had told him about. Merlin looked hesitant, saying the place was overgrown and unsafe to exit as the rain created muddy movement in the valley.

"It seems *La Niña* year is *La Bruja* year, more treacherous than most," Maddie said. "That witch can distort anything, including probably the weather. But she won't be allowed to cloud us out more than she already has. We will expose her from under that *Diabolito* Mask of hers and send her off on her *bruja* broomstick. May she crash and burn."

Merlin reluctantly directed the car through the thick, muddy ground. We got stuck. Merlin managed somehow to manoeuvre the 4x4 by using the slope of the descending mountain on which the chapel stood. Maybe Amilcar was coaxing us out of the mucky meandering path. We could do with some blessings from above. Especially Merlin, who really was in a predicament. He raised his eyes as we passed the chapel above us, kissing the large but simple cross he wore on a steel chain around his neck. The chain, I realised, was usually hidden from sight. I wondered why. Perhaps the reason was that it was long enough to get in his way while working. The necklace could be of some risk when dealing with machinery and be dangerous. Life threatening perhaps. I pulled my thoughts back together.

Why did my mind visit these weird places?

Any trigger could cause me to think in an unexpected direction, even if there was no obvious point.

We managed to make it out of the back gate. The river was higher than before as we traversed it. I hoped from now on we would take the regular route. I think everyone felt the same as nobody spoke when we crossed the angry river. At one point, the large car moved seemingly without grip as if it was about to float downstream.

I recalled the time I was in Petra in Jordan when the rains came. I sheltered in a hotel as I witnessed cars and sheep being swept down the torrential river that the waters had formed on the usually dry and dusty road. There was no stopping it, no way to save the sheep. The cars would end up crashing and the animals dead. My stomach turned at the memory. Then my brain recalled Winston's tragic story as he lost his wife and girls. I felt sick and paralysed.

Please, God, I prayed from my corner in the backseat.

Save our Souls.

My brain silently sent out the morse code. After a few seconds, the car reconnected with the riverbed gripping it, and we had firm ground under our tyres.

Thank you, God!

I remembered then my mother's words, 'You may ask Vivi but always be gracious enough to say thank you when your prayer is answered.'

Humphrey asked Merlin to stop the car when we were safe and on higher, albeit very muddy land. We all got out but stayed near the car. Maddie lit a cigarette, inhaling deeply. I just stood there looking back at where we had come from. My legs felt weak. We should never have taken the risk. I looked at Humphrey, whose caramel skin was almost pale. Merlin looked like he was about to be sick.

Then Humphrey spoke, first to Maddie and me, saying, "Vivi and Maddie. Forgive me. I took the decision to explore this route without taking Merlin's expertise into account. I instructed him rather than ask him. The power distance in this part of the world is large. I should have realised and should not have been so sure of myself and my plan. What we did was dangerous, and I put everyone's life at risk. We will not retake this route again. Theo would never have agreed to it. Now we are safe, please accept my apologies. No decision will be made without everyone's consent in future, and I will include the experience of those who know the land whether they normally take instructions or give them."

I could see Humphrey was shaken.

He continued to speak in gentle tones to Merlin. He translated what he'd just said to us in Spanish, adding that Merlin was part of our team and equal in our quest to unveil the truth. And that Merlin had both the duty and the responsibility to disregard orders that may put us at peril. Merlin nodded and bowed his head.

"*Nosotros descubriremos la verdad juntos,*" We will uncover the truth together, Humphrey said.

Merlin raised his head and looked at us all. He demeanour now calm and robust somehow. His role as an individual had been validated. Merlin stood like a reborn man before us. Humphrey had the strength to acknowledge he had made a grave mistake. Merlin held out his hand to Humphrey, which he took. They looked at each other.

Two equal men on a mutual quest.

It was the first time I had seen Merlin smile with confidence. Like a free man. We were overcome with emotion at witnessing Humphrey's humble way and Merlin's magnificent metamorphosis. We clambered back into the mud-covered car. We did not take the road to *Si Como No* but went to Quepos.

Nobody questioned Merlin when he said we needed to clean the car before continuing on our way. After twenty minutes' drive, we arrived at the car wash. Maddie and I got out. Humphrey and Merlin stayed in the car as it moved through the semi-automated car wash circuit. Maddie wandered over to the small shop and went inside, saying she needed cigarettes and chocolate.

"Anyone could be forgiven for needing nicotine and sugar after that frightening experience," she said.

I was still wobbly on my feet and took a seat outside on the shop's simple cement bench. My mind wandered, alone in my own little world as I bathed in the soothing sunshine.

Thank God, we survived, and we were not washed downstream, never to return.

We were here to wash off the mud from the car. But even so, the exterior of the vehicle would still be scratched. Happily, the damage was just on the surface. No actual harm had been done. Just some grooves. No grooves, no music...

"No puede ser!"

I woke up from my musings. I opened my eyes and closed them again. The sun was bright, and my eyes were not prepared to instantly let the rays abuse my retina. I shut them again and used my hand to shield my eyes from the light. A figure of a man who looked blurred around the edges stood some meters away from me. With the sun behind him, I could not see who he was. My eyes were trying to adjust and focus.

"Bibi! Que haces aquí?"

Slowly my eyes adjusted, but I already knew... "Eddie!"

I found my balance as I got up from the bench where I had been contemplating. Eddie came forward, steadied me, and gave me a massive hug. After a while, I stepped back out of his embrace. It was the first time I saw his handsome face again after all these years.

He was a man now and more solid like a grown-up.

The last time I'd seen Eduardo, he had not filled out yet. He surfed and played football all his life, but he was not a fully matured male back then. Now, standing before me as a grown-up man, Eddie's body was toned, and his kind eyes twinkled in his tanned face. He still had a full head of curly dark hair in which glimmers of silver were reflected in the late morning sun.

"*Siempre el Eduardo el Guapo*," I said. Still the same handsome Eduardo. "What a complete joy to see you, Ed."

I hugged him again and realised that Maddie, Humphrey, and Merlin were observing us from next to the now gleaming car. There was no evidence of any of the distress or potential cataclysmic disaster that we had just managed to avoid.

All looked squeaky clean and hunky-dory, as General Salim would have said. Oh Lord, why think of him now, and why did I send him an email a few days ago? He would think I was still crazy about him... my world was all a whirl sometimes.

They were all smiling as they could see I connected again

with an old acquaintance, whatever our history was. I took Eduardo by the hand.

"*Ven conmigo*, come with me. Let me introduce you to my friends."

"*Hola,* Merlin!" Eduardo said as he greeted Merlin with what looked like a bit of dance of digits and palms ending in a click of the fingers.

"*Pura Vida.*"

"*Pura Vida* Mai*,*" Merlin answered, smiling broadly at Eduardo.

Clearly Eddie and Merlin already knew each other. There seemed to be a bond between them.

I then introduced Humphrey and Maddie, saying, "This is my long lost friend, Eduardo."

"*Un placer de conocerle*," Humphrey said.

"The pleasure is mine," Eduardo responded. "Join me for a coffee and some *pasteles*," he said as he led the way into the house behind the garage and the shop.

We followed him into his home and settled into the living room. The party wall that connected the house to the business on the roadside was solid. In contrast, the opposite side of the room was predominantly glass, allowing for a great view over The Pacific and Cathedral Point in the distance. A picture that allowed you to breathe.

I inhaled deeply as I remembered the first time I came to Costa Rica and met Eduardo. On my first night at *Si Como No*, I arrived at the bar, and a guy was digging into a freezer and filling an ice bucket.

He heard me arriving and said, "*Un momentito*," as he struggled to dislodge the frozen cubes from the bigger block.

As he straightened up from halfway inside the freezer, he picked up the silver coloured container, which had drops of water running down the sides. He took a hammer to it and chiselled out the ice he needed. He straightened himself up and rolled his shoulders as if he were uncoiling himself from his previous confined position. As he stretched his posture, the guy turned and looked at me.

"*Buenas tardes,*" he said as the setting sun coloured the sky behind me.

"*Hola,*" I smiled at him.

What a stunningly beautiful boy, I thought.

He wore a white polo shirt and a jade amulet attached to a leather string. The dark Mayan pendant sat just below his Adam's apple, where his neck joined his torso. His eyes lit up when he looked at me and offered me a drink.

We somehow connected.

As the days went by, Eduardo and I spent time together and eventually, he came to the UK. I met his mother, Nina, and recalled the same cement style bench in their house as I had sat on today. That was Eduardo's bed. He slept on concrete. That never left my mind. His mother was the one who would always bid farewell with the words *Vaya con Dios,* the exact words that Amilcar had said before our final goodbye.

Even with his humble beginnings, Eduardo was grand in the way a gentle soul was, and he knew what he liked and who he was.

Eduardo hailed from the Boruca tribe, the proud indigenous people of Costa Rica. When he visited me in London, he brought me a fantastic tropical cedarwood, hand-carved Boruca mask. He brought me one with flowers, frogs, and birds. Eddie told me that the history and traditions of *Boruca* masks began over five hundred years ago during the Spanish Conquest. *Diablito*, or Little Devil, masks were created to scare the Spanish invaders off. The Spanish observed uncircumcised natives with faces of devilish images and other animal figures and assumed they worshipped the devil.

The Boruca people feel a great sense of pride, Eddie told me, in knowing that they were triumphant in keeping the Spanish from conquering their land and spirit. He went on to tell me that Boruca was built on the wisdom and faith of the elders; it had been passed down over centuries. They were proud people. Having survived the Spanish conquistadors in the 1500s, their sense of identity was intact. However, Catholicism did enter as a religion and took hold, as evidenced in Eduardo's mother, a staunch catholic. When Eduardo's father passed, she took Eddie and his brother up the Pacific Coast and settled in Quepos. And that was where I met him again all those years later.

When Eddie was in England, I worked for a large hotel chain. One day I had a course called *Seven Habits of Highly Effective People*. I was fascinated by a particular item on the emotional bank account, as they called it. The crux of the learning was that one person may think they were doing something good for another, but the recipient did not experience it in the same way. You assume you are making an emotional deposit. However, you may be making a withdrawal from the other person's emotional bank account.

When I came home that evening, Eddie asked me what I had done during the day. I told him the insight we learned. Eddie and I were due to go back into London town to watch a movie. Having just come from there, I was shattered and not in the mood to go back into the West End. However, I thought Ed would enjoy a movie in the newest cinema. I should not take that experience away from him just because I was tired.

But then, I recalled the insight of the day, and I said to Ed, "Do you want to go into town?"

"Sure," he said.

I then told him about the example of the mother and her son from the seminar that day, and I said, "If you want to go, we will have fun, but if you prefer something else, just tell me."

Eduardo looked at me and simply said, "I am really a bit of a homeboy."

On that day, we lived what we had learnt.

We rented *Underwater World* with Kevin Costner, which Ed said was his favourite movie, and we ordered pizza. I will never forget him comfortably installed on one sofa and me on the other. From where I was lying, digesting the pizza, I looked down on his soft brown curls. He turned his head to look at me with his gentle eyes and adoring smile, and I knew we understood each other.

Eduardo offered us a seat, and moments later, a lovely girl in her early twenties came out.

"This is my daughter Sylvia," he said. She was so like her father. It was uncanny.

"*Encantada* Sylvia," I greeted her.

When she spotted Merlin, she skipped up to him. "*Tio mio*," she said. Merlin embraced her warmly, and Eduardo smiled.

"Merlin is my late wife's brother," Eduardo said. "I am sorry you did not meet Esmeralda. We lost her a few years ago to dengue fever. No one ever survives it twice. May her soul rest in peace."

He paused and then attempted a smile. "I know Sylvia's mother would have been happy of our reunion," he said as he stood next to Sylvia with his arm around her. "My girl represents all the goodness of her mother, and she is my greatest blessing."

Sylvia looked up at her dad, who gently kissed her on the top of her hair. Eduardo said, "Sylvia makes the best Costa Rican coffee." Sylvia gave us a bright smile and went off to the kitchen, followed by Merlin, who said he would lend a hand.

While at *Casa Eduardo*, Theo called. We told him we were still in Quepos and would be at *Si Como No* in an hour or two. He said that the timing was perfect and he would meet us there. After an hour or so at Eddie's house, he cordially invited us to Sylvia's wedding. It was to take place the following week at *Si Como No*. Eddie had worked there for so long before opening his car wash business and still had friends there. The owner, too, respected Eddie. There was a natural bond of loyalty and respect between them. Sylvia beamed and said she would love us to attend.

"It is a lovely and generous invitation," I said, "We would not miss it for the world."

We exchanged numbers, said our farewells, and set off up the road to *Si Como No*.

Merlin was more talkative now and chatted to Humphrey in the front of the car while Maddie teased me.

"With respect, darling Viv," Maddie said as we arrived at *Si Como No*. "Let Humphrey, Merlin and me deal with the spy devices. We are doing logistical duties, and you can just chill in the sunshine and cool down in the pool until we return from *Casa Curtis*. Also, if we run a little late, you will be there for when Theo arrives."

I was perfectly happy to avoid the one hundred and two steps in the heat of the day and opted for the pool with grace. Around an hour and a half later, Humphrey and Maddie returned. They told me the house had been rigged up. Maddie had placed her spy pens at strategic locations, including a plant pot in the third, locked bedroom. Humphrey's contraption was a lot more sophisticated as far as I could make out, and it was linked to his iPad. He could view comings and goings from multiple angles.

Both Maddie and Humphrey joined me only minutes before Theo appeared. With not a cloud in the sky, we congregated in the pool and ordered some much needed *Caipiriñas*.

Evil Death

I watched the roof of the House on the Bluff from the edge of the pool. That whole place was full of recording equipment, and Theo didn't even know. Once again, I felt disloyal, and I felt sick to my core. How many times were we not going to tell Theo? The first time was when Maddie and I went to Marbella. The second time was when Maddie and I did not tell Theo we suspected Cristina. Now Maddie, Humphrey and I had the house rigged up with cameras which Theo was unaware of. We must come clean. Even if it jeopardised exposing Cristina. It was not our right to carry on like this.

I looked at Humphrey as he stood at the side of the pool, still dripping. His swimming trunks, with their purple and turquoise sea turtles clambering over his gorgeous bum, stuck to his thighs as he dried his dark curls with a large white towel.

A taller, darker version of Michelangelo's David.

Once he had worked through his issues, I was sure I would find it impossible to resist him. But for now, that was not worth thinking about.

Humphrey draped the towel over his shoulder like a toga,

then pulled his iPad out of his rucksack. I knew he could see the inside of the house via the cameras; the very same place that I'd just been looking at from the pool. However, I could see only the exterior of the building.

The inside perception was always infinitely more revealing than the outside, I pondered.

Theo was in the pool too, and he swam up to me. "Are you okay, Viv? You seem preoccupied."

"Theo, no, I am not okay. I need to tell you something. We should have told you before. We thought we were doing the right thing to bring some clarity, but I am just feeling now that we are stirring up murky waters even further, and it will only lead to more trouble. What if it blows up in our faces, and you won't forgive us? I can't bear it anymore."

"Whoa, calm down, chica. What is going on with you? Let's get out of the pool and talk about what's on your mind. I have an hour or so before I pick up Cristina from the House on the Bluff. She said she needed to do some cleaning as you girls have moved out. So, I dropped her there before I came here. I didn't mention it as I know Maddie and Cristina don't see eye to eye, so why disturb the peace?"

"Theo, I need to tell you. Merlin talked to Humphrey the night you were on the call with Bing. Merlin didn't say much at first, but he eventually confided in Humphrey. When you caught him loading the car, it seems he was being bribed by Cristina to smuggle out the art in the house so she could sell it on."

"Hang on, Viv. That's first a massive accusation of Cristina, even if you girls don't like her. And secondly, there were no artefacts in the crates. Not that it made any sense to me, but what you are telling me logically does not make any sense."

"Theo, let us go over to Humphrey and Maddie."

Humphrey called us. "Theo, Viv, come over. This is important."

My gut tightened. I had no idea what level on the seismic Richter scale this eruption would measure, but it would blow up. Of that, I was sure. As Theo and I climbed the steps out of the pool, Maddie came over to join us.

"Theo, we need to tell you something. We thought we should investigate to be sure of our facts."

"What is going on here?" Theo asked. Then he turned to Humphrey and me. "All three of you are up to something I should know about, but don't? That's a first for me. And not one that feels entirely right. Hope you have not gone and done anything stupid." Theo's eyes rested on Humphrey for a bit longer. "What is going on?" Theo asked again. His voice was now steely calm.

Humphrey simply placed the iPad on the table, with the camera rolling. It showed the empty living room in the House on the Bluff. Then Merlin walked across the screen with one of the crates. He put it down.

"What the hell is Merlin doing at the house? Why has he got a crate? I need to go down there and see. More importantly, why are you filming? What is going on?"

Merlin disappeared out of sight. Just as Theo was about to storm off to Cathedral Point, I said, "Wait, Theo. Look at this." Across the living room walked Cristina. She was holding some artefacts and putting them into a cleaning bucket.

"What the hell?!" Theo said.

Cristina then shouted at Merlin, telling him that he was

useless. Merlin simply stood there. Cristina then yelled, "*Ayúdame!*" Merlin walked over to help Cristina as instructed, placing a crate in the middle of the dark hardwood floor. It was empty. Cristina took a large cushion from the sofa and slipped it out of its cover. She moved out of sight, but she could be heard telling Merlin to open it. Now Theo was looking on and no longer attempting to move.

Merlin was in the frame, and he was holding the cloth case wide open. Cristina had her back to the camera and was clearly trying to fit something into the cover. She was cussing and telling Merlin to hold still. Eventually, she moved around as she slipped the item into the pouch. A glimpse was enough for Theo to see what was going on. In the split second before the artwork disappeared out of sight, Theo recognised the only precious artefact permanently displayed up at the chapel on the hill at *La Hacienda*.

Theo was witnessing Cristina stealing the sacred vessel in which Theo had placed his brother Amilcar's ashes.

I recalled how Theo had the urn held right next to his heart as we made our way, on horseback, up to the chapel. Theo had placed the ashes in the exquisite bowl as they lifted and floated off over the plantation and the Pacific towards paradise.

"Humphrey, come with me! Now!" Theo grabbed his keys and, still in his wet shorts, set off up the steps, followed in hot pursuit by Humphrey.

"No one could have done anything worse, Mads," I said. "This is not just opportunistic stealing; this is a violation of all boundaries. Cristina has disrespected Amilcar, and Theo will make her pay for that dearly. Cristina might have been Theo's first frolic, but Amilcar was Theo's entire family. God only knows what is going to happen now."

"Don't take your eyes of the recording," Maddie said as she got her phone out of her bag and started to film the recording. "Just in case. What is happening here is pivotal."

Merlin was seen pleading with Cristina to stop what she was doing. She told him that he should be the one to worry about and that those were not her fingerprints on the storage room key or on the crates. He should be trembling in his *botas*. We then heard her laughter. Shrill and sadistic.

Cristina came back into the frame, now brandishing a machete.

She ordered Merlin to pick up the crate with the jade and golden bowl in it. Merlin stood motionless. Cristina placed the blade under his chin, tilting his head up.

"Hágalo!" Do it!

Merlin slowly lifted the crate. His shoulders slumped, he then disappeared out of sight. Cristina followed with what looked like cleaning buckets and materials. Still, we knew better by now, having seen her put other precious pieces of art into the plastic to hide them.

"How can we see what is going on? I think we have lost them."

Maddie looked at the iPad and pressed a button. The camera switched to the locked bedroom where Maddie had left the blinds open. The place looked like before. It was hard to detect what was going on. Maddie figured out the system. With the next press of the button, another camera placed over the front door porch area panned out, allowing for a view of the steps, the lift area, and the surrounding tree canopy. The crate and the cleaning materials had been placed on the cogwheel lift platform, and Merlin was seen arguing with Cristina. She shouted profanities at him and then went back inside. Merlin was seen walking down the steps. Cristina came out holding the machete and closed the door behind her.

At that moment, we heard Theo shouting as he was making his way up the steps. He sounded like a man possessed. Cristina stopped dead in her tracks as she backed away, moving towards the lift. Now the camera showed Humphrey and Theo coming into view.

"Puta Oportunista!" Theo shouted as he made his way towards Cristina.

She held out the machete like a sword. Humphrey blocked Theo from going to her. Cristina moved onto the square metal platform of the elevator. Theo pushed Humphrey off him just as Cristina pressed the large tomato-red button on the lift. The crate and the cleaning buckets wobbled. Brandishing the machete above her, the knife blade caught the last of the sun's rays as the lift chugged into motion, and she disappeared down the shaft. Theo and Humphrey turned around to make haste down the steps to try and catch her at the bottom but stopped suddenly when they heard Cristina's scream of terror.

The lift had gone into a freefall under the combined weight of Cristina's body, the buckets and the crate which held the green and gold bowl of ashes.

The speed at which the platform hit the ground created such an impact that whoever was on it would automatically and stratospherically be propelled off it. Cristina, along with the bowl, crates, and buckets, was vomited off the square metal plate into the jungle below. The sounds of her shrill shrieks cut through the sky like acid as she flew to her fate.

A witch out of control with no broom to hang on to.

Mere moments later, Cristina's cry was silenced. The sharp screech that pierced the air had felt like it would never stop. Until it did. The decibels of finite silence pounded in our ears.

Theo and Humphrey ran down the steps. I looked at Maddie.

"Let's go, Mads", I said

We didn't worry about taking anything with us and left all our belongings by the pool. We scrambled up the steps at *Si Como No* to the entrance and ran along the tarmac road and headed off down the track to Cathedral Point. We could hear Theo and Humphrey shouting 'Cristina!' as we approached the parking where Merlin sat in the car. He was trying to call the police. Merlin pointed in the direction, in which Theo and Humphrey had gone. Towards the beach.

Out of breath, we followed the track, slipping as we went on loose pebbles and rocks.

"Theo!" Maddie shouted.

"Cristina," Theo howled.

After a while, the calling of Cristina's name stopped.

Maddie and I spotted Humphrey and Theo on the fringe where the jungle meets the ocean and where the sand turned from golden to black.

And there she was. Queen of the jungle, mother of illegal trade, lying lifeless on top of black rock. The machete was stuck in the black volcanic sand at an angle; Like a spear that had conquered. Bold and proud, softly glowing in the setting sun.

Cristina lay defeated, slumped on her stomach, embracing the stone. Maddie and I stood back as Theo lifted her body. Cristina fell to one side with her face to the heavens. Blood flowed from her eyes, her guts, and her glory.

Theo fell to the ground, his hands in his hair.

Maddie and I kept our distance. I felt sick and vomited on the black sand. Maddie held my hair in a ponytail and steadied me. She didn't speak.

Before long, we heard the dogs coming down the track. *La Policia* shouting. The blades of a helicopter cut the air.

There was no doubt. Cristina was dead, along with her shenanigans, her lies and manipulations, her crimes, exploitations, and greed. At that moment, Cristina had ceased to exist. Her fate had been sealed.

Maktoob, as they say in the Arab World. What is written will be. And it was. Cristina was no more.

One Funeral and A Marriage

The funeral took place within the next week. Theo attended it alone. He went to ensure that Cristina was genuinely dead, I think, not to pay his respects. She had violated the sanctity of Amilcar.

Reporters gathered outside the church in Quepos. Chauffeur-driven, gleaming black Mercedes cars lined the road. Men in black stood side by side, their heads bowed. Hats had been removed and were tucked under their arms. I could not help but think about the way that Theo held his beer. Under his armpit and close to his heart.

There were only men at the funeral. The reporters were savvy enough not to film them. An unspoken fear and respect allowed the men to remain faceless as we watched the ceremony via the local tv station. All the mafia males looked the same. Polished, black leather shoes stood side by side. They observed the arrival of the coffin from a distance. Looking on in silence. Some greeted each other without making a sound. Then I spotted Theo. He stood between the men, wearing the same style of clothes. Donned in black.

With his hat off, his blond angelic locks starkly contrasted with the dark-haired men. Theo appeared to be one of them. Cristina had united them all. With her goods. Some must have been relieved that their secrets never got out. Others were no doubt already missing the access to her glory. Cristina could no longer manipulate nor satisfy. No more payments of hush money. No more fruits from her loins.

After the brief ceremony, the drivers opened the car doors for their bosses. They slammed shut one by one. In quick succession, the men in black sped off, away from the side-line and back into the shade. Safe in the knowledge that La Puta Principal was securely sealed. Six feet under.

I remembered the film *Four Weddings and a Funeral*.

Today was the marriage of Sylvia and Alejandro. Since we were now staying at *Si Como No*, all we had to do to join the party was turn up in our festive gear later that afternoon. The staff at the hotel were preparing for the event. Colourfully painted oxcarts were wheeled in to be placed under the large palm leaf covered atrium where the wedding reception was going to take place. The *carretas* were custom designed to hold the chafing dishes. I have always wondered where the name for the large, industrial-looking, stainless steel food containers came from. When I asked Dr Google, I learned that '*chafing*' is derived from *chauffer*, meaning *to heat* in French. I love these little nuggets of knowledge.

I was not a fan of extensive buffets. I preferred boutique selections of food rather than the large dishes that people dig into. I'd witnessed people destroying and plundering buffets during my travels simply because the food was included in their rate. Whole plates of items would be piled up only to be left untouched and discarded like foxes who kill hens, leaving them for dead without any apparent purpose. Then again, to be evil or callous, a moral code is needed that can be violated and against which, as far as I know, only humans have. Foxes should be excused.

Pillage, rape, indulgence, and destruction were all human traits that emerged during Big Buffets.

The oxcarts, had originally been used to move the coffee, sugarcane, and corn. They carried merchandise from the central mountains of Costa Rica to the Pacific. It was the Spanish who brought in the idea of using an oxcart for transportation. Still, the European design got stuck in the mud in Costa Rica. So, an indigenous Aztec disc was incorporated into a solid wood wheel bound by a metal ring that could cut through the soil. Even though the colonisers introduced the vibrantly painted *carretas*, they were now the national labour symbol of Costa Rica and the pride and joy of the nation. I must say I found that interesting. I guess even if you fend off the intrusion, some of the hallmarks eventually wear off on you.

The traditions and ways of working and thinking that were first rejected and considered a threat to the local culture became the symbol of pride. As was the case with the Catholic religion that came with the Spanish and the oxcart. Naturally, I wasn't suggesting that invading other peoples' territory would be acceptable. However, whenever a merging of cultures occurred, due to whatever reason, sometimes bridges would be built. The purity was disturbed; There was no doubt about that. As a result, hybrids emerged. Over time an alien antagonistic influence could lead to new avenues for idea development, collaboration, understanding and, who knows, perhaps even world peace?

A controversial subject, I realised, though nonetheless worth a ponder.

"Viv, where is your head at?" Maddie asked me.

"Oh, nothing really, just thinking about oxcarts, invasions, and the mixing up of cultures."

"As always, interesting thoughts in that mind of yours, Buss. We were all blended, but I think we have turned out as fine cocktails with exciting and unpredictable flavours. Talking of which, let's have one of those Mimosas that became *Piñasas* or whatever Theo called them. By the way, do you know why this tropical über fruit is called pineapple, Viv?" Without giving me any chance to contemplate the possible answer, Maddie continued. "*Ananas comosus* originated in South America, where early European explorers named it after its resemblance to a pinecone. How juicy is that nugget of information, *Niña Piña*?"

"Blimey Mads, you are in an incredibly exuberant mood this morning. Happy to see that, of course. Seems you are coming out of your cocoon. Any sadness or madness has evaporated. Maybe your jet lag is well and truly behind you."

I gave her an understanding look. The spell on Theo and the ongoing strain on Maddie and Theo as a couple had been broken. I knew that Maddie felt relieved, or perhaps I could go as far as to say, released.

Evil had killed itself by doing evil. How could that be considered a bad thing?

"Viv. Come on! You keep glazing over. We have a breakfast meeting to get to. *Piña* and bubbles. It must be done. Today is a day of celebration. Let's get our skates on."

We went across the breakfast deck to find Humphrey, Theo,

Wai, and Nab sitting at a large table.

"*Buenos días Bika!*" Wai said as he came towards me, embracing me warmly. "How great to see you."

I introduced him to Maddie, who he hugged too.

"Maddie is from Berlin," I said.

"Ah, a fellow Berliner. My companions at the Berlin Philharmonic Orchestra nominated me as an Honorary Berliner. A great pleasure to meet you." Maddie smiled and did not put Wai straight on the meaning of *Berliner*.

"Wai plays the flute exquisitely," I told her.

"I will be performing at Sylvia and Alejandro's wedding. So, you will be able to make up your own mind," Wai smiled.

We chatted easily together, and somehow the pieces of the puzzle seemed to fall into place. Maddie was the practical one. She was bright, energetic, expressive, and had the clarity of mind. Her sense of logic saw through complex situations. Theo had a cool head. He managed well in crises to take an objective look at what was going on, understand it all and provide us with a way out.

I was good at seeing synergies and opportunities strategically. Wai was a musician and knew how to sequence the notes, the rhythm, and the tune of any creation. He and Nab were also involved in The Loving Little Lids Foundation. Like Theo, both men had known Amilcar well, and ensured we all acted according to Amilcar's wishes. And Humphrey had an outsider's eye, a visual mind, a balanced point of view, a kind heart and considered, creative ideas.

All in all, our little impromptu gathering set the scene for our alliance that would lift us to new horizons.

Each person with their speciality as well as individual

experiences, characters, and strengths. Like the different spokes on a wheel. Each of us served another function. By working together, we would each make the wheel spin around and go places. Perhaps it was the fact we would be attending a wedding celebration later that brought one of my favourite poets to mind. The Lebanese author of *The Poet,* Khalil Gibran, had such beautiful nuggets of wisdom that could clarify entire situations. Einstein too had that ability in more succinct ways.

My brain danced off as the others continued talking over *huevos fritos*, beans, and bubbly. My recollection was a bit patchy though the phrases came back to me. I had once recited the poem during a play we performed at Hotel Management School. It related to intercultural nuances and traditions. We were given the task of performing a play with characters from different cultures and being inspired by arts, creativity, poetry, and painting. We were encouraged to improvise and use our creative license as we felt fit. We had certain pillars and structures to give our production form like a skeleton provides the framework to a body. Still, the rest was interpretation, interaction, and emotion.

It was the most touching and incredible assignment.

We bonded with new friends that we had never even known before. We related better through that initiative that Ms Braun gave us. She was our *Cultural Queen* and *Intuitive Tutor*. I felt that embedding cultural awareness and understanding in early adulthood was the keystone in our emotional arch. The wedge-shaped stone at the apex of an entrance could bear the entire weight of the structure.

Interesting that you could relate life to the principles of architecture.

The capstone in the arch keeps the building blocks in place. The pillars that stood apart held up the temple's roof. The poem emerged from where it had been stored for over some thirty years. I have that sort of a mind. Anything that's engraved into my brain will remain forever etched in it. That included poems I performed at primary school, tables one through ten, and certain songs and nursery rhymes.

The fountain of repetition never forgets.

Personally speaking, I loved that I didn't need a calculator to work out what seven times five adds up to. I knew that in today's world, children were told to think rather than regurgitate. I must say I thought there was some merit in cramming it in sometimes; it gave way to instant recall.

I still know, word for word, the song we sang during our summer camp performance on the day our parents picked us up. I was wearing my pink polka dot sunglasses and a bright yellow raincoat. I carried a transparent brolly which I twirled as it leaned on my shoulder, as the children in our class performed on the small stage. I was ten years old at the time.

At the drop of a hat, I could still sing: '*Aux Champs-Elysées, aux Champs-Elysées, Au soleil, sous la pluie, à midi ou à minuit, Il y a tout ce que vous voulez aux Champs-Elysées*'. That brought me immeasurable joy. Recollection through programming. Controversial, perhaps. I like free-thinking, but instant-recall of golden nuggets wedged in the apex of my mind, I have found to be a blessing and a joy. I realised I was lucky as what had been engraved in my mind were typically matters of usefulness or happy memories. Some people may have had horrific instant-recall moments. Just like the ones I knew that Maddie had.

It was so lovely of Eduardo to invite us. And fantastic that the wedding was taking place at *Si Como No*, where I felt so at home and happy. The marriage poem was triggered in my head as I thought of the ceremony, we would soon be attending that afternoon.

'You are born together, and together you shall be forevermore. You shall be together when the white wings of death scatter your days. You shall be together even in the silent memory of God. But let there be spaces in your togetherness. Let the winds of the heavens dance between you. Stand together yet not too near together: For the pillars of the temple stand apart.'

I thought of Amilcar. The poem, as far as I could see, could be interpreted beyond the context of marriage. Maybe we were not born together, but Amilcar, Theo and I, as well as Wai and Nab, were certainly brought together. And Maddie, too. I felt so strongly that Amilcar was still with us.

Forever connected and together.

"Viv?" I refocussed as I felt Humphrey's strong hand softly touching me. His milk chocolate skin contrasted against mine. It reminded me of my friend Ellie, who I met when I had lived in Holland. Her father was Moroccan, her mother was highly Germanic.

Ellie used to shock me terribly when she would joke that her mother was like Eva Braun.

She was utterly unique in every way. She pulled unmentionable punches and was utterly hilarious. Later she would send me letters when I lived in Switzerland, writing on them:

'*Vite facteur, parceque l'amour n'attend pas*,' Quick postman, because love doesn't wait.

She once arrived at my parents' house with three other

girlfriends. They were all topless, wearing motorbike helmets, just for fun and the *Shock Factor*. She was original, kind, and outrageous. We used to go on holiday to the south of France with a gaggle of us. She always wore white. No matter what. She was delighted that she tanned easily when her blond blood was overruled by her more *sang exotic,* the blood from her father's side. With her tanned limbs, Ellie used to touch mine, saying, *'Black and white. Reunited.'*

Now it was Humphrey who touched my hand, reminding me of Ellie as she teased me for my much paler skin and lack of deep tan.

"Where did you go, girl? I have been watching you, and while you looked happy enough, you were definitely not on planet earth," Humphrey said.

"I am not the only one who noticed, it seems," Maddie smiled. "Viv has been on a trip all morning. Off on the winds of thought. Where did they take you, Viv?"

"Drink up, Vivi," Theo said. "I can't recall topping up your glass of champers before. I guess there is always a first time. What's up?"

All eyes were now on me and gentle smiles from everyone around the table.

I spoke, "We should look at what we are good at. Where we want to be. Where we feel at home. What makes us tick. Which role do we wish to play? How we see our lives and what pillar we intend to be to keep the roof of our business up."

"Vivi, the oracle," Humphrey said. "From the Daisy Oracle to something infinitely broader. You are a person who nudges brains and hearts, Viv. You raise some valuable questions for us all. Personally speaking, I have been stalling myself from looking clearly. But I think I'm just living in a bit of a haze. I travel from here and there and enjoy myself. But I am not taking a stance or revisiting what matters. That, I realise, is the same as being in denial. I am going to take on the challenge, whatever the outcome. Time to take stock and readjust the squeaky wheels to go places I choose. Your musings nudged me. I will review your questions and come up with true answers to guide me going forward. And if I can contribute in anyway, it will be my honour and pleasure."

"You are one of us Humphrey," Theo said and raised his glass to Humphrey.

We all put some more food on our plates as the birds sang and other breakfasters came and went. A monkey jumped from the bamboo balustrade onto Wai's shoulder and leaned down to steal a half-open banana next to Nab's plate.

"Cheeky monkey," Wai said.

Maddie topped up my coffee mug, "I think you are right, Viv. We must ask ourselves these questions. Much as they may confront us. I am very conscious that there is nothing that I would love more than to be here in Costa Rica. With you all especially." She looked at Theo warmly, lovingly and with grace. "But I also know that I have my girls in Europe who still need me around for at least some of the time."

After another sip or two, Maddie continued, "I cannot ever depend on anyone else again, apart from myself. I escaped from Ethiopia, where I started as an independent young woman, but I lost that status. While I was not against wedlock, the word itself contains the word *'lock'*, which really is a bit of a giveaway," she said. "That is how I see marriage. Restriction, oppression, constant compromise, pain, hurt and sorrow. I pray with all my heart that this wedding today will be a good one, loving and long-lasting. For me personally, however, I no longer believe in the bond of marriage. That may sound bitter, and I understand I have my issues to face and deal with. However, I know that I can love, share, care, and be, but not to the detriment of losing myself. My motto is interdependence with allowances for symbiotic synergies. Where oxygen and space are abundant and where the connection is strong, without being strained." She looked at Theo.

"I understand, Maddie," Theo said.

She got up and went over to Theo, who was sitting two seats away from her. Theo pushed his chair back as Maddie sat on his lap and kissed his blond locks. The love in Maddie's eyes amplified as her Liza Minelli's looked at him, her pupils widening. Theo topped up his coffee cup and handed it to Maddie.

She sipped from the cup of understanding and resonance, The Cup of Cornucopia.

Wedding Witness

We took our seats under the palm-covered Atrium as the guests streamed in. Fairy lights crisscrossed the ceiling underneath the palm roof and bright tropical flowers, including Birds of Paradise, covered the bamboo pylons that supported the structure.

The beauty of the lush jungle around the venue provided a natural backdrop that needed no enhancement. It was vibrant, fresh, and perfect. Mother nature at her best. Long wooden tables were laid out. The colourful *carretas* were lined up, boasting colourful salads, rice and the *Assado de Boda,* the wedding stew.

Wai played his flute. I recognised the tune as James Galway's *Song of the Seashore.* It was beautiful to see the Pacific through the trees. He then went on to perform *Danny Boy*, which had to be one of my all-time favourites.

I used to play the flute when I was much younger. We started on the simple recorder. Then when we could read music, our parents thought we had advanced enough we were allowed to progress. My brother moved on to the guitar. I chose the flute.

I was enchanted by the way Wai played. The exquisite symphony of the birds could be heard in between the pieces of music. When the skies opened, the rain only added to the rhythm of nature. As the first lightning bolt struck, Sylvia and Alejandro arrived already wed and holding hands. They beamed as they came down the steps into the decorated and covered, barn-like area, with no walls, just bamboo balustrades. Sylvia looked beautiful in her fabulous white lace dress, and Alejandro was handsome in his new tuxedo. Humphrey was taking photographs. He had offered that to Eddie, who was very touched.

In a way, I think it was a blessing that Tica Sylvia was marrying Tico Alejandro.

Intercultural marriages gave new insights to people, though they could also be tricky. Two of my friends married Jordanians. Nadine and Elsabé said they did not realise they would be marrying the entire family, not just the husbands. That was one of their biggest challenges. As my dear friend, and Pussy Posse member, Priss, found out first-hand. Arabs have a strong connection with their mothers and listen to them in pretty much all matters, and certainly in the case of marriage. That was why Priss didn't marry her Emirati Beau in the end. He had been promised to his first cousin at birth. He proposed that she could be his second wife. Naturally, she declined.

To marry two women may not have been an option in Catholic Costa Rica. Still, the similarities between the Arab world and the Latino one, were significant. Mothers tend to do everything for their sons. Laundry, cooking, cleaning, and whatnot. Men looked for spouses to fill that spot. Machismo was Arabic, as well as Latino. Another similarity was that both Arab Men and Latin Lovers typically were jealous; They needed a lot of attention. Infidelity was a common occurrence. I recalled our first trip to Amman. Our Jordanian friends told us about Man Caves, where West Amani males seduced and bedded women out of wedlock.

They have rampant affairs, which they were vocal and proud of amongst their male peers.

I thought about Sylvia, who lost her mother to Dengue Fever and Alejandro, an orphan. If his mother really had been Cristina, I was categorically sure she would not have done his laundry, cooking, nor cleaning. He seemed like such a friendly and gentle person. Solid as a rock, though soft and kind on the inside. I did not know him. But Merlin spoke of him in that way, as did Eduardo.

I was happy to see the couple beaming and joyful amid all their friends.

After a variety of mixed drinks, we settled down for dinner. Hollowed out coconuts served as cocktail glasses with bamboo straws and a little banana leaf, hand-painted parasols with the guest's name painted on it. We had seen the hotel staff working on them earlier. Each employee had about ten empty soft-drink bottles in front of them. Each held an opened umbrella with the parasol pole dangling into the bottle and the opened brolly sitting on top. With a list of names, the associates were painting the names on each one. The bottles were then placed underneath the fan attached to one of the trees to help the parasols to dry faster. The blower unit was strong, and the little umbrellas spun around in the bottles as if they were mini helicopters waiting to take off. It was a painstaking job. One I would not have liked.

I loved the effect but could not fathom the idea of such pernickety work.

Once I was in Holland in Enkhuizen, where they had a Ship in a Bottle Museum. The lady explained to my beau and me how the artists painted every detail on each little matchstick and tiny thread loop. It was so painful to listen to. I felt sick at the thought of having to perform such work in that much detail. I guess I was a broader stroke kind of person. However, I knew that detailed attention made the difference between good and great. I personally choked on fidgety work.

Having said that, I also knew that a simple detail could make a stratospheric difference. I recalled the little brown paper bags we filled with sand a lit candle in them. They were so atmospheric.

Effective simplicity. That was what resonated with me.

The Wedding Party was in full swing. The rain didn't stop. Fresh fish and barbecued food were prepared on a grill that was the size of a church door. We ate and drank to our hearts' content. The conversation flowed, and we were happy. Then the Carnaval began. Silly hats, glowsticks, giant glasses, whistles all appeared seemingly out of nowhere as everyone got dressed up. After Wai finished performing his delightful tunes and the people gathered for dancing, there was a DJ playing music. Then, a full-blown comparsa band played the percussion on stage. They wore bright neon colours and set the tone for the party.

We danced the night away.

When we were all a little worse for wear, the music was turned down. The main light in the room was dimmed, and only the fairy lights glowed above our heads. We made our way back to our seats or any empty seat, I should say. Even the rowdiest of wedding party attendees had now quietened down. The *Si Como No* team leapt into action, giving everyone a fresh glass of champagne. Wai disappeared, returning moments later with the notes of Debussy's *Clair de Lune* gently gliding through the air.

I looked at Humphrey. He put his hand in mine and kissed my forehead.

"I couldn't think of anything I would rather do than spend this special moment here with you. But I think this is a real photo moment for these lovely people. I will be back as soon as I can." Off he went, with his lens in tow.

As Wai played on, the peaceful sounds gave a sense of balanced gravity to the party crowd that minutes before were going crazy on the dancefloor.

Alejandro and Sylvia had been dancing. When Alejandro took off his dicky bow, I noticed that it was not the type you tie yourself but an elasticated ready-to-go one. Alejandro scooped Sylvia's hair up and put it in a ponytail using his bow-tie as a scrunchy. Sylvia, with her mop of magnificence lifted off her shoulders, looked at her husband adoringly.

The Look of Love.

The scene was serene and quiet as Alejandro spoke to the crowd in Spanish.

"Era huérfano," Alejandro said. *I was an orphan.*

Not a sound could be heard, apart from the frogs and the crickets noisily proclaiming their nocturnal existence from the undergrowth beneath the venue that stood on stilts above the forest floor.

Alejandro looked up at the sky. I translated the words for

Maddie as she sat close to me, so she may be able to understand his every word.

"I grew up without a mother or a father. I didn't know whether they were dead or alive. What I do know, however, was that they must have been good people because even though my youth was difficult and I spent time in different homes, I ended up where I am now. Nothing comes from nothing. And I believe it must be from the parents I never knew because I am quite sure I do not deserve my wife Sylvia on my own merit."

At this time, I saw Eduardo walking towards Alejandro, who smiled and laid a hand on his arm, politely gesturing to Eduardo not to interrupt him. I saw Eddie wipe away a tear. He was an emotional, gentle man who clearly cared about Alejandro. Sylvia got up from her chair and held her husband's left hand while Alejandro held the microphone in his right one.

Maddie was practically sitting on my lap; she urged, "Keep on telling me what he said." Alejandro continued.

"I had no family until I met Eduardo. He gave me a job when I needed one."

Some of the people in the crowd clapped their hands, expressing their respect for Eduardo. Alejandro shot Eddie a look of gratitude. Eddie smiled back at Alejandro.

"When Eduardo gave me that job, he actually gave me my life."

Alejandro took the glass of water Sylvia gave him, let go of her hand just long enough to take a sip before she slipped his back into hers.

"I am now a married man and have the love of my life Sylvia right here next to my heart."

He bent down to kiss her hand. Sylvia beamed up at him, though she was clearly overcome.

Then Alejandro said, "Today, I have not only married my love, but this is also the day I acknowledge I have a father. I am no longer an orphan. I have a family. I belong."

"Oh my God, Maddie, what an amazing young man that Alejandro is," I said.

"Any father would be proud of such a guy," Maddie agreed.

Turning to Theo, Maddie said, "Isn't he just one of the most amazing young men you would ever be fortunate enough to meet? This guy will be etched in my mind forever. If I ever think my life is tough. I will remember that kindness and positivity can still prevail. Alejandro lived the hardest of lives without the care of his parents. Yet he is living proof that you can still muster the strength to be a full, loving and most extraordinary individual."

"Es Verdad," Theo said. That is true. "Eduardo should be proud of him. If I had a daughter who married a man like that, I would be truly grateful and blessed too."

As Alejandro completed his heartfelt but straightforward speech, he continued to hold Sylvia's hand. He picked up the glass of champagne which had been placed before him.

"Salud, amor y dinero," he toasted. Health, love, and money.

He raised his glass to everyone and separately to Eduardo. Then he turned to Sylvia, sealing his toast with a kiss. Alejandro held Sylvia in the crook of his arm next to his heart. He had his glass of champagne close to his chest, almost under his armpit.

Oh, my Lord, just like his father...

Busy Brain

I opened the doors to our apartment's extensive balcony. The gentle oxygen dense air wafted in. The Pacific greeted me in the distance, softly swelling and subsiding, like a regular pulse at ease. I walked onto the terrace and sat in the rocking chair, enjoying the familiar and fabulous scenery.

Birdsong and greenery; what else could anyone need first thing in the morning? Apart from a coffee, perhaps.

I thought about the first time I arrived at *Si Como No* and how I met Eddie at the bar. We'd become close friends though we had lost touch for years until a week or so ago. I was so happy we reconnected, and I would ensure that we would stay in touch now.

My mind jumped to my girlfriends: Hélène, Annie and Priscilla. We had a reunion coming up around the date of the summer solstice. That would be in about six or seven weeks, around the 21st of June. We hadn't yet decided where to meet.

We had agreed in the beginning to have a Girl Gathering twice a year, and we had done so pretty much every year since we formed the Pussy Posse.

I remembered being out of touch for a while with my Posse when I was going through a hard time with General Salim, not knowing if he was dead or alive. That was a very dark time. I had isolated myself and, on reflection, was totally absorbed in grief and confusion. I didn't even want to connect with my girlfriends. I was in emotional survival mode, and I didn't handle that challenge well, if the truth be told. The girls were there for me, I knew that, but all I had on my mind was the man I cared for, who had gone silent on me. I was in an emotional pit.

When I was finally ready to reach out to them, they gave me the sweetest hard time saying that it was precisely when we were in need that we should be and would be there for each other.

We renewed our vows at that time and committed to staying in touch.

I made a conscious note to reach out to my girls over the next few days. I was not in an emotional turmoil. I considered life's priorities, which were fundamentally focused around those who mattered to me. In my case they included my family, the Pussy Posse and Maddie and Theo, naturally.

I thought about last night and about the warmth, pride and joy that spilt out of Eddie during the wedding reception. It was like lava flowing slowly down the slopes of a volcano rather than an eruptive spectacle. Eddie had depth, the kindest loving heart, and a sense of self. He was strong and sensitive. Having lost his wife, he had now gained a son in Alejandro. In turn, Alejandro had gained a family in Eduardo and Sylvia. Indeed, that was an excellent outcome for both Alejandro and Sylvia as well as for Eddie. A happy new beginning, I told myself. One that should not be tinkered with and simply be left alone. My mind didn't take the bait.

What if Alejandro was Theo's son?

Didn't I have a responsibility to tell Theo what I'd witnessed at the wedding?

It was not only that Alejandro held his drink in the same unique, endearing way that Theo did. Merlin, too, had told me he was convinced that Cristina was Alejandro's birth mother. As for Theo, Cristina had told him some thirty years ago that she was pregnant with his child. Theo had given her money and offered support. Still, after that, Theo had never heard from her again. Until all those years later, when he saw Cristina again, on the arm of *El Comandante*. No future reference was ever made to a possible son, and Theo never broached the subject with her.

I got up to fix myself a coffee. I had to work out what to do. Maddie was still sleeping. I set myself the task of calling on my own heart and mind rather than running off to Maddie to tap into her Ever Ready Logic and nimble investigative mind.

Subtle nuances were at play, and a stream of consciousness was needed. Or rather, a subconsciousness flow allowing anything to emerge and present itself. Like in a dreamlike state or trance without the rigorous framework of rationality.

Just let any thought bubble up, I told myself.

How would Theo feel if he knew Alejandro was his offspring?

Theo grew up with a mad and perhaps even bad dad. I was not the one to judge, but it was clear that his father had disrupted Theo's life. Then again, the blond boy survived the Dutch enforced arrival into Latin America. He had stood out like a sore thumb, but over time Theo became *Ticofied*. Theo was now part of Costa Rica's people, heritage, and future, like Catholicism and the oxcart. Somehow fate had played its hand three decades ago, securing Theo's next generations, even if Theo was still unaware of that reality.

How crazy.

A man may be oblivious that he had fathered a son, but a mother never could be.

Although planting a seed only takes seconds, carrying a baby takes nine months. The juxtaposition between transiency and relative longevity in the very same situation was interesting, I thought. Mothers know the truth. Fathers may not. The knowing lies with the female. But what if the mother was a snake, like Cristina? Of course, she knew she had given birth to a baby. She appeared to have dumped Alejandro, milking him for all he was worth before moving on to satisfy her insatiable greed. Leaving Alejandro to move from home to home and from one orphanage to the next.

How hard-hearted could a mother be?

I had no point of reference in that regard. I was blessed with both a loving mother as well as a father. I counted my blessings.

I changed the position of the wooden rocking chair on the balcony and sat back down in it, sipping my coffee. From the far end of the terrace, I could see the blue corrugated roof of the House on the Bluff. That poor, beautiful home. Its location was heavenly and to die for. Literally, it had seen the death of Curtis Coffee's son Arturo, a wonderful young man by all accounts. It was unclear whether it had been a fall or the venom of a snake that had caused Arturo's passing. My brain labelled that event as *unjust*. Then Cristina brandished a machete instead of having a broom to fly away on. She had crashed and burned as recently as a few days ago.

In her case, it was her own venom that brought about her

fall; injustice.

When Arturo had passed away; justice.

And then Amilcar, the best of souls, had passed; injustice.

My mind was on a roll, ignoring my request not to be so judgemental and stop labelling events based on emotions.

You aren't a judge or jury; life is a flow, as you know.

I got up to splash my face with some water. It broke my thought loop. Clearly, my busy brain was looking to express itself and was not ready to lie back down in its cradle. It wanted answers and was raising questions.

If there were Loving Little Lids that fit the jar, we should surely try and match them? We have the jars; we have the lids. Let's pair them up and move on from the mess and discombobulated fragmented phase to find balance.

Getting life into synch was needed.

All patterns in nature made sense. The Golden Ratio lay at the heart of everything that was in balance. You would be fibbing if you didn't acknowledge that truth. And building on fact was indeed always the best policy though the concept was subjective, in my opinion. Your reality differs from mine. But in nature, there is an universal understanding. I opened my laptop and refreshed my mind on one of the rules of Mother Nature. The golden ratio was sometimes called the divine proportion due to its frequency in the natural world. The number of petals on a flower, for instance, will often be a Fibonacci number. The seeds of sunflowers and pinecones twist in opposing spirals of Fibonacci numbers. Even the sides of an unpeeled banana would usually be a Fibonacci number.

Just like with the pineapple, I thought.

The symbol of hospitality. Thanks to centuries of pillaging

and colonising, the pineapple had travelled far and wide. It came to represent something more than a tasty fruit. Beyond merely being a symbol of welcoming, the pineapple had dark Imperial roots, too. Like Catholicism and oxcarts, though, they were enforced upon the Ticos while pineapples were wilfully exported by the *Conquistadores*. There was a big difference between willingly doing something and having it shoved down your throat.

The choice is freedom.

I recalled the time when Eddie took me to his grandfather's piece of land. It was a fair drive from Quepos. We went with his friend Stacey who was a boy. I was expecting a girl with that name, but it seemed it was a gender-neutral name as Stacey was all man. Dark, strong and Tico. An old guy was sitting by the rickety entrance fence. It had come off its hinges and was wedged in the mud. Leaning at an angle against the wobbly post that tentatively and temporarily offered some sort of support. Like a crutch that itself was broken. With the next rains, I imagined the fence would slide face down into the mud, just like Arturo had on that fateful day.

Oh, come on, Viv! Get a grip on that mulling, bubbling brain of yours.

I remembered the pineapples on Eddie's *abuelo's* plot growing relatively close to the ground. Lined up like little robust overweight soldiers standing to attention side by side.

The pineapples' gold and green coloured armour full of spikes suggested they were impenetrable. They stood together, imposingly, with an apparent mission to scare off intruders who might bruise, or worse, eat them. If you had never tasted a pineapple on first seeing them, you would surely choose to leave them alone. They looked hostile. But once you were introduced to their inside and the delicate sweet and juicy flesh, the colour of primroses in the spring, the flavours would never leave your tantalised palette.

Stacey holding his machete, inspected the most succulent looking specimen. With his American baseball cap back to front on his handsome head, he smiled at Eddie and me, raising his eyebrows as if to say, *Will this baby do?* Eddie nodded. With that, the razor-sharp machete sliced the fruit where it was connected to the ground. It was like witnessing a murder minus the splattering of blood. As the Pineapple Parade stood close together, the two piñas on either side were murdered in the process. As a result, the three chopped pineapples would leave a significant space where the culling had taken place.

It sent my brain back to the time when I was exchanging my milk teeth. I once bit into an apple, and my two front teeth stood side by side wedged in the fruit. I was taken aback as I looked at my little ivories firmly fixed in the pale Granny Smith as blood trickled down, colouring the light flesh pink. One tooth was grey. I had fallen over when I was little and damaged it. My mother told me I was a wonderful person for having the two teeth come out simultaneously. She told me they would grow back together and therefore be aligned and straight, giving me a wonderful smile. She also told me I was lucky that we were given another chance and that my grey tooth would be replaced by a lovely white one. Thinking back, my mother often complimented us for the things we did well. We were praised equally for matters we had no control over whatsoever, like losing one's teeth or getting a bright white one back in return. My British grandfather, who was staying with us in Holland at the time, pulled out his clean white starched handkerchief. With aplomb, he opened it up by shaking it twice. He positioned me on his lap and smiled at me, pretending he was Dracula as he cleaned me up.

'There Little Miss Gap in the Fence. All done.'

Stacey took one of the fruits as I observed the gap where the three pineapples had once been.

Stacey stripped the pale victim of its spiky armour and laid it bare on the top of a chopped tree trunk. With the machete, he undressed it, cut out the pale flesh, then slid it onto the end of the Swiss penknife he'd unhooked from the belt that held up his combat Bermudas.

Slaughter in Paradise. Another juxtaposition to ponder.

The hard and the easy, the bad and the good, the problem and the solution, mostly held hands. Interesting.

When we were little and got stung by a stinging nettle, we knew that the Dock leaf grew right next to the nettle that caused the sting in the first place. My grandfather showed us that they release moist sap by rubbing the dock leaves vigorously, which was cooling and soothed the skin. The poison and the antidote offered right next to each other, courtesy of Mother Nature. I thought it was a doc leaf, as in doctor, that made you better. Had we not been taught; we would never have known. Some things were simply handed down from generation to generation.

Little nuggets of knowledge for comfort and survival.

With my mind back on the pineapple parade, I relived the scene with Stacey and Eddie in my mind's eye. Each *piña* stood proudly with its impressive headgear enhancing its height. It reminded me of when Captain James and I were watching the changing of the guards in London. The remarkable men sitting on horseback in their scarlet tunics and high furry hats.

"Why do those guys wear those Grizzly bears on their heads?" I asked James.

"You are not far off, Viv. Those are called *Bearskins*. The Imperial Guard were Napoleon's elite troops hand-picked for bravery and experience. The infantry wore bearskin headdresses as a status symbol to make themselves look taller and more fearsome in battle. Anything a bloke could do to make any part of his body look taller, longer, wider or more impressive, he will do," he said as he winked at me.

I remembered telling James the story about when the conquistadores first arrived on mounted horses in Latin America. To the Incas, the sight of Pizarro's conquistadors passing through their land was extraordinary. They had never seen people carried by their animals before. Some thought they were gods, part human, part beast. James smiled. I guess he knew the story. He was knowledgeable, but he never behaved like a know-it-all.

He simply absorbed what I was saying, took my hand and said, "Time for Tea."

As if the memory triggered a reaction, I boiled the kettle and made a cup of camomile tea. I heard that Maddie had got up in the room next door. Minutes later, I heard her turn on the shower. It was good that I'd worked out what I would do without having Maddie as a sounding board. She was an excellent person to reflect thoughts off. Still, today, my method was in the madness, the surreal and the unconventional. By allowing for the free flow of ideas and for my slightly eccentric hallmark absurdity to roam unbridled, I

got there in the end.
   My colourful cocktail mind was made up.
   I would tell Theo.

Write it Forward

I opened my laptop to send a message to Annie, Hélène, and Priscilla when a new one pinged its way into my inbox. *Oh my God.* It was General Salim.

'Hello Sunshine, how nice to hear from you some time ago now. Sorry I did not reply earlier. I was looking at a plot of land to build an Eco-Hotel. Thought of you, of course. Couldn't think of anyone better to lead that project. Saw your message in my inbox and was happy to hear from you. Long-time, Miss Vivi. A very long time indeed. I hope you are keeping well. And hope we have a valid reason to reconnect sometime soon. The skies are less bright without your sunshine breaking through them regularly. I have come to realise that. Even though I am old, sick, and tired, the thought of you gives me a spring in my step. Thank you for your warm rays of joy and your message. Hope to be in touch soon. From my dunes of gold to your hills of green.

Yours, Salim x.'

I sat on the bed with my laptop open, staring at the screen. When I opened my inbox and saw a message that read, '*S calling V*', my stomach had done a somersault, and I'd felt dizzy. I completely forgot that I had sent Salim a message when Theo left *La Hacienda* to pick up Maddie from the airport. I'd been feeling a bit boisterous and recalcitrant with a devil may care attitude. I remembered it now.

I opened my sent emails and scrolled until I found the entry to HQ@Hospitality MENA.com.

My email read:

'*Hola Salim, you crossed my mind and skipped across my heart. I am in the lush loveliness of Costa Rica. Checking in with you as it has been a while. From my hills of green to your dunes of gold, besos, Vivi xxx.*'

Exuberant, I thought. Perhaps almost flirtatious. What was I thinking!

An Eco-Hotel?

Now that would be something that would tickle my fancy or tickle my fanny, as Priss used to joke. I think of General Salim and the email I've just received. I would, of course, love to see him again. Some things never die. Apart from the obsession with him. That seemed to have dissipated now. Thank God! I wouldn't mind working with him for a while on the Eco-Hotel he talked about. Maybe I would tell Salim I would be planning a visit and take it from there. My current strategic work on 'Levant Region Tourism, a Collaborative Approach' was ending. Although I must say in my spare time, I was really enjoying writing my book. I made steady progress in between working, travelling and recent adventures.

Perhaps I should include some of these bizarre happenings in my writings, I thought.

If nothing else, it would be nice to be able to re-read chapters of my life at a later stage and remember the fantastic times I'd been lucky enough to live. I never intended to write a novel, but when I talked to Annie, who was contemplating doing it herself, things simply developed from thereon in. I recalled sitting with Annie in my house in Amsterdam when we discussed her thoughts on midlife crisis activities.

"When you come to our age Viv, you either write or run."

"What do you mean?"

"Well, when you get to your mid-forties or fifties, it seems you either write your story or run a marathon. That's how it goes. Menopausal muffin top women write, sipping wine and fitter females run in skimpy lycra outfits, drinking water. What would you rather?"

"I wasn't planning on doing either apart from the wine bit. Though having said that, thinking about it, I have written the odd poem or chapter."

"Really? What did you write about?"

"Hang on, let me check my sent messages. Whenever I do something that is just for me, I mail it to myself. Let me see if I can find it."

"You're a weirdo, Viv. Never knew you put pen to paper or fingertips to the keyboard before."

"I find it a relief to write. Somehow the words spill out more eloquently when I write, and the movie plays in my mind's eye. I can see the whole thing play out like in a film."

Annie looked at me, her head at an angle, "Can't believe I didn't know that about you, Viv. We have been friends forever, and I had no clue. I would love to hear what you wrote."

"Hang on, here it is. It's several years ago but feels like yesterday. The paragraph is a bit raunchy. It's about General Salim."

"Good God, Girl! Let's hear it!"

"Okay, but don't judge me, Annie. I wrote it for my own eyes and heart only. This was never intended to be shared with anyone, not even with the Pussy Posse, but here we go."

"Don't mind me," Annie laughed. "Pretend I am not here. And remember, I am open-minded. Do you recall that time when I invited the Über driver up to my Fulham pad? My flatmate found my knick-knocks in the empty cocktail glass the following morning. Emma started her day surveying the aftermath of our impromptu sexual exploits while I was still fast asleep. Mr Well Hung is no doubt still driving other ladies back to their homes, with or without a bonus."

"You are the Goddess of Outrageous Behaviour, Annie. That is the ultimate compliment, as you know."

"Cheers, Viv. Appreciate your words," Annie laughed. "Now, let me have that saucy story of yours."

I looked over my writings and musings put down in words when I was still in the thick of infatuation. And boy was I in deep. I remembered Annie was the closest of my friends and began to read my tale;

'Come, I want to lie with you.' It sounded almost biblical. It was what I wanted, too. I waited for this moment, to see Salim again and to spend time together. We lay down on the bed and talked a bit. I told Salim about my day, my time with the dolphins, the cheeky goat who made its way into my garden and watched me as I swam naked in the private pool. I told him I thought he was reincarnated as a pushy goat, coming to check up on me.

He said, 'It was me, and now I am coming back to get what I saw in the sunshine and to enjoy all of it after dark.' He rolled out of the chatting mode position and was ready to move into a different type of communication altogether. He kissed me for some time and then slipped off his dish-dash. He was smiling down on me while working me with his nimble fingers. Salim locked his black eyes onto mine. We were in the missionary position. Very appropriate, I chuckled to myself. It had been Salim's mission to get me into bed. Mission accomplished. Salim hovered above me and slowly came into me, making sure I was okay. When he felt comfortable that I was, too, he picked up the pace.

As he increased the rhythm of his thrusts, he kept looking at me with those dark eyes and whispered, 'Last night was good. Did you enjoy it? Would you like something else to remember me by?'

'Yes, I would,' I whispered.

'Your wish is my command and my utter pleasure,' he breathed.

While still expertly working me, he asked, 'Have you ever had a threesome?'"

Annie interrupted me, "What the hell Viv? You raunchy bloody mare! Where did you draw that juicy interlude from? I am both shocked and delighted."

"It's inspired by events but stirred like a cocktail and blurred like when you've had too many."

"You saucy moo, you," Annie said, looking flabbergasted.

Anyhow, that was how I kicked off with my writing. I started with that chapter and wrote from then on. Every now and then, I would sit down, let my mind wander, and allow my fingers to do the talking on my lightweight Apple. Whether on a plane, in bed, at my dining table. By the pool, with a morning cup of coffee in Amman or a sundowner in Europe. I put down in words whatever bubbled up in my heart and mind. I found it therapeutic. A bit like how someone may pick up their knitting needles when they have some downtime. I found myself looking forward to it and finding pockets of time to put the proverbial pen to paper.

Spilling out thoughts, memories, fantasies, frustrations, emotions, and most of all, realisations.

Before I started writing, I used to love taking photographs. I felt an overwhelming sense of satisfaction from taking pictures. The compositions, destinations, people, and nature captured on film were precious treasures to me. I have bags filled with photos. I thought I'd lost them until recently when they were found in storage behind the eaves of my parents' house in Kent. The top of the chimney stack had come off the centuries' old house when the gales pounded the part of England where my parents lived. Due to work, the eaves had to be cleared, and my long lost treasure was found. I was reunited with the photos I thought were lost forever. My heart swelled as I looked through sacks, bags, and boxes. I found a few postcards from my mother among the loot, which she sent to me when I was at the hotel school on the mountain in Switzerland. I loved the fact that her neat handwriting would forever be etched in my mind. I thought about whose handwriting I was able to recognise. Annie's and Hélène's but not Priss's. I guess she was younger than us and more of an online kind of girl, a millennial.

One of the greatest surprises and delights on the day that my treasured letters were returned to me was a note from Captain James. It was written on Her Majesty's Yacht's headed paper and dated the 2nd of November 1992, Bab al Mendez, Saudi Arabia. At sea. I recognised James' writing. He always wrote using the same black fountain pen, his elegantly connected letters with paced spaces between lines full of humour with subtle and delightful innuendo.

The letter read, *'We are worried about you since we have not heard from you for a while.'*

CJ went on to tell me about a horrific event that happened to two of his officers. They had gone downtown in Jeddah and were late back to the ship, which never usually happened, so James expected something to be amiss. Just as James was about to send out a search party, the two officers returned pale as sheets, shaking, and looking like they'd seen a ghost. James took them to the Officers' Mess to talk in private and sat them down, along with his number two. It turned out that the men had witnessed a public execution. Having been spotted on the scene, some extreme person had grabbed the men by the scruff of their necks. He had shoved the two naval officers in front of the face of the person who was about to be executed. Seconds later, the guillotine fell, slicing the head off and splashing the dead man's blood into the faces of Coxton and Frasier. As they were thought to be Christians, the two naval officers were thrust in to the field of vision of the convicted Islamic man. It was the last thing he saw before he died. This was rumoured to be the ultimate insult for Muslims. I don't know whether that was true or not. Still, the horrific event left James' men scarred after that fateful visit to downtown Jedda in the early nineties. Apart from news on events in Saudi, James had tucked some photographs into the envelope. One of him on a polo pony in Malta, the other with Mike and the Men, all in uniform on the deck of Queenie's Royal Dinghy, now decommissioned.

I thought about my handsome Captain James.

Now, he was a character I'd like to see in a movie someday.

Blond-haired, intelligent eyes, tall and athletic, and a smile that said, "*Come hither.*"

Finding those treasured memories was extremely valuable to me.

Never get stale, I reminded myself. Keep living this luscious life.

I decided to use the present to write my future. If you are already able to feel, live and imagine, you can bend the energy to sculpt the life you want to live. Apparently, simply imagining your future is not good enough. You need to see it and feel it. That can only be done if you act, think, and breathe as if what you desire already exists. The theory said that if your wish for something, you're projecting your desire from a position of lack. And if you do that, your brain will simply perpetuate that thought and manifest lack.

So, the mind needs to believe, feel, and know that what you genuinely want already exists. All the energy there ever was and ever will be, already is.

Therefore, the energy simply needs to follow the figment of your heartfelt and convinced imagination. I love that philosophy, and I started to live it as I wrote my book. I imagined having a trilogy that was treated for film and translated into seven languages. I sent some of my chapters to three London agents. I was a first-time author with no track record. They replied to me and declined, albeit in a charming way. But I already knew that my books would see the light of day. That was not being cocky. That was just based on feeling and knowing that it would be.

Recently, the first miracle had happened.

I had met a brilliant book and film agent via an unexpected route. An introduction was made via my best friend, the most competent lawyer in the Middle East. He had a client, who had a contact, who knew a friend… And the connection was made.

I was having lunch in one of my favourite places in Amman when I got the call. The lady agent and I spoke for a while. We instantly hit it off. She had grown up in the Middle East and experienced similar adventures. By the end of the call, she said, "Vivika, please send me your sample chapters."

I sent them to her that night, and the following day around six in the morning, I woke up to a WhatsApp message which said, *'Love it. A real page-turner. I can see an eight-part series and a great book. Can you commit to a trilogy? If so, I would love to sign you up.'*

And that was how I met Susannah.

Been with Ben

Humphrey held the photographs in a pile of neat envelopes in his hand. Merlin was taking him into Quepos to print off the pics of the wedding. Humphrey's photography gear was digital. He did not have the needed equipment to print the pictures. We talked about it the day before and had agreed that Sylvia and Alejandro, as well as Eddie, would probably like hard copies as well as a digital record of their delightful wedding. We decided to make the wedding photos available online as well. Sylvia and Alejandro could send it to friends via a link.

My job was to stick the pics in an album. I found a nice A4 sized notebook in the *Si Como No* gift shop. It was made of banana paper with a colourful cover. It was covered in little embossed gold, and jade coloured pineapples with a label that sat in its own little pocket.

I wrote 'Sylvia y Alejandro - *La Boda Maravillosa*,' The Brilliant Wedding, along with the date@SiComoNo.

The rain was coming down. It had been almost sunny earlier, and then very wet all morning. I had the privilege of seeing a double rainbow while drinking my second cup of coffee; That had proved to be the perfect omen for me in the past. I hoped it was again a sign of confident positivity to deliver a poignant day in Paradise.

We were at *La Hacienda*. I realised I had missed that place. I enjoyed being at *Si Como No*, but I felt ready to get back to some sort of working life. I had been on a perpetual break apart from my tourism assignment and writing, which I consider a joy.

While I hated routine, I did like purpose.

It was time for me to pull my boots up and get going with a project that gave me a spring in my step and a fire in my belly. An initiative that fuelled the soul.

Humphrey interrupted my line of thought, "You have *mission* written all over your face," he said. "Here. Careful. I know you don't like anything lukewarm."

"Thank you, Humphrey, you marvellous man. I appreciate receiving the perfect brew from you."

"You are the ultimate blend for me, Vivi. I would love to go with you on a journey to explore the Blue zone in Nicoya, see some exploding volcanoes and bathe in the hot waters of Tabacón. I think you would love it."

"Oh, it's paradise there," I said. "With the tropical flowers, the exquisite birds, and the conical cone of Arenal, the place is like the Garden of Eden. The lizard I saw there was called a *Jesus Christ Lizard,* apparently as it can run over water. How more heavenly can you get? You are right, H; it is a truly wonderful place."

"When did you go?" Humphrey asked.

"Quite some years ago. I was with my ex-toy-boy-and-still-very-good-friend Ben. He had been incredibly ill with glandular fever, apparently an exceptionally horrific case of it. The specialists were all over him as his situation was extreme and rare. I was in Costa Rica at the time and sent him a two-page letter by fax. I knew he was bedbound for six days and not able to move. I decided to bundle all my love and good vibes to send to him in hospital in London. I tried to transport his brain and take him on a journey of all the beautiful things waiting for him. Basically, saying that if he made it through, I would take him to Costa Rica. It may have been a bit of an odd thing because, at the time, Ben was going out with a gorgeous Italian girl who is now is the mother of their four children. However, at the time, the message, and prayers I sent to Ben were derived from my love for him as an amazing person. I genuinely believe in the power of positivity. Therefore, it is energy and can be projected and sent from wherever and directly delivered to where needed. Apart from my thoughts in wishing him well, I thought a written message would do Ben good. At the time I sent the fax, it was two o'clock in the morning in the UK. Ben had just mustered the will to go to the loo for the first time in almost a week. The nurse helped him, and when he was safely back in bed, she gave him my letter that had been painfully pushed out of the fax machine. Communications were still diabolically slow in those days. A fax was considered the quickest in terms of getting written messages across. That is hard to imagine in our more mobile existences where instant was no longer refers to an instant soup or cup of coffee.

Having described the splendid scene in Costa Rica to Ben, my final sentence said, '*Make it through this Benzidickylicious, and I will take you to Costa Rica.*' And that was what I did."

"Lucky chap," Humphrey said. "So, you were no longer going out with him, but you stayed great friends even when he was dating someone else?"

"Yes, I know some people may find that odd. But I think it is stranger to let go of someone you have shared part of your life with. Especially if you are still plain sailing, just perhaps not in the dating boat anymore."

"That is a novel way of looking at it, I guess," Humphrey said. "You are rather refreshing, Viv. And unusual in a charming kind of way."

I went over to Humphrey and put my arms around his waist. "You are the refreshing one, H. You are a genuinely superlative, delightful individual.

"Finish your story about your Beau Ben but tell me on the double hammock."

He tipped backwards into the hammock that hung from one of those portable contraptions you could move around. I balanced myself next to him and continued my story.

"It was a crazy trip. We got so lost trying to get from San José to Arenal that it took us seven hours to finally arrive. Although I usually have a good sense of direction, I had driven for three hours on this day, and I ended up twenty minutes from the hotel where we had started from. I was so frustrated. However, Ben and I decided to press on. The trip should have taken just three and a half hours, so it really was a bummer, to put it mildly. When we were on the right road, at last, the sun set just as we got into the mountainous area. The road was full of sharp bends. A car was weaving ahead with its lights on in front of us. I decided to set off in hot pursuit of this vehicle and followed in its wake; my plan was to use it as a beacon rather than snake our own way through the dark. It seemed like a good idea, and I really pressed hard to catch up with the car.

What happened after that was utterly bizarre.

The driver of the car in front noticed me wanting to stick to him. He then switched his headlights off so I could not see him. Whether he kept on driving, I don't know. Until this day, I think those guys were on a drug run and felt we were following them to apprehend them and their illegal narcotics or some other illegal trade. My plan of pursuit was foiled.

We crawled onwards through the mountains. After seven long hours, we eventually arrived at the *Cabanas Arenal*, where we were lucky enough to get the last room. The receptionist had booked it for us when we left San José. She said we were fortunate as hotels were booked up, even though the rainy season had commenced.

The place had a good reputation, though the only available cabana had ripped mosquito nets. The place was literally buzzing with the biting insects. I looked at Ben and knew we couldn't stay in that accommodation. Ben was still recovering from his terrible illness. The mosquitos may have been carrying the dreaded Dengue Fever. We decided to find another place to stay. However, this proved impossible. We were utterly exhausted by now, hungry, and disappointed that the hotel that was booked for us wasn't up to what we needed. Even if Ben had not been ill, we would not have stayed.

You could only get Dengue Fever once. The second time you die. The trick was to avoid getting it in the first place.

The rain was torrential, the muddy dirt road was unlit and as it snaked ahead of us. After some time on the road seeking a place to stay, I spotted a sign with a large 'H' through the sheet of rain. It pointed up a steep driveway. I had no idea what we would find. As we drove up, the electronic gate was closed. I looked at Ben. He was always so full of life, but he was now frail and slumped in his seat. I imagined a role reversal with me being Joseph and him Mary seeking an Inn. My mission was to find a room, any room if it was free of mosquitos at a refuge that would accommodate us.

I jumped out of the car, making my way up the slippery cobblestones, almost falling over, until I reached the intercom to ask for someone to open the gates. I pressed the buzzer, but no one reacted. I tried again, and still nothing. I returned to the car, sopping wet, and honked the horn loudly. Ben was in no fit state and had his head against the car door, looking increasingly like the life was draining out of him. I was now distraught. I tried the intercom again. Someone, praise the Lord, answered. They told me the hotel was fully booked and that there was no room. I pleaded with them until, in the end, the chap told me there was one Swiss Style Villa. I had no idea what that meant. I didn't hesitate and said I would take it. The saviour's voice told me the villa still needed cleaning. He said to come to the check-in desk and suggested having dinner while the accommodation was being cleaned. I agreed to everything the saviour said while thanking my lucky stars and all the angels in the Costa Rican sky."

"Jeez," Humphrey said. "Was your Ben-bloke, okay?"

"No, not really. He was in a total mess. I thought perhaps some food would do him good, so we went for dinner at the restaurant *Vista Arenal*. Though the volcano could not actually be seen as the weather was so bad. Ben and I sat and had a warm drink and some *tapas*. Slowly Ben started to feel a bit better. As he turned a corner and I was feeling a glimmer of hope that I had not single-handedly killed him off, the waiter came over to us. He invited us to sit by the window. The people who'd booked that table were about to leave.

It was the premium table, with the best view of the volcano. Apparently.

We accepted the waiter's kind invitation to sit at La Mesa con Vista, the table with a view, though I was unsure why we moved as the rain was still coming down in sheets. Nonetheless, Ben and I went to sit by the window. As soon as we did, the rain lessened, and by the time our food arrived, the downpour had stopped. After that, a tiny spark of orange sprayed like a firework in the night sky, which steadily increased, ending in a tremendous display of Erupting Arenal. It was as if our efforts were being rewarded as Mother Nature performed her dance of power and beauty. I looked at Ben, who replied with a gentle smile. He was clearly still exhausted though he was happy too, in a non-energetic sort of way.

'Let's go to bed', I said to Ben."

I clocked Humphrey shifting in his seat uncomfortably.

"No, numpty, I did not sleep with Ben! It was just that there was only one bed in that villa. A massive one. I opened the curtains, then I pushed the huge bed towards the floor to ceiling window. It took quite some doing as Ben was in no condition to help me. I wedged the massive bed along, inch by inch until it stood with a full view of the volcano. We lay on our sleeping island looking at Arenal, which was showing off its fire-throwing antics against a backdrop of blackness. Ben looked at me and smiled as he slowly raised his thumb before falling into a sleep or recovery snooze. I stayed awake most of the night in total awe of the display outside the window; I also wanted to keep an eye on Ben. He woke up every now and then, appreciated a minute or two of the fireworks and then dropped off again."

"Wow, Viv, that must have been quite a trip."

"It was a hell of an adventure, blending the good, the bad and the beautiful. After our challenging night, which ended in an incredible crescendo, we had blue skies the next day. Ben and I went to the hot springs the following morning, and we felt we were in paradise. The hot springs from the belly of the volcano were full of minerals and ancient goodness.

After that, we went on our way to Lake Arenal. Ben was driving. He felt buoyant and much better, and he said he'd love to take the wheel. I was encouraged. He must have been feeling better. My seatbelt was bothering me. So, I took it off. Stupid, of course. Anyhow, we were going down the black volcanic sand dirt road when we hit a pothole at speed. The car flipped over and crashed. I was propelled over the backseat into the trunk of the 4x4. Ben was still in his place behind the wheel, locked in position by his seatbelt. The passenger side doors were smacked in the face of the unsuspecting tarmac. The car was severely damaged and all the windows shattered. The light weight 4x4 was a wreck. The laptop and camera were propelled from the car landed in the long grass on the side of the track.

As I looked up at the sky through the missing glass which lay in pieces shattered all over my body, I heard Ben saying, 'Viv, are you okay? Viv. Viv!'

I spoke in the same staccato tones as Ben. "Ben, Ben, are you okay?"

"Viv!"

"Ben!"

We repeated each other's names. We could not speak in complete sentences. We were in shock and monosyllabic. We called each other's names repeatedly. Back and forth. Just to know the other was alive. The car was a write-off. Miraculously, Ben and I were okay.

By the time we had established that we were both still on God's planet, some locals stopped and came to our rescue in a passing car. They helped us out and arranged for a tow truck. Ben and I were shattered and shocked but, against all odds, miraculously intact apart from one massive bruise on my left arm. Thank God. I was so lucky we didn't get killed, Humphrey. Ben is still one of my very best friends to this day, as is his wonderful wife, Wendilia."

I looked at Humphrey. I couldn't quite figure out his expression. He looked thoughtful or was it distress I could see in his face? Perhaps he remembered Daphne and Anthony and the awful fatal accident. It was a fine line between life and death.

If you were lucky enough to survive such an event, you needed to live life to the full and be consciously grateful. Always. We'd both always done that, but afterwards, Ben and I lived even more consciously and with gratitude, following that fateful day.

I left the hammock to clear the church door table in La Hacienda's lobby and laid out the photos Humphrey had taken at the beautiful wedding. There were at least a hundred pictures. The exuberant energy danced off the oversized prints. I loved having photos that were larger than standard size. It allowed you to step into them more readily and experience the moment all over again. My eye was drawn to a particular image that

Humphrey had seamlessly captured.

Alejandro had his left arm around Sylvia and his *'Copa de champán,* tucked close to his chest, almost under his arm.

"I need to talk to Theo," I said to Humphrey. "He needs to know."

El Padre

As Theo sauntered into *La Hacienda*'s Lobby, holding Maddie's hand, he said, "*Buenos días amigos*. A great morning to you. I have some good news. My Maddie has agreed to fly her daughters in for a while so they can spend some time as a family, and then I can meet them too. Hopefully, they will think I am a decent sort of bloke. Perhaps not father material but nonetheless, a good uncle. '*Tio Theo*', I fancy that. I can only imagine what beautiful young women magnificent Maddie has put on this planet. She clearly is the most amazing mum, and these young ladies are blessed with a parent like her."

"Yes, it's time for Emmanuelle and Eshe to see their mother. And to be introduced to their possible part-time home," Maddie said as she looked at Theo lovingly.

Theo and Maddie had been getting on like a house on fire ever since Cristina was no more. The vicious spell of vindictiveness made way for a new level of lightness in their being. It was undeniable. Those two were meant to be together.

Theo and Maddie looked at the wedding photos. "These are great," Theo said. "Sylvia and her husband will be so pleased with them. Alejandro seems like a very decent chap, and I am happy Eddie has the son he never had."

"Amazing shots, Humphrey," Maddie said. "How lucky are these two young loves to have the blessing of a Hollywood professional to photograph their wedding. I reckon you could use them to sell weddings in Costa Rica. Those shots are so natural. The couple looks so at ease and right in each other's company. And the place looks utterly spectacular. I am sure *Si Como No* will want to post some of your photos on their website too."

"Well, thank you, guys. Your generous praise is much appreciated. It was my sincere pleasure and privilege to experience that wonderful wedding. Allow me to take care of coffee," Humphrey said as he went through to the kitchen.

I knew he was making himself scarce on purpose. Maddie shot me a look, to which I responded silently. There was no other time than now. I swallowed.

Eat that frog. It was the title of a book I read once. It said that you should simply deal with the most challenging thing of the day first, as it would not disappear. The sooner you ate that frog, the sooner you were able to make the most of the day ahead.

I remember doing exactly that when I needed to tell some news to the owners of a beautiful Lodge where I lived years ago in the English countryside. I had only been in their place for ten months when I got posted abroad. I felt terrible about it. These people were friendly. They had been on honeymoon in Petra when nobody even knew about Jordan. Janice and William were terrific people. I had once walked their puppy spaniels, who'd then broken loose and had killed around a hundred chickens that belonged to the local farmer, just outside Buckingham. They paid for the dead chickens and never made me feel bad that the puppies hadn't been on the lead.

He was an investment banker. She was the daughter of a famous British Fashion icon. They had three children: Petal, Daisy and Bamboo. They were utterly charming, down to earth and in some ways only, slightly eccentric. The cousins of the children were called Planet, Electra, and Mars. We used to play football on their full-blown soccer lawn. They had one field full of wildflowers and another one that looked like a mini Versailles. They had sunken trampolines that you did not have to climb onto and horses that roamed free around the house. Janice and William were fantastic. I hated the thought of having to tell them that I needed to renege on my contract and move on.

Eat that frog, I told myself. Otherwise, it will simply stare you in the face.

Eventually, I just launched right in.

"Theo, I don't know how to tell you this," I started. I picked up the photo of Sylvia and Alejandro and gave it to him, "But I think Eddie was not the only one who added a son to his family."

"That is a nice pic, Viv. Humphrey did a great job of capturing the evening."

"Have a beer," I said to Theo as I took a bottle out of the mini-fridge.

"*Hermana mia*, it is before noon. I think that is pushing it. And anyway, Humphrey is fixing us coffees."

"Indulge me. Hold this beer and look at the pics."

Theo did as I said.

"You are a bit of a weirdo, Viv, but hey, whatever floats your boat."

Before long, Theo was holding his beer in his endearing way and natural resting position.

"Now, look at Alejandro again," I instructed him. "What strikes you?"

"Cut to the chase Viv," Theo said. "You are trying to tell me something. What is it? You are my sister. Don't give me the long road."

"I think Alejandro is your boy," I said. "I think he is your son."

"What is going on here?" Theo asked as he turned first to look at me and then at Maddie.

"Look at the way he holds his champagne," I said, showing Theo the picture while pointing at the way Theo was holding his beer. "He is the son Cristina told you about before you left for Switzerland. It is true. But you never knew. This photo is living proof."

Theo looked at Maddie.

"I think it's true, Theo," Maddie said.

"Let us call Merlin," I said. "We cannot be sure, but the evidence suggests that Alejandro, who thinks he is an orphan, actually has a father who we believe is you!"

Theo looked at the photo and sat down on one of the twelve colourful chairs around the table.

"Hang on, girls. You are flying off like one of those colourful parrots. Taking off into the skies of the Garden of Eden."

Theo turned to Maddie, who had taken a seat next to him.

"And, as for you, Mads. You are usually not so emotionally extreme as Viv. What happened to you and your logic? You seem to have taken to the skies of fantasy too."

Humphrey came in with coffee. "Fancy a cup of strong brew, Theo?" he asked.

"I am not sure coffee is going to cut it, big H," Theo answered. "I was not expecting to wake up to this. But I won't turn my back on what my little sister is suggesting without investigating it further. Whatever is going on here. Call Merlin and have him bring Alejandro to the house. Check with Eduardo first. I need the young man to come to *La Hacienda* to observe him and take it from there. I am not often confused, but I can say that I am at least a little thrown with what you girls are suggesting. But life can be unexpected. *Pura Vida!*"

Before I called Merlin, I put a call into Eddie. I explained our theory, and he was, as you can imagine, utterly flummoxed. Additionally, he was worried. He did not want to hurt Alejandro though he knew that the truth of possibly having a father was no small matter. But if indeed he did, then Alejandro would be entitled to the truth.

Having spoken to Eddie, I suggested he should connect with Theo and Merlin. I felt a real sense of purpose. Theo agreed to invite both Sylvia and Alejandro to quote for some jobs at *La Hacienda* under the premise of a potential work contract. Eddie had given Alejandro an opportunity at the car wash. He had wanted to support him and, at the same time, make doubly sure that Alejandro was the right man to take care of his daughter Sylvia. Alejandro won over Eddie's heart in every way and jumped over every conceivable hurdle. As the couple were now married, Eddie said he would fully support the idea of them both fleeing the nest and broadening their horizons. If both were able to work at *La Hacienda*, Eddie would support that opportunity.

El Padre

Over the next few days, Merlin and Theo interviewed Alejandro, and I met with Sylvia. She was creative and organised; she'd be a tremendous support in promoting the coffee business. She quickly understood the concept behind the Coffee Crop promotion mailing and got excited at the prospect. Sylvia suggested using discarded coffee beans that didn't cut the mustard and mixing them in with a natural resin from one of the local trees to create a natural wax seal to close the *Smell the Coffee* promotional personalised mail to targeted clients. Sylvia had a marketing mind, and that was exactly what we needed to allow the coffee business to take off. She suggested the finishing touch to be the imprint of the fingertip of the person closing the letter. It reminded me of the wax sealed invitations I received back in the day when I attended the parties on the visiting British Naval ships in Amsterdam.

I thought of Captain James in heaven and sent him a hug from my heart.

I explained to Sylvia about the Loving Little Lids Foundation. She immediately said that contacting those clients and *Si Como No* guests would be a great start in connecting with potential buyers.

She was logical, pragmatic, creative and proactive. Perfect!

Theo and Merlin seemed full of beans after they met with Alejandro.

The newlywed couple were hired and offered the House on the Bluff to live in if they wanted to. Positivity was palpable. Theo had a glint in his eye and Alejandro a smile on his face. There seemed to be an unspoken affinity and an undeniable energy that needed no further defining or contextualising. Not at this point anyway. Sometimes events just need to be allowed to happen and take on a shape organically without force. Like the river meanders and finds its way, life too should flow freely from the source to the sea.

Humphrey proposed an inauguration picture with the green coffee plantation behind us. Sylvia put her arm around my waist in a newfound friendship. Just then, both Eddie and Merlin appeared and joined us. Eddie stood next to me with his hand on my shoulder, and Merlin was next to Maddie. The House on the Bluff was behind us. The *Guaria Morada,* spilt over the balustrade. In that magical spot, we both framed and celebrated our togetherness.

The flower, a type of orchid that bloomed between January and April, was no longer the mighty purple splendour it had been when I first arrived. But I knew it would grow stronger, grow deeper and blossom again. It clearly loved its perfectly pitched elevation at *La Hacienda*. Dr Google told me that according to Costa Rican tradition, the orchid evokes peace and love and hope for the future. The flower only had a subtle fragrance as it was filled with dreams yet to be fulfilled.

And finally, Dr G told me it was designated as Costa Rica's national flower on the 15th of June 1939.

That was today. Father's Day. What were the chances of that, Theo?

Fate made it clear to me. The time had come for my *Robin Hood hearted hermano* to take up the role he was now ready for. To be *El Padre*. Fathers' Day would never be the same at *La Hacienda*.

My brain took the highspeed train of imagination.

Under *El Comandante*, there were never any celebrations. Under *El Padre*, things would be very different. My joyous heart celebrated all the goodness in the air. Until I spoke to Theo.

"Isn't it amazing, *hermano mio*. All these events and how life unfolds?"

"It is indeed, *hermana mia*. But we cannot assume all this is the simple truth born out of complex circumstances and dramatic developments. People have their own agenda. They may construe realities that are, in essence, a Fata Morgana. Some situations appear to be real only because people want them to be. If there are the smallest of hints, possibilities, or coincidences that they may be, stories become facts.

You know me. I need to be sure of anything I do. You are family without being my blood. You, and now Maddie, are the only exceptions to the rule. As is my brother, Amilcar, may God rest his soul. But that is where it stops. For everything else, I need evidence. I am open to any opportunity life throws at me, no matter how unexpected or seemingly unlikely. I know that you love me, Viv, and that you are excited about the possibility of me having a son. You never fail to warm the ravines of my heart with your loving optimism. I know you want the very best for me. You and Maddie make me believe in good. But not in miracles. I have seen too many gullible people, crooks and criminals trying to make illusion become a reality. I need proof. The observation that Alejandro holds a glass of Champagne, the way I tend to hold my beer, is not a DNA deliverable."

"But Theo, wouldn't it be amazing if Alejandro is yours?"

"Viv, *que será, será*. Whatever will be, will be. I will simply consider Alejandro a new worker to help Merlin on the land at *La Hacienda*. If I sense that there is a likely hint of truth to the story, I will act. I will pluck a hair from his head, take the saliva from his mouth or blood from his veins. At that time,

I will do what is needed if I choose to. Let's not pussyfoot around and get on with the business Amilcar gave to us. Our very own family business."

He pulled me in under the crook of his arm.

"*Eres mi familia.* You are my family. My real family. *Mi Familia de Verdad.*"

Portugal Potential

Priscilla was the one who took the *touro* by the horns.
I read her email that she'd sent to all the Pussy Posse members:

'Pussies. Priss here. And when I say here, I mean Portugal. This is where I hope we will meet around our mid-year at the summer solstice for our sisterhood celebration. I know you own a rental accommodation just outside Lisbon darling Annie, but I have gone further south and have to say, I love it. I took a sabbatical from work. I am trying to get pregnant. I don't think I want the father of my one and only child to be a conservative Arab or an arrogant ex-pat, so I was planning some time in Portugal. With over five hundred years of Arab influence, the potential father will blend European and Arab cultures. That, my dearest Pussies is my idea of the ideal man. Not someone who marries his cousin.

Not that I am envisioning marriage. My mission is insemination. Why should I take the artificial route? That seems a waste of good sex and unnecessary expenses if you are fortunate enough to afford it. I have my turkey baster on hand if real sex is not on the cards. Refined, educated, hot-blooded, cool-minded, fun-loving, peace-seeking, adventure-orientated and good-looking; That is the type of man I want. Not too much to ask for. A hybrid of the best of Europe and the Arabian world. It all started with my search for a daddy, but on closer investigation, this may well be my spot to live my forever life and future place to call home. On my recent exploratory trip to the Algarve, I found the place to be nothing short of incredible. Viv, Algarve is derived from Al Gharb, 'The West' in Arabic, but you probably knew that. I know your heart lies in the Middle East, yet you miss Europe, so consider me your un-asked-scout to find the perfect combination for a potential pad for you. That way, you don't need to keep careering around and jumping across continents and tectonic plates. Exciting as that may be. Thank you, by the way, for sending us a pic of that coffee plantation where you are staying. Bloody fantastic set-up. With your say so, I will take part of the time during my sabbatical Sperm-Meets-Egg-Mission to market the hell out of that excellent looking coffee that you rave about. Bring me a pack back, will you Viv when you come for our reunion. Yes, of course, bring some for our sisters Annie and Hélène. When we fill one of our cups, we fill them all.

So, with your permission, lovely ladies, I vote for Portugal, which, by the way, comes from 'burtuqal', the classic name for orange in Arabic. Though I wasn't with you guys in Jordan when you gave birth to the Pussy Posse, I am so glad you invited me to be part of this awesomeness. I would like you to taste Arabia in the most western part of Europe. This was the end of the old world before Vasco di Gama and Columbus crossed the Atlantic to where you were now, Viv. In Central America. Get your bootie back over here. I know you mentioned a possible stint back in the Middle East. Would love to hear about your Eco-Hotel plans and, bloody hell, if you finish a book, I want to have a role in it as an Aussie Queen with a baby beau. On that note, I think the signs are all around me. On every electricity pole and power tower and on the traditional wooden wheels, there are stork nests. This morning I saw a field full of storks feeding their baby birds. It was just outside Aljusur, meaning the roots in Arabic. I looked it up. This is clearly a sign that I should lay down some roots here and have a beautiful child.

Anyway, please confirm. Flights to either Lisbon or Faro. I have a great friend with a gorgeous Aston Martin. He will not be the father of my children as he is blond but a great guy, and funnily enough, he's from the cradle of civilisation in the Middle East. I am not entirely sure how clean he is, though he acts like a gentleman. Amin offered to pick any friend of mine, from anywhere they land and bring them to me. He said he would do so in style.

I met him at the fish market. Funny how life happens. He is a friend of mine now. One of my first. That's how life goes!

No need for massive updates via email. Want to hear all when we meet. Just send Yes, Si, Aiwa or whatever you say in Dutch, Ja I think, via WhatsApp. I will book a boutique hotel Villa Vista that my friend Amin knows. His name is Amin, but I call him Amen as in the song It's Raining Men, Amen! His friend Luiz who owns the hotel, got in touch with me. Seems like a lovely chap. Dark hair. Good start. Dates for our get together I suggest mid-June for five days or a week if you can manage. Amin oversees the classic car rally. He and his buddy Luiz are heavily involved in F1 and the classic car rally. If I were to simply suggest the possibility of us being interested, I know he will invite us. Like you, Viv, I hate roaring engines unless built into a man I want to ride.

On the other hand, Annie loves the speed and skill and is fast car-obsessed, so you may like to get a little closer to this guy and have him test your oil levels, hahaha. On the face of it, he has a well-versed measuring dipstick built-in, or should I say dickstick, hehehe. As for Hélène, my darling, you will be interested in knowing that there are some eligible young wealthy bachelors on the coast. One of them is a friend of Amin, and he runs a beautiful bar on stilts overlooking the sand dunes and the Atlantic Ocean beyond. He is so lovely. A bit naughty, but you would not have it any other way. He is brilliant but again blond. He reminded me of that chap, Lex, who you used to go out with. That pic you showed me of you and him in your first year after a game of tennis always stuck with me. His grin and your smile were both so happy and infectious. Happiness can happen again, but it is time to seek it out a little more proactively. The highest achievement in life is happiness, with or without blokes. Let's take a mid-year stock of life and see how we can tweak and optimise it. You are brilliant sounding boards; we can bounce ideas and thoughts off each other when we get together. Making life the best it can be is both our right and our obligation.

For me, I have decided that I want to go for a baby. That way, you will be aunties, and if I make you all honorary fairy godmothers, my newborn will never need anything. One mad mum and three fabulous females to rock his cradle and his world. I realise I may be too old by now, but I am younger than you, darlings. Hypothetically, it's still possible. For now, my eggs have not yet been fertilised, and Bloody Mary's are on the breakfast menu. Talking of which, did you know that the wines in Portugal are the finest you can imagine? No offence, but I think I have a massive opportunity to market the hell out of them too. Coffee from Costa Rica and wine from Portugal. What better products to let my creativity loose on?

You will be my sampling panel and inspiration. You always are. In every way. Say Yes to Portugal, my perfect and precious pussies. I will do the rest.'

"Hey Viv, good morning to you," Theo said as he came over to me and hugged me. "What was that smile on your face? I was watching you from the doorway reading something on your laptop and saw a look of affection coming over you. Who is the lucky sender?"

"You remember Annie and Hélène?"

"Of course, I will always remember when you guys stayed in Costa Rica together, and we met here. Great, they met Amilcar too. Costa Rica is an important part of your life Viv, and it is nice that they experienced a bit of why you love it here so much."

"Apart from you, it is the oxygen, Theo. The fact is that not everything is predictable or organised. This place is paradise on earth. The volcanos, the ocean, the power of the rain, the abundance of flowers, fruits, and friends. I love it, and I will always come back. But I have a sneaky suspicion that I need to pop over to Portugal. I was just reading a message from Priss. She is promoting the idea of southern Europe for our get together. I need to get myself back over the pond one of these days.

I am interested in talking to Priss about marketing the coffee too. She is an advertising goddess and has expressed an interest. We can pay her in kind as she loves coffee until we really ramp up our revenue stream. She is worth her weight in gold. Hope you get to meet her one of these days. She is looking to get preggers by an Arab European hybrid man with dark hair and great talents. Knowing Priss, she will find the one and do the deed. She is something else, that Aussie Queen. I frankly hope she can deliver some offspring. The world needs more of her."

"Would love to meet her someday, Viv. Sounds like you are Europe bound, and that is understood. Mad Mads will have her girls come soon, and we can span the globe and focus on angles that will work for all and the business. All being in one place all the time makes no sense. A bit like those pillars you spoke about. Holding up a roof. They need space between them. Though I will miss you."

I sat down to reply to Priss. I sipped my fresh guava juice and looked out over the coffee plantation. The fact that Amilcar had left the estate to Theo and me was overwhelming; Surreal, really. That my name was now on the deeds still didn't feel real. All I felt was that I must do my best. And enjoy the blessings that had come my way. For now, I felt the best thing to do was to go ahead with Portugal and meet up with my nearest and dearest girlfriends. I would gain perspective and insights that would allow me to be more effective and constructive. I thought that by being in the very place where ideas were needed, I would be inspired.

I decided to reply to Priss and The Posse straight away.

Priss, Portugal is on! Marvellous call. Thank you for your energy, suggestion, and initiative. I will be leaving the new world that Columbus 'discovered' (let's face it, Paradise was already inhabited before Egg Man made his way over here) and returning to the Old World, where Vasco di Gama sailed from back in the day.

I have, in fact, been to Sagres, the most western point of Europe, where the slave trade used to be buoyant. I recalled feeling the austere beauty but also ominous past when I went there. It was a cloudy and breezy day. The exposed fort and rugged cliffs plunged into the sea with the Atlantic beating against them. I recalled it as impressive and humbling. Raw and real. And as you know, anything genuine that gives energy is my kind of tonic. Just like you Lovelies; My fellow feline Pussies. Can't wait to see you all in Portugal. Will check flights and send you my timings. Faro airport? If that is best, I will fly via Amsterdam and perhaps join Hélène on the same flight. Love those little new Fiat 500s. Is it big enough to squeeze us all in for our trips to the beach? Roof down. Sun on our faces. Laughing our guts out. Until we cry and can't breathe. I can see us now. Can't wait!'

As I pressed *send*, I felt a surge of happiness at the thought of seeing *My Girls* soon. How could you almost forget just how much you needed each other until you connected again.

The blessings of eternal friendships.

The type of connections where you tapped into the source of goodness, and it filled you to the brim, making your soul smile.

I went online and booked my flight. Soon, I would be Portugal bound.

Parting Words

Costa Rica stayed with me as I travelled East to meet the Pussy Posse in the West. I said goodbye to Maddie and Theo, knowing that we were connected over email and phone. Our friendships were forged on the Mountain of Love, and until this day, I adored those two very different individuals. They would always be part of my life.

When I said goodbye to Humphrey, it was warm but not passionate. Handsome and tall, he stood in front of me.

"Well, Viv. What to say. I have had the most awesome time getting to know you. I feel like we have met in a former life as I am so comfortable with you. Thank you for making such an important appearance and walking onto my Stage of Life. I feel I am ready to work through the things in my life I need to. And to come out stronger. You made me see there is still work to do and gave me the confidence and courage to resolve past issues and embrace the promise of what is yet to come."

"Spoken like the pro you are, dearest Humphrey. I am so happy to have met you, and I know for sure we will meet again. Don't know where don't know when."

"But I know we'll meet some sunny day again," Humphrey finished. "Vera Lynn got it right in terms of timeless lyrics. And that is what you are, Viv. Timeless and legendary. I will always fondly remember our special times in these hills of green. Like you, I always have and will always come back to Costa Rica. Let's agree to let each other know when we do, so we can keep weaving valuable great times into the episodes of our separate movies."

"You will forever be a very special chapter in my book. In a hero role, Handsome Humphrey."

Big H pulled me into him and put his arms around me. His taut torso snug against mine, he rested his chin on my head and exhaled.

Holding me there, he said, "Some people I will never forget. I lost Daphne as my partner. I hope I will never lose you as my friend. Though you know you mean rather more than that to me. Time will tell our story. One chapter at a time. And as for that novel you are writing, Viv, when you are ready, share it with me. My Rolodex is deep and wide. I pretty much know everyone in the film and music world. From Motown to Sony, and everyone in between. I would love to make your story come to life. Knowing I will feature in it gives me great pleasure."

He kissed my hair and said, "Merlin is waiting to take you to Quepos airstrip. I will be thinking of you as you bump over the jungle on your way to San José."

He stepped back and smiled. "I can see that scene in the movie. I imagine taking you to that pathetic excuse of an airport lounge; An open-air structure with a simple roof to keep the rain off. The coffee is brewing, and the fresh banana bread is laid out on a colourful, painted plate next to the disposable cups. Made of coffee paper, of course, in line with Costa Rica's epic ecological principles. As we sit next to each other on the simple wicker couch, I sip my drink and eat my cake, not really tasting anything. My tastebuds are dulled by the fact we are about to part. Somehow, for me, the zest has gone out of life.

The small Cessna plane arrives and lands on the dirt landing strip of black volcanic pulverised rock. The aircraft comes to a stop and turns round to be ready for take-off. The chap who brews the coffee and takes care of the shabby lounge goes to the plane to collect any rubbish. He gives the pilot a cup of coffee and a piece of banana bread. He signals to you to get on the scales holding your luggage. They need to ascertain how heavy each person and their bags are to distribute the weight. A few other people turn up and go through the same procedure. The coffee and logistics guy asks you to take the seat next to the pilot.

It starts to rain.

You hug me and climb up the rickety metal steps and bend your head as you board the tiny plane. The Captain is in place, and you greet him. Pilots always fly with the windows open on this journey, and he is smoking a cigarette out of his. You slide your window open too and look at me standing on the other side of the parted glass. The rain is coming down more strongly now than when we first arrived. I come in to kiss you through the open window, and you kiss me back. You can't see that I am crying as the rain soaks my coconut skin as I stand there forlorn, knowing if I stifle you, you will never come back. And that is all I long for. For you to return to me."

His scene-setting was heartfelt.

"Humphrey."

"Come here," Humphrey said as he pulled me into his arms and closed them around me.

My throat felt twisted as my tears dampened his pink cotton shirt. He put the palms of his strong hands gently over my ears and tilted my head.

"Viv, you have a life to live and a story to write. I will be in yours, and you will be in mine. Be the gorgeous girl I adore, and leave me with the memory of your smile. I will never forget the joy you bring. You made me realise you can only be happy when you are in harmony with yourself. And you, *Pura Vida* Viv, are one of the few people I know who has her own number. You know who you are.

Parting is such sweet sorrow, that I shall say goodnight till it be morrow," Humphrey said, as he gave me a final goodbye hug.

"From Vera Lynn to Shakespeare. You move seamlessly between songs and poetry. We will add film. Can't wait to work on that project with you. In the meantime, let's visualise and believe in the very best life can offer. Anyone blessed with the miracle of life better set out to make it marvellous and stay connected to good energy. Which is what you are, Humphrey; Pure and good energy."

Europe Bound

After a bumpy and wet flight over the green lungs of Costa Rica, I landed in San José. A taxi took me to Santa Maria International Airport, where I boarded the flight to Amsterdam. Good old KLM. The flight was uneventful. I slept.

I spent two nights at my place in Amsterdam and connected with Hélène. We managed a zoom call with Annie and Priss and received directions on where we would be meeting. Priss gave us the details of a lovely looking boutique hotel, Villa Vista, which lies in Luz's foothills. As the name suggested, it had a great view of the green sloping hillside and the startlingly deep blue Atlantic beyond. Apparently, the property only had six rooms, and we would be occupying four of them. Management told Priss that we would likely have the whole place to ourselves. I couldn't wait to hang out and catch up. Apparently, Priss enjoyed speaking with the owner and was their ongoing communication. I wondered what that was all about...

I told Priss that though it would be a stylish arrival to be picked up in an Aston Martin, I had booked a Fiat 500. Hélène had one of those in Amsterdam, and I enjoyed zooming around in it. It was an easy kind of a car with a hint of attitude, especially in the convertible model, which I had booked.

Both Hélène and I slept on the less than three-hour flight from Amsterdam to Faro. Me, because I was still a bit messed up due to jet lag and Hélène because she had a midnight romp with someone she met earlier during lunch. That turned into dinner and ended up in a wild summer night between the sheets.

Hélène, despite her amorous adventure, as always, was immaculately turned out when the taxi arrived to pick us up to go to the airport. With a cigarette between her glossed lips, as was her hallmark, she hooted with laughter when she recounted the events of the day before. It reminded me of when we first arrived in Amman all those years ago when she hit it off with Michel, the wealthy Jordanian.

Hélène still smoked and has never stopped wearing silk, continuing to use men at her pleasure. And theirs. Mostly.

On arrival, we picked up the bright white Fiat with its cherry coloured drop back roof from the car rental company.

"Unlimited mileage?" the efficient Portuguese agent asked.

"Absolutely," I confirmed.

"Any additional insurance for total security?"

"Absolutely not," I replied.

"Quite right, too," Hélène piped up. "We are not here to be safe. We are here with the Pussy Posse to take you, Portuguese guys, for the ride of your life, we can assure you. With the Pussies in Portugal, may I suggest that you take out insurance, not us?"

She laughed as she pulled out a smoke from the pack in her bag.

"You are not allowed to smoke," the agent said as his cheeks blushed.

He was clearly impressed with the blond diva who stood beside me.

"*Oh Bruno, Querido*," she said, reading his name tag. "Just one little puff of smoke will not cause anyone any harm. You eat so much pork in Portugal; I would almost call it *Pork-ugal*. That meat is much worse than any smoke of mine."

With that, she pulled her lighter out of her bag. As she tried to ignite her slim Panatela, the automatic door slid open, and new tourists entered. The breeze extinguished the flame. Quick as flash Bruno took the lighter from Hélène and, protecting the flame with his other hand, lit her up. Hélène hovered the tip of her cigarette above the lighter and drew long and hard on the slim cigarillo.

"*Obrigada, Bruno. Multo obrigada.*"

She touched his hand and exhaled. Bruno was transfixed.

I took the key off the desk where it lay, ready and waiting. We said goodbye and settled into the fabulous little Fiat.

"Only four kilometres on the clock," I said.

"Good. We don't want anyone else's cast-offs. Not in men. Nor in cars."

"Hm." I said, as I opened the door for Hélène, and helped her with her luggage. She had too many bags to manage the manoeuvre by herself. "How are you going to overcome that challenge as we age?"

"I just go younger and younger. Less hassle. More muscle."

With that, Hélène stubbed out her slim cigar next to the car. She smiled at me as the remains of her cigarillo still smouldered on the ground. In many ways, she was the epitome of elegance, yet she was utterly politically and environmentally outrageously incorrect in others.

"Shall we?"

"We shall," I said.

I got in the car, turned the key, opened the roof, and revved the little engine.

"Show me Villa Vista, *Bella Mia*," I said as we followed instructions from the GPS's female voice guiding us towards Priss and Annie, a mere hour away.

Villa Vista

Hélène and I arrived at the gates of Villa Vista. I jumped out and pressed the intercom at the entrance.

"They should have put the button where you don't have to leave the car," Hélène remarked.

"You will need to adjust, my dear Princess. We are in the Algarve, not Las Vegas. Things are slower here, a little less slick than Dubai and Monaco or indeed LA, but there is a charm in that."

"*Bom dia*" came through the intercom, and having said who we were, the electronic doors opened gracefully. I was charmed to see storks sculpted into the gates.

Was this another omen for Priss or new things to come?

In Costa Rica, I had seen creatures and flowers incorporated into the majestic gates of *La Hacienda*. Maybe storks were the equivalent in this neck of the woods. On either side of the gate, a magnificent *V* was engraved into a lighter metal.

"V for Vivica and V for Vacation," Hélène said. "And if I am lucky, *V* for Virility with a capital of enormous proportions. *Virility*. Think about it, Viv. What a word. Imagine that one powerful word encapsulates strength, energy, and a strong sex drive. What more could a girl wish for?"

"You are outrageous, Hélène. Outrageous but undeniably good for my health. My Queen of Good Energy."

"You are my dextrose energy, Viv. You know that. No Virile Viking could ever take your place or that of Annie or Priss."

"Jolly glad to hear that. No men can please us Pussies more than The Posse can. So happy we are going to be together for the next few days."

The Fiat 500 made its way up the sloping driveway. The lush green lawn was interspersed with olive and fig trees and an ancient kind of aqueduct, a blond stone structure that traversed the land. Before arriving, I checked out the website and learned that this modern art boutique hotel, categorised as a five star and *individual,* stood on the ground of an ancient farm where cows used to graze against the backdrop of the Atlantic ocean. As we found out later, the son of the former farming family was in charge of the hotel and of a few other assets.

The impressive driveway led up to Villa Vista, which stood proudly amidst the flowers and the grass, as sprinklers danced from all sides to keep the vegetation green during early summer when the rains had dried up. It was almost as green as Costa Rica but several shades lighter and less intense. It was a toned-down version of where I had just recently come from.

"Careful!" Hélène shouted. "Where is your mind at Viv? You could have killed that woman."

Taken aback, I realised Hélène was right. I had drifted off into my thoughts and almost scooped up one of the hotel workers on a golf buggy. She did look bemused and signalled us quite defensively to follow her to the car park, which was out of sight and hidden behind the trees. Having parked, I had not even gotten out before apologising profusely for almost driving her off the road. As the roof was open, I simply stood on my car seat and said how sorry I was. Ridiculous really. I should have simply gotten out. Hélène was laughing at me as she fumbled around in her bag for something, anything, to smoke.

"I like the car," Hélène said. "Obviously, as it is the same as mine, minus the roof. But with the hood down, smoking becomes impossible. So now I need to inhale my air, my personal toxic oxygen." She lit up her cigarette and got out of the Fiat.

I lifted out our luggage through the open roof.

"Ja, give it to me," the victimised woman said. She looked Portuguese but had a distinctly German twang and expression to her accent. "I will handle ze bags."

Oh Lord, she reminds me of Frau Helga Hauss, who interviewed me a gazillion years ago when I landed my unwanted job in cosmetics. She was German too and made every 'th' sound like a 'z' or an 's'.

"Viv, for goodness' sake. Stick with the programme; you are so ridiculously absent."

The golf cart lady took hold of the luggage as I tumbled it out of the top of the car. While managing our far too heavy suitcases, she looked at us reproachfully.

"Zees are very heavy. Zat is not good."

"Let me help you with those," I offered.

Had Hélène not flirted our way out of paying for some thirty kilos of extra weight at Schiphol airport, we would have paid the equivalent of both flights in luggage.

Happily, the beau on check-in was susceptible to Hélène's

innuendos and flirtations, and when he hesitated, she held his hand and said, "Put your hand on my heart and tell me you can feel my heart race. Please don't do that to me. You are too handsome to leave a taste in my mouth that is anything less than divine. Allow me to bring all the things I need with me. I know I can't take you. But if I could, I would. You are een heerlijk gebakje, which translates as a delicious tempting pastry or words to that effect.

It did the trick. We paid nothing, and the agent gave us some vouchers to use before our flight.

"Viv! For goodness' sake."

I looked up, and the woman was now standing with her arms on her hips, looking at me.

"I sink you really need a holiday. You have a head full of sings. My name is Renata. I do everysing in zis hotel. I will take your bags to zee reception. Follow me zer."

"My Lord. I just got a massive telling off from Renegade Renata," I said.

"Too true, Viv. Getting up and standing on your car seat and talking to Renegade Renata through the open roof. She gave it to you straight. But to be fair, you did almost mow her over on the way up and really, you did make quite an odd first impression. No wonder RR is not impressed. Hope you can change the perception of Matron and Manager. As she said, she does it all."

We strolled up to the reception area, where we were greeted by an outstandingly good looking man.

"He is rather Silver Foxy," Hélène whispered in my ear.

I had to admit. The guy really was quite extraordinarily handsome.

"Viviiiiiiii, Hélèèène!" Priss came storming around the corner with Annie in tow. "Finally, you are here. Annie and I have been sipping the most beautiful Portuguese wines from Luiz's estate. We were sampling them in readiness for your arrival."

Priss looked at Luiz, the demi-god. I was momentarily transported to the lightning in the Costa Rica sky. The electricity between Priss and Luiz was tangible. I was transfixed. Until Priss launched her arms around me, hugging me as if we hadn't seen each other for years. Annie and Hélène hugged, and then we changed like musical chairs.

Luiz waited for our loud screeches and joyful voices to subside and then said, "There are some Portuguese delicacies set out for you on the top terrace. From there, you will be able to enjoy the breeze and catch your breath. But perhaps you would like to freshen up first."

"No, no," Annie said. "First things first. And that means to catch up over some *Vinho Verde*. Water and washing can wait. We can't, can we, Priss?"

"We absolutely cannot!" Priss said. "I have waited so long to be together, and now we are!"

Luiz smiled at us all, and I noticed his dark brown eyes resting on Priss, "As you wish, Ms Priscilla. Your wish is my command."

I remembered hearing that expression before as I felt a twinge in my stomach thinking of General Salim. Gosh, he really could still stir me even when my mind was on other things with my nearest and dearest girlfriends.

Priss beamed at Luiz, "You are the gentleman I never met. Thank you, Luiz."

He smiled and led the way up the circular staircase that gave way to an expansive whitewashed terrace surrounded by glass that allowed for the far-reaching views of the ocean, to be seen even when sitting down.

"Tapa Time," Priss said as she took the wine from the ice bucket. "Luiz chilled this especially for you."

"Let me help you," Annie said as she poured our glasses rather too full even for a green wine.

"After we have some refreshments, we can go down to the beach. Renata booked a table for us at Tabu. Apparently, the *ceviche* is to die for, and the fried squid, not the one in batter, is totally delicious. If you can still find a space that is after these lovely little delicacies that have been set out for us."

We never made it to the beach or to Tabu. We simply enjoyed each other's company while nearing Midsummer's Eve.

I thought of James up in heaven, whom I would forever associate with the summer solstice since that was the night we first met all those years ago. Even though he was no longer on God's planet, I still felt connected. His energy, thoughts, and humour I could still tap into.

Life was transient, poignant, and sometimes painful but utterly unique, baffling, thrilling, and miraculous.

I looked at three of my closest girlfriends and remembered Maddie back in Costa Rica. I had no doubt that she too would become part of the Pussy Posse eventually. In my heart and mind, she already was. With my jewels of girlfriends in one place, I observed them happily smiling, chatting, talking, and hugging. We would always be together no matter where we were in the world. Safe in that knowledge, I thanked God for all my blessings, past and new. For my girls, I counted each of their blessings twice.

What a great start to our Posse meet-up in Portugal.

"Saùde!" I said, raising my glass.

The girls stopped chatting and raised theirs.

"*Para um reencontro maravilhoso em Portugal*," Priss added. "To a great reunion in Portugal."

Life's a Beach

The next day was somewhat of a challenge. We had intended to wake up early but only managed to get out of bed around eleven. Breakfast was laid out on a large table on the ground floor terrace overlooking the gardens that sloped down on each side of the rising driveway, where I had almost knocked Renegade Renata off her Germanic socks the day before.

"You are long sleeping," Renata said as she came to our table, bearing a large thermos of coffee in one hand and fresh orange juice in the other. "You have ze choice of ozzer juices, but zis area was known for oranges, so I sink you will want zis." She didn't wait for our responses and just poured the burnt orange elixir into our tall glasses.

The suco de laranja was delicious. It was going to take me some time to wrap my head around the Portuguese language. It was like Spanish, yet very different. Additionally, in this most southern part of Portugal, the language got *swallowed,* as Priss told us.

"I should really be learning the language in Lisbon, but I rather like learning the lingo from certain locals like Luiz," she said. "So, I will just look forward to swallowing whatever he has for me." She winked at us.

"Broody mare," Annie laughed. "Does Luiz even know you have set your sights on him? Poor unsuspecting Portuguese Prince. The claws of Puss Priss are ready to nail down her Papa Prey."

At that moment, Luiz arrived. Whether he had heard what Annie just said was not relevant. It was all done in a well-meaning spirit, and the good energy around the table at noon-o-clock was alive and kicking.

"*Bom dia senhoras*," Luiz greeted us. "Priss asked me to suggest an activity for today, and, with your permission, your carriages await. Not the traditional horse-drawn one on this occasion but nonetheless vintage. Please feel free to meet in the parking lot behind the hedge whenever you have finished your breakfast. Perhaps bring your swimming costumes too. The towels are already packed."

With that, he smiled at us then discreetly left us to finish our breakfast or brunch, I should say.

"He is a keeper, Priss," I said. "A man with initiative, kind, good looking, pro-active, doesn't need the limelight, has style. What's the catch?"

"I am not sure yet," Priss said. "I don't think he's been married, and my buddy Amin or Amen, bless that guy for introducing me to Luiz, said that Luiz is his closest friend. And to take my time. Not that I can spend too much time. Clock ticking and all that. But for this week, I won't be making babies anyway, so we can just enjoy, explore, and have fun. I appreciate Luiz. He seems so perfect. But as you say, what's the catch?"

We asked Renegade Renata for one more round of coffee

before getting our gear. "You have had too much caffeine," she said. "Yesterday zer was a lot of alcohol and now too much coffee. You are making your life a danger to yourselves."

I heard Hélène whisper, "I would not have it any other way!" as we all tried to suppress our laughter at the hilarity. Matron had spoken, and we behaved like schoolgirls, just as we would have done all those years ago when we first met. We celebrated our childlike silliness. Why not? Enjoy what strikes you as funny, and don't entertain what you find boring. A simple principle.

I went with Annie, and Hélène hopped in with Priss in the car that Luiz was driving. We jumped into two jeeps. My brother Martin would have died to drive one of those. They were classic Defenders. They were immaculate and fully original.

"*Olá,*" I said to our driver.

I thought it was strange that Luiz did not introduce us to the person, but maybe he was his chauffeur and simply doing a job.

"Olá to you too," came from the front seat.

I sat baffled in the back. That voice sounded familiar... Could it be? Surely not.

"Bash?" I stammered, my heart racing, while my mind was telling me that I was behaving bizarrely and that I needed to get a grip.

"It is I," the voice from the front confirmed. "Your very own Bash. Get out of the back, and I will meet you outside for a long-overdue hug."

I tumbled out of the car and into his open arms.

"I thought you were wanted?" I managed to ask him.

"I hope I still am. We never finished where we left off," Bash said, as he smiled his riotously roguish grin. "We have to catch up. But let me get you to the beach first, or we will be here in the parking all afternoon. As for me, wherever we are is a good place to reconnect since our Spanish chapter, but for the others, I think they would prefer the hidden beach where Luiz and I will take you. Plenty of rugged rocks there for a pew in the sun and a drink in hand. In the meantime, jump up next to me in front. If you don't mind, Hélène? Has it really been thirty years? I missed you at the recent reunion on the Mountain of Love. Lex did too. He did not stop talking about you. Before we go, I need a hug from you too."

While Bash was saying hi to Hélène, his phone rang; it was Luiz.

"Let's get going *habeibi*, we need half an hour to drive to our beach. Slightly west from here and down some smugglers' paths. I brought the gear we need, and you will only have to get your gorgeous selves down and back up the cliff. A bit of a descent and a climb, but with some *vino* in your *sangue*, I am sure you will not notice or at least will soon enough forget."

With that, he put the Defender into gear, and we set off to go to the beach for what Bash described as a "Lazy Beach Afternoon". There was no doubt that off-roaders were needed. We parked both cars in a remote place, where another vehicle was being unloaded. A team of three chaps took equipment and prepared all the gear for lunch on the beach.

I was dying to hear about how what, and why I was seeing Bash again, but I appreciated not knowing everything here and now in my older age. There was a time and place, and neither had yet come.

The team of guys were all young and virile enough to please

even the most demanding feline like Hélène. She observed the young men as she inhaled deeply, full of appreciation.

"What a most satisfying landscape you have," she murmured to no one in particular. "All-natural goodness in one place. This is very good for my health."

I locked arms with Hélène since we had nothing to carry.

"You lovely cougar," I said. "You never change your spots."

"My G-spot still seems to hit the mark," Hélène hooted as one of the young men was looking at her.

Clearly, sexual energy did not require proximity. Not in Hélène's case, anyway. I smiled as I thought of her already plotting an encounter down on the beach below, which I considered seemed an awfully long way, especially in flip-flops. Eventually, we made it down the steep cliff. Thistles and grasses were growing in purples and golden hues. The plants were rugged and rough yet still managed to look delicate and pretty. I guess we all have elements of both. Some of us fare better than others, depending on the circumstance. And how wonderful to know where you could bloom. My personal best conditions were a blend of the Middle East, Europe, and Costa Rica. Three in one. That would be my optimum idea of heaven on earth and the best place to blossom.

"Viv, not again! Stay with the day and leave your trances for when you are no longer with your Besties," Hélène said.

"I may have been dreaming about where I would like to have my forever home or at least one of them, but you, my dear, are possibly even worse. I know you are plotting to have one, if not all these boys, for dessert. Preferably raw and served in their own juices. You are incorrigible, and I love that about you."

We stood with our bare feet in the surf. Priss was wearing

a bikini that showed off her svelte figure. With her dark hair and pale blue eyes, she looked like an Irish Princess. Her skin was the colour of cream, and her body the shape of a perfect hourglass.

"Come on, you," she challenged us. "I know the Atlantic is utterly freezing and that the waves are pretty challenging, but we need to brace ourselves. When have we ever not?"

With that, she dived through a swelling wave like the surfers used to do in Costa Rica, lying in wake for the big rollers.

"Oh, *Deus*!" Priss cried. "Bloody Nora, that is so cold!"

"How do you think we are going to come in now?" Annie said. Then, she dived head-on into the next wave.

What to do? Best get it over and done with. I launched myself in. Hélène dismissed our idiocy and strolled out of the surf onto the beach for a smoke.

When we were all back on the sand, I asked Priss, "You seem to know quite a bit of the old local lingo. Did you skill up before you came here?"

"Not really, but I am picking it up as I go along. If I want to be able to engage with those potential Portuguese Papas, I need to be able to communicate."

"Talking of papas, how long have you known Luiz at Villa Vista?" I asked her.

"I met him last week when I came to check out the hotel. Luiz is a friend of Amin; I had no idea that you guys went to school together. And it seems I missed out on a chapter that you must fill me in on Viv. I noticed you call him Bash. Will want to hear all my lovely sparkle Viv. Over a bottle or two. What a jolly tiny world we live in. But I am no longer surprised at coincidences. Nothing in life is linear. Not least destiny. Both

Amin, or Bash, and Luiz are gorgeous rogues. But it is Luiz who I really like especially."

"I think the feeling is entirely mutual from his side, Priss," Annie said.

"*Ja,* the dextrose energy between you and him could be cut with a knife," Hélène added. "Talk about sparks flying."

Priss laughed it off. "We will see whether there is any mileage to be had from a liaison with Luiz. Who knows? I certainly could do a lot worse in the daddy department."

"I don't know about you lovely ladies," Annie began. "But I am starving. Must have been the icy water and our marathon chat."

"What are the Luiz and Bash doing over there by that cliff?" I asked.

The two men were facing the rock, and each had a white plastic bellowing bag attached to their swimming shorts. We had not noticed them earlier and only now observed what they were doing. After a while, they returned brandishing their bags which now held weight in them and were no longer blowing in the wind.

"Time to get out of the sea. We will have our lunch as the tide is coming in. Hope you all like mussels?"

Luiz and Bash walked up onto the beach, and we joined them. One of the boys, Andres, had set up some rocks and large stones to protect the small fire he made from the breeze coming off the ocean. He and one of the other chaps started to clean the shells to take off the beards.

"Let me help you with that," Hélène said as she appeared with a silk scarf around her blond bob and a cigarette in hand.

Her cream and dark blue sarong showed off her slim legs as

she took a seat on the rock. Andres sent the younger guy to get a towel for Hélène to sit on. Not so much for her comfort as for his. She was, after all, very easy on the eye. A joy to behold on a sunny afternoon on the Atlantic.

Bash and I found a spot to catch up.

"What are you doing in this part of the world, Bash? I realise there may be things I am not privy to, nor that I wish to know. So, limit the things that will not contribute to positive energy. But I do want to hear about you and how you are. Why Portugal?"

"Look around you, Viv. What is there not to like? The place is untouched apart from the beaches on the south. I like the fact that there are plenty of places to hide. Lying low in the shade is my newfound solution. Marbella is noisy, wild, brash and blingy. Every underworld character has set up home there. I really enjoyed living there but as you know, whether I do right or wrong, somehow, I always find myself in the thick of problems. I have not yet worked out whether they are self-inflicted or partly due to my background and roots. Everybody trusts a blond-haired, blue-eyed boy, which I am. But no one trusts an Arab, which is also what I am. It is all very controversial.

My conclusion was to move away from the hotspot and cool down and keep my nose clean. Literally. Enough of the running. Enough of the white powder. Portugal is the right spot for that. This part of the world increasingly sees wealth moving in between the pine trees, hidden in coves, surrounded by nature and away from prying eyes. Things are quieter here. And I like it. I feel like I am getting to know who I am a bit more. I used to be a tool for others.

For the first time since we were in Switzerland, where I felt happy and protected, I am starting to feel the same way here. I can even do things that interest me. You know my fascination with cars. I managed to move most of them here from Marbella. Don't ask me how. But they are like the children I never had. When I grew up, my dad was a dealer of high-quality cars in Iraq, and I guess it is in my blood. I will show you my matchbox collection first and then take you for a ride in some of my classics if you allow me."

"Blimey, Bash. You have had quite a ride. I am so happy you are okay. But I never got to see you at Malaga airport with Maddie and Bing because Interpol had intercepted you. I wrote you a letter when Theo asked me to come to Costa Rica after all had gone pear-shaped in Ronda. After that, I never heard from you. Theo and Amilcar told me that you would be okay but that I should not put myself with you. I know that may be a bit straight-talking, but that was their advice. As you can imagine, I was torn."

"Habibti Viv. Both Amilcar and Theo were right. Much as I am so delighted to see you and attracted beyond measure to take you all the way on the drive of your life in my Aston Martin and beyond, I caution you. I will not be able to contain my flirtations with you. I adore you. You always made me laugh at school, and you still do. I love your spirit and your way. But I am a rogue and a scallywag, as you once called me. With this, I consider you warned. Maybe you will be able to resist me, but the feeling is not mutual. Be on guard for me as a lover but open your arms to me as a friend. And let me grow to understand that women can be true friends too, like the amazing friendship I have with Luiz. I will be honoured if you can be someone solid in my life. Forever as a deep and valued friend. But as I said. I need your help."

"I would love to be your *Forever Friend* and *Not Ever Lover*," I laughed.

"Those are possibly some of the most valuable words I have ever heard, Vivi habibti. I will treasure them and you." He hugged me and then filled up our glasses with more excellent Portuguese wine.

"Tell me about Luiz, Bash. Seems he and Priss are getting on well."

"I met Luiz when I brought my cars over here. He was a classic car enthusiast with an extraordinary collection which frankly speaking only matches mine in this part of the world. He had a network of observers who spotted classics he would like to add to his collection. He, like me, was brought up with cars. His dad, who recently passed, was a well-known collector. Luiz had heard about my olive golden Aston Martin. A classic in a league of its own. I was able to drive it across the border from Spain, which was mere hours away. One day I was visited by someone who I knew and was introduced to Luiz. He is a timid and honourable man who keeps himself to himself because of his wealth. I am noisy and loud. He is quiet and elegant. We balance each other out.

Our cars are now in two different places. One collection is under Luiz's villa just west of Faro and the others are at my home not a million miles from here. Luiz also keeps a few around the back, beyond the parking at Villa Vista, in case he fancies a drive when he is there, which is not all the time."

"Luiz certainly seems to be around at the moment, and it is so nice that he is joining us even if he must have lots going on."

"I think the *Priscilla Factor* is playing a role here," Bash grinned. "Females throw themselves at Luiz for his wealth and good looks. He is continuously hunted and therefore stays away. He hates it. We get on because we genuinely like each other, and we don't need anything from each other."

"I was asking Priss what the catch was with Luiz. She said she didn't know. She really likes him but has been around long enough to consider the potential relationship too good to be true."

"Luiz is an only child. From a wealthy, prominent family. He grew up in the lap of luxury. As I said, he's always cautious about peoples' motives. Since his father's death, he has been alone, apart from having me and his cars. He always wanted to be a father. Never a sugar daddy. When he finds that special girl, I think things will go forward quickly. Maybe it is Priss."

"Lunch is served," Annie said as she scrambled across the black rocks that the ocean had deposited on the part of the beach where Bash and I were talking.

"Coming," I said, as Bash jumped up and gave me a hand and pulled me up. "We must have been talking for a long time Bashikins. I am totally stiff."

"I was stiff even before we sat down. Rock hard, I can tell you."

"We decided on friendship, Bash. Keep your *jojo* in your surfers, and let's go for some food."

"Creamy mussels," Bash said and winked at me, "Now that is my idea of a great afternoon snack."

No matter what, Bash was a perpetual flirt. His innuendos and cheeky smiles were par for the course. I enjoyed being around him. But had already decided I would never be with him.

The ocean harvest was abundant. The large succulent mussels

cooked in local white wine and herbs from the hillside were finished with a dash of cream. Luiz broke the fresh bread, and we indulged in the sea food feast, with the juices trickling down our chins. Priss was wearing Luiz's sweater around her shoulders. The cool summer breeze picked up, and the waves started to roll in. The spray from the ocean landed in a gentle vapour on our smiling faces.

"I think you may need some sunscreen, darling Viv," Bash said. "Let me apply some cream. I am the best at that."

Everyone laughed, and Luiz pulled Priss a little closer and popped a mussel into her mouth. We were relaxed in each other's company. And happy. I was grateful that I knew without a shadow of a doubt what true happiness felt like. It was a place within me that I would always respect and protect.

Happiness is life's ultimate success.

"Viv darling, are you still with us?" Annie asked me.

I reconnected with my surroundings.

"Move your bootie and come with me to put these babies back in the sea."

Luiz joined the conversation, saying, "Am so happy to hear you say that, Annie. When we harvest the mussels, inevitably, some of the tiny shells are gathered as well. And we always put back the babies too. Babies matter to our future."

He looked at Priss and Annie, and I took the white plastic bags, now again blowing in the wind as the big mussels no longer weighed them down.

We released the little clams back into the cold Atlantic, where they could grow and flourish. And bring forth the next generation.

Forever Connected

Bash rang me saying he wanted to see me.

"It is your final day in Portugal. I know that you girls will want to continue your chats until you too have to say goodbye to each other. It is amazing to see how you seamlessly connect, chat, laugh and have such a great time together. Over the past days, whenever I have joined you, it struck me how special your friendship is. And how easily you go from laughing to crying and back again. You pussies are really a Perfect Posse. Seeing you connect like that made me extra happy knowing that I feel the same with Luiz. We may only be two, but it is not about quantity in friendships. I have come to realize that.

I need to meet a potential client today. He is a well-known Spanish football professional who wants a Heavenly Hide Away Home, away from prying eyes and paparazzi and I know just the place. I will meet him later today as he must fly back for an important match later. Please can I come early morning Viv, to say goodbye?"

I was happy to see Bash and to be able to say goodbye. He was special to me.

I heard the engine before I saw the silhouette of the supercar as it came undulating up the driveway. Even on that short stretch, Bash gave it full throttle. That was simply in his nature. Being quiet was impossible for Bash. He loved noise and attention. Perhaps to keep a lid on any feelings that might be heard otherwise.

In the case of the classic Aston Martin, the noise was more of a roar, fine-tuned by the Quincy Jones of internal combustion. Each Aston Martin model was individually engineered to give it an unmistakeably recognisable tuned sound, just like a musical instrument. I was fascinated by the knowledge and the expertise needed to achieve the exact, hallmark reverberation. But the roar of the engine did nothing for me, apart from announcing that my dear friend Bash had arrived.

I stepped down from the terrace that spanned the width of my room and walked across the lawn. I hoped Renegade Renata was not observing my movements from Reception, as she would frown upon my impertinence to cross the freshly watered grass in a diagonal line. The girls were still asleep. As Bash switched off the engine, I arrived beside him.

"I had to see you before you go," Bash said. "I have been thinking about what I said to you that you shouldn't be with me. But Viv, the past few days have been so good, I wish I could retract my words. I think I want to be with you."

"Come here, nutter," I said as I pulled Bash into me.

He held on to me like the clams and mussels hung onto the cliff. I realised he had let his guard down. I was a safe space for him, just like Portugal. I did not judge him, and that, I realised, was what he wanted. I remembered what Theo and Amilcar, God rest his soul, had told me. Words to the effect that Bash was not a bad guy; he had a good heart, but he should not be my guy. I realised now that they had been right.

"Hang on," Bash said as he stooped into the Aston Martin to retrieve something. "Here, these are for you."

Bash handed me a bunch of three large pink petalled flowers tied together with a ribbon and a jewel of a ladybird in the centre of one of the flowers.

"These beauties will die in a week or so," he said. "But Lady Luck will always be with you. She is made of one large ruby and surrounded by little diamonds. The little black marks on her back are the remains of the giant black diamond I smuggled for my father from Iraq. I told him it was lost. He went ballistic, but I am glad I did as I needed some funds from time to time, and the black beauty saw me through."

He looked at me and then at the floor.

"What's on your mind Bash," I encouraged him.

"I know I want to be with you, but I am not good for you. This way, I hope you will think of me and associate me with good luck and energy. Because that is what I believe you see in me, and that is what I thirst for. For someone to see me as I am, even though I am just learning to understand who that person truly is. Thank you, Vivi, for the past few days. I find it hard to face my demons and let my guard down, but I realise that I will never find myself if I don't. And will never be able to live my own life. I know you girls have one final day together, so I wanted to see you and say goodbye. And give you this."

He took the gem-studded ladybird brooch out of the heart of the flower. He blew off the pollen and kissed it.

"Here you are habibti Vivi. With all my love," he said as he pinned it on to my linen top.

I swallowed hard. Bash really was a kind softy at heart. One who was damaged and was now seeking his truth. I felt privileged that we were connected and had no doubt that we would meet again, probably in Portugal, as he was not at liberty to travel unless it was courtesy of Interpol.

Bash hugged me one last time.

"You will always be my girl because it was you who made me realise, I can be my own man, and I love you for that."

I felt as if a Boa Constrictor was coiling around my throat.

"I love you too, Bash," I croaked.

With that, Bash kissed me on my cheek. He looked at me one more time, his eyes damp, and slid into the car.

"Say goodbye to the girls for me," Bash said. "Take care my girl." He then revved his engine more loudly than ever and swung the olive golden exquisite set of wheels around and set off down the drive.

Renegade Renata must have been watching. The gates were already open. Bash accelerated his Aston Martin DB6 Vintage down the last stretch and swung out of sight. When I returned through the reception area, Renata, for once, looked empathetic. She didn't reprimand me for violating the rules of crossing the lawn.

Everyone has a heart, after all, I thought. *No matter however strong, loud, or harsh an exterior might be. We all have our stories, and some need to bear more than most. I hoped for the very best for Bash.*

I thought about our trip to *Sagres*, on one of the days we spent together. We managed to catch the sunset that people talked about. The Romans considered it a magical place where the sunset was much more significant than anywhere else. They believed the sun sank hissing into the Atlantic, marking the edge of their world.

Luiz had asked whether we wanted to watch the sunset. Even though we had just spent the afternoon walking, chatting, drinking, and eating, we didn't want to waste a moment of this togetherness. We set off to a point just beyond Sagres and sat with blankets wrapped around us, and a brandy in hand, watching the most dramatic sunset. Sitting on the rugged cliff, with winds coming in off the Atlantic ocean, we huddled together and simply sat, drinking in the beauty of the setting sun over the resplendent sea.

It was pitch dark when we finally left *Cabo de São Vicente*, Cape St. Vincent, the south-westernmost point of Portugal and mainland Europe. It struck me that the Romans and Phoenicians really recognised a good thing when they saw it. Magical and sacred. How much better could life get?

One day we went for a picnic in the countryside, surrounded by cork trees and exquisite wildflowers. We lay on our backs on the grass, paddled in the stream and caught up on our lives over the past months. We each had the time to talk about our highlights and our low points and to exchange views and thoughts. I told the girls about Maddie and my time in Spain, the passing of dear Amilcar, whom Hélène and Annie fondly remembered. And the story of Bash, the Costa Rica trip, meeting dear Humphrey and why I did not pursue a relationship with him. As well as discussing ideas on the developing coffee business, and the books I was writing. I assured them all Pussies would have a role as well as in any eight part series. I had to solemnly promise Priss.

On the way back, we once again, took the country roads. The pretty winding track crossed underneath the motorway overhead. I preferred to take the slow route. Especially now. I wanted to stretch out our time together as much as possible. As usual, having the Pussy Posse together had been spectacular though there was somehow a more poignant feeling that was starting to take root inside of me. We were all much older now. The years brought experiences and added to our lives. All our characters were different, yet still very much aligned.

Our differences led to synergies. Our multi-cultured backgrounds fuelled a more satisfying existence, and our sense of belonging felt more solid and sacred than ever.

When the girls woke up on the last day, and after I had said my goodbye to Bash, we ate our breakfast in the sunshine. Luiz kindly said he would take us up to *Monchique* on our last day, saying that his Princess and her friends deserved a royal goodbye.

The natural mineral water found in *Serra de Monchique* had been known since the presence of the Romans in the Iberian Peninsula. Archaeological remains referred to the water as sacred.

As we drove up into the hills, I felt a soothing of my soul as the energy came over me now that I had previously only felt in Costa Rica. Even within a twenty-five-minute drive, we were now worlds away from the beach life. Monchique was the old spa resort where the Portuguese royals used to escape the heat in summer. Luiz stopped to buy us each a bottle of water.

"PH 9.5," he said. "The best water in the world for anything.

It cleanses and heals you."

We sipped in silence as the car climbed to the top of the hill where Luiz stopped in a small village called *Foia*. He invited us into a fabulous restaurant. The panorama was breathtaking. We stood side by side as we took in the natural beauty. After a while, we sat down and ordered fabulous food, accompanied by gorgeous young Portuguese Vinho Verde. As I gazed out over hills of green and the ocean in the distance, I thought of Maddie.

I looked at each one of my dearests of girlfriends. They were chatting away. Luiz was holding Priss' hand. Safe in the knowledge that we would always be close, I raised my glass. All pussies followed suit.

"May awesomeness prevail, dearest Pussies."

"Until the next time, darling Viv. Bring on the Movie. We all want to be in it!" Priss said.

"To Pussies Galore," I said. "We are and will be Forever Connected."

"Forever Connected," the Pussy Posse purred as we clinked our glasses with shining eyes.

Full of love for each other, we were grateful for our adventures and the lives we shared through thick and thin.

Through sick and sin.

Forever.

Interview with the Author

Helen Van Wengen (Britt Holland) is a citizen of the world. That sense of wonder, sharing and positivity in the joy of cultural exchanges has been poured into a series of books which in part reflect different aspects of Helen's own remarkable life.

Born in Holland, Helen's childhood was in the Netherlands, with frequent visits to the UK, before she travelled to Switzerland to study hospitality at one of the world's top Hospitality Management Schools. There, Helen was introduced to friends and cultures as they lived, learned, and forged strong global friendships.

This experience shaped the young woman's life forever and set her on a journey that would see her work in the hotel industry worldwide, particularly in Europe and the Middle East and in Central America and Asia.

Now living between Jordan and Amsterdam, Helen is engaged in multiple projects, ranging from hospitality and tourism to social enterprise initiatives that drive profit for purpose, people, and planet. Helen believes in aspirational outcomes with a positive spirit. With her upbeat nature, Helen knows that miracles happen every day.

And on meeting Helen, it is the positivity that shines through. A positivity which has enabled her to boldly reflect on complex, wonderful and sometimes frankly hilarious parts of her life for a series of fun but savvy books which have echoes of *Eat Pray Love, Sex and the City and Four Weddings and a Funeral.*

Helen said: "The journey of writing these books has been so transformational because when I am writing, I feel as though I really am there while at the same time being able to reflect on situations and emotions I write about. And in some cases, remember as the words pour out.

"There have been times that I have cried and laughed, and those elements are all in the books".

"The books are not autobiographical, but there is so much of myself and my own experiences in the characters."

And the process of writing the books she said has fuelled and developed her soul and given her great joy.

Between The Sheets is a fascinating read, full of love, drama, sex and intrigue, supported by strong female characters that give the work a sense of empowered authenticity.

Helen said: "I love how my writing has connected my heart and mind to the past, made me more conscious of each day and allows my excitement of tomorrow to spill over on to the pages of my books. As a result of writing, I reconnected with amazing friends with whom, in some cases, I lost touch. One dear friend described my books as 'a magic carpet ride' that sparked a tear, a smile, and triggered thoughts she had forgotten all about. Touching other peoples' lives in positive ways matters to me. I will continue to live and write stories for others as well as myself. Living life is a privilege and one I embrace.

Also by Britt Holland

Between the Sheets
A story about life, lust and love

Vivika no longer feels like her former bubbly self. She was stuck in a rut. Overworked and exhausted. When a British naval ship docks in the port of Amsterdam, Vivika is compelled to attend a cocktail reception. Vivika isn't looking to be swept off her feet by the Captain of Her Majesty's Ship, *Carlington*. She can't help noticing that he seems able to manage her like no man has before. He intrigues her, but before long he sets sail.

When Vivika starts working for a luxury hotel chain with resorts in the Middle East, she soon realises she's joined a sinking ship. The owner, a prominent Arab businessman, is at loggerheads with the management company, and pins all his hopes and demands on Vivika.

With an ego larger than Burj Khalifa and a temperament more explosive than Vesuvius, His Excellency General Salim, does not take no for an answer. He stirs her in ways she didn't deem possible. With her loyalties divided between company and owner, Vivika plots her course. She negotiates the waves of passion, pain, and loss.

Will she survive the high Arabian seas with her true north intact?

Mountains of Love
A story of memories, past loves and new adventures

Vivika, the high-flying, fun-loving hospitality professional from *Between the Sheets*, attends The Grand Reunion in the Swiss Alps. Here she had lived, loved and learnt with her fellow students three decades earlier. Vivika wonders whether her old flame, Bash will attend. More than memories are rekindled on the Mountain of Love. Vivika's adventures take a turn for the worse when she is linked to an illegal trade network. Can she continue to believe in Bash, or is it time to smell the coffee? As circumstances unfold, Vivika encounters pain and gain, and sets out to write her own future.

Printed in Great Britain
by Amazon